AIRSHIP 27 PRODUCTIONS

Motor City Manhunt
© 2016 R.A. Jones & Michael Lail

Published by Airship 27 Productions
www.airship27.com
www.airship27hangar.com

Cover and interior illustrations © 2016 Jesus Antonio Hernandez Rodriguez

Editor: Ron Fortier
Associate Editor: Gordon Dymowski
Marketing and Promotions Manager: Michael Vance
Production and design by Rob Davis.

ISBN-13: 978-0692622766 (Airship 27)
ISBN-10: 0692622764

Printed in the United States of America

10 9 8 7 6 5 4 3 2 1

R.A. JONES & MICHAEL VANCE

CHAPTER ONE

September, 1927
Los Angeles, California
Population 1,238,000
Chief Export: Schlock

It was like a shotgun blast of metal, rubber and glass.

Frantic, the mousey, middle-aged man in a light grey suit, straw hat, and black-rimmed glasses clutched the steering wheel of his '25 Ford Model T convertible as he careened into the on-coming, scattering blast of flivvers, trucks, and vans. Behind his glasses, his brown eyes were wide with terror. His face as white as death, he gritted his teeth.

Horns blared as vehicles screamed by him and drivers leaned out of the windows of their motorcars to shake their fists, screaming obscenities.

Terrified men, women and children on the sidewalks scattered like leaves.

He heard none of it.

Then he struck a pothole.

The Model T convertible lurched up, careening wildly to his left. The impact jerked his hands off of the steering wheel, his butt off of the driver's seat, knocked his glasses crooked on his face, and drove his straw hat and head through the motorcar's canvas roof.

The hat seemed glued to his head.

It was.

His face now florid with blood and covered with flop sweat, he found the wheel and seized it using his knees like a pair of pliers.

He side swiped a taxi that careened past him onto a sidewalk and smashed through the shop window of a tobacconist.

The shin of his right leg accidentally hit the toggle switch on the dashboard that raised the canvas roof. Unlatched from the chassis, the roof slowly began to pull his knees free from the steering wheel as it lifted him higher and higher.

Behind him by a good ten yards, Sam Washburn, the director of this two-reeler being filmed for the Hal Roach Studio, yelled "Cut!"

The careening cars and trucks and vans on the huge silver screen in front of the Model T blinked and vanished. Other lights came on, illuminating the sound stage around the unmoving stunt car.

"Get me out of this thing!" the comedian snapped as he struggled to free his head from the canvas roof. His legs were churning in the air as if he was running.

"Fantastic! Terrific! Stupendous! You're the best, Mr. L!" exclaimed the director. "We'll have you free in just a sec."

The cinematographer beside Washburn stopped grinding the handle on his camera as crew members pulled the comedian from the Ford's partially raised roof and then out of the Model T.

"Charlie Chaplin ain't got nothin' on me!" grinned the comedian as he landed on his feet.

"Except maybe 20 million fans," the director muttered as he turned away.

+++

On a real city street nearby, an identical '25 Ford convertible smashed through a first, then a second, and finally a third wooden workhorse on the Hollywood street before striking the huge pothole.

A large '24 Dodge truck with a bed full of hay that was right on the Model T's rear bumper followed through the explosion of debris behind the Ford.

A woman with a terrified, small child wrapped around her thigh on an adjacent sidewalk screamed without sound and pointed to stunt double Michael Yellowstone, the young man in a light gray suit, straw hat, and black-rimmed glasses whose head had been driven up through the canvas roof of the car.

The Ford careened madly as it swerved in and out of oncoming traffic as Michael tried to miss each vehicle by steering with his knees. Its canvas top began to rise higher and higher, carrying Yellowstone with it.

His legs swinging in larger and larger arcs as the top rose, the Osage Indian finally threw the weight of his body up and over the edge of the Model T's canvas roof which, in turn, was pulled farther up and back with him from the car's chassis.

In the blink of an eye, Yellowstone did a full back somersault that tore his head free of the accordioned canvas top of the convertible and carried him, tumbling, onto the hood of the hay truck, then over its windshield, then up over the truck's cabin to land on his butt in the hay in the truck's bed.

Careful not to move a muscle, he sat until he heard a distant shout of "Cut!", then exhaled.

The young director of the film's second unit was by his side before Yellowstone had even climbed down from the truck, his gratitude and respect obvious from the expression on his face.

"That's why they call you 'One Take', Yellowstone!" he enthusiastically exclaimed. "That was just perfect, just darn perfect!"

"Glad you liked it, son," the Osage Indian said with veiled sarcasm. "Maybe someday, you'll even let *me* do the slow burn."

"Help yourself to donuts and coffee," said the director, ignoring the stunt man's remark. "Then Mr. Washburn needs you at the back projection screen on stage six in fifteen."

+++

The comedian in the big, black-rimmed glasses and the straw hat climbed up into the bed of the hay truck that had replaced the '25 Ford convertible in front of the rear projection screen as Yellowstone climbed out of the vehicle. The comedian crawled onto the hay, and sat down. He stuck several blades of the yellow straw in his mouth, mugged his relief and then chagrin for the camera, and shrugged his shoulders. He spit the hay out.

"Cut!" yelled Washburn. "Genius, pure genius, Mr. L."

"Could you reasonably expect less?" said the comedian as he rose from the hay.

"Not reasonably," said Yellowstone as he watched from his position next to the truck but out of camera range. Michael waited patiently as the director walked to the hay-filled truck where he stood by the tailgate and the comedian climbed out of the truck.

"You're amazing, Yellowstone!" the comedian effervesced. "You're..."

Yellowstone looked away from the actor and down at the actress who had played the child wrapped around her mother's thigh on the sidewalk earlier. She was tugging at his left pants leg with her left hand; in her right was an autograph book and a short pencil.

"Excuse me," he said to the comedian, and squatted down by the girl.

Yellowstone knew better than most that the motion picture camera was illusion in a box.

He was well aware that, at a distance, it disguised the differences between himself and the comedian; the stunt man was three inches taller; his was the muscular, athletic body of an Olympic swimmer or marathon runner compared to the actor's average build; the camera hid his dull bronze skin, his square jaw, high cheekbones, and broad nose; the stray bang of black hair that most often feathered his forehead was hidden under the straw hat.

Most of the people who saw this film would never notice the difference. That was the magic.

So he pointed a thumb at the comedian.

"I think you probably want him," he grinned.

"Uh-uh," said the little girl. "You."

"Well, it looks like you've got yourself a fan!" interjected the comedian as Yellowstone signed her book. "About time! As I was saying, you're the best stunt man in the flickers, Yellowstone. You have a job with me anytime you want it."

Yellowstone rose to his full height as he watched the little girl skip away, waving her trophy autograph book at anyone on the set.

"The best stand-in who *was* in the flickers, Mr. L," corrected Yellowstone, pressing both of his hands hard against the small of his back. "That was my first and last autograph. I'm just getting too old for this nonsense."

"You're kidding! What are you, twenty-five? Twenty-six?"

"I'm thirty years old, partner... and I'm calling it quits."

CHAPTER TWO

July, 1935: Detroit
"City of the Straits"
Population 1,575,000
Chief Exports: grain, flour, hogs, cattle, beef, hides,
sheep, wool, cotton, coal, iron and steel
Motor Cars

"It's hot as Hades in here," said police Lt. Jack Hill as he plopped down in a tufted leather chair, threw his legs up, and dropped the heels of his black brogans down on the edge of Rebekah Nixon's desk. "I thought it was sweltering outside, especially for Detroit, but this is murder."

The small, oscillating fan that swung slowly back and forth on one of the book shelves behind the Assistant District Attorney did nothing but churn the heat.

"What," answered Rebekah without looking up from the document she was working on, "you got air-conditioning in the 3rd Precinct Station, do yah? What a swell. I thought you'd be used to this by now."

Hill grinned as he scrutinized the not unattractive woman of thirty-five years sitting across from him. Her slightly severe features would prevent her from being described by men as pretty. Other men: not him.

Rebekah wore her dark brown hair swept back and tied in a knot at the back of her head, and her piercing green eyes matched Hill's own in intensity, though not in color. Another thing that kept her from looking as attractive as she might otherwise be came from her deliberate desire and effort to maintain the utmost of professional appearances at all times: minimal make-up, usually gray or black business suit dresses, shoes with relatively low heels.

It was no different for today. He loved her anyway.

At thirty-eight years of age, Hill knew that he wasn't exactly Clark Gable either, although his 5'10" frame carried 170 pounds of lean muscle and he wasn't exactly butt ugly. He wore his dirty blond hair slightly long for the day, slicked back from his forehead and creeping just a bit over his ears and the back of his collar.

His eyes were brown, large and intense, becoming even more so when he was agitated or angry; his ears stuck out slightly from his head, and his square jaw jutted out and tapered to a prominent, cleft chin.

Rebekah looked up.

"But, then, again, Jack, I see the police department can't even afford uniforms for its detectives. You could at least wear a tie, sweetheart."

Rebekah looked back down.

Hill said, "Touche."

As a detective, he wasn't required to wear a uniform, except for formal occasions, and preferred what he happened to be wearing: a blue, short sleeved shirt with a pocket over his left breast, and khakis. The pocket was for his ever-present open package of Lucky Strike cigarettes, one of which he now lit with a Zippo lighter he carried in his front, right, pants pocket. He seldom sported a hat. Even the light sport coat he wore was primarily to hide from sight the revolver he carried in a shoulder holster.

Rebekah looked up again, her eyes weary from overwork.

"And get your clodhoppers off of my desk," she said. "Show the respect deserved by the first female Assistant District Attorney in America, mister."

"Yes, mommy." He looked around her plain office for a moment before finishing his thought. "Not much of an office to respect compared to the D.A.'s digs. What, about a third the size? And where's your secretary, anyway?"

"It may not be much for now, but I'll be in the D.A.'s office before you know it," Rebekah smiled and closed the file in front of her. "Then it's the office of the Attorney General of Michigan for me, and finally Attorney General of the United States."

"Yeah, yeah, yeah; I've heard it all before," Hill said, continuing the banter that partially defined their relationship. He looked at his wrist watch. "It's about 7:30 p.m. How about you knock off 'early' for a change, dump this dive, and we go catch a quick bite and some Jazz at Baker's Keyboard Lounge. Then take in the movie at the Fox. I hear they're showing *Gold Diggers of 1935*."

Rebekah dropped her ink pen on the stack of legal documents, pushed her chair back from her desk and stood up, stretching her arms over her head. As she stepped around the desk, she picked up her purse from a chair next to the wall nearest her.

"Sorry, lover, but I'll have to take a rain check. I'm beat. But I will let you walk a lady out."

"Really?" Hill responded as he dropped his legs from her desk to the floor. "Where is she?"

"Just when I had hope for you, you have to go say something like a troglodyte again," she quipped, stopped by his side, and wrapped both hands around his left bicep. "Get up, old man, and walk me down the hall before I forget I'm a lady and kick your butt."

Hill laughed and stood up.

"Does a lady keep her love affair with a handsome, rugged, police lieutenant a secret just because it might be a potential conflict of interest and all? Inquiring minds want to know."

Rebekah slapped him on his butt.

"Get moving, big boy, out the door and down the hall. Ladies don't kiss and tell until there's a ring on their pinkie. Besides, a little mystery adds some spice to an otherwise boring relationship with a cheap, over-the-hill flatfoot."

As they began their walk down the long hallway of the massive Detroit Courthouse that faced the large plaza named Campus Martius between the Grand Circus Park and the river, Hill adjusted his long stride to match Rebekah's smaller steps, and playfully wrapped his arm around the small of her back. She shoved it away.

"What part of mystery do you not understand, Jack? Someone might see us."

"Welllll, I know it's no mystery that we share our uncompromising attitude towards the scum you generously call criminals. We both believe a man is guilty until proven innocent rather than the other way around. Isn't that enough to base a love affair on, buttercup?"

"What attitude? I'm neither that cynical about my fellow human beings nor that inflexible in the administration of the law, Jack."

"Right. Your hard-headed attitude about crime and criminals coupled with that passion that you carry over from your work into your personal life is what attracted me to you in the first place. But, have it your way. I'll change the subject for the sake of peace on the home front. Tell me – were you this tough as a little girl, Assistant D. A. Nixon?"

"I was an only child. My mom died when I was only three. After that, I was raised mostly by nannies and servants, and grew up trying to win the affection of a father who always seemed more interested in making money and becoming a Judge on the Supreme Court of Michigan than in playing mumbly-peg with his little freckle-faced daughter."

"Tell me more," the detective said softly, realizing he had inadvertently opened a door the woman usually kept tightly latched.

"So I decided to win him over with my achievements, instead," she continued. "That was what drove me to pursue the same career in law that he had. Unfortunately, my pursuit of a 'man's' life and career instead of the role of wife and mother simply put even more space between us."

"Obviously, that didn't stop you – which makes you just as stubborn as I am."

"Apparently. Rather than discouraging me, his disapproval of my goals and the disapproval I got from most other men--including you--just served as incentive for me to strive even harder to succeed as a prosecuting attorney.

"That led me to leave Detroit and take a job in Chicago, where I worked on an organized crime task force. When I was offered this job back in Detroit, it didn't take much to convince me to take it.

"And voila – here I am! Take me or leave me. Anything else you want to know, detective?"

"Just one...the date you'll marry me," Hill said earnestly.

"You've proven your point to your old man, Rebekah. Now it's time to start thinking about yourself; about that wife and mother job instead of this nonsense with the law."

Rebekah stopped so abruptly that Hill walked past her by several feet. He turned. The fire in her eyes was matched only by the set of her jaw. Without saying a word, she pushed past him to the exit, shoved the door open, and walked through it, glancing back only briefly to see if the detective was following her.

"Wait!" Hill yelled and was at and through the door even before it could swing back closed. In less than a half dozen heartbeats, he had grabbed, stopped, and turned her around to face him at the top of the steps that lead to the street.

"Let...me...go," she said in a whisper that chilled him to the bone. "I've told you at least a dozen times that I will not quit this job. You neither understand nor care what sacrifices I've had to make to get here, or how much harder than a man I had to work to get where I am and to stay there."

His own blood now racing hot through his veins, and knowing it would set her off, Hill verbally lit her fuse.

"Sure, sure. You think you worked any harder than all those lawyers who *didn't* have a father who's a retired Supreme Court judge?"

He regretted the words the instant they left his mouth. He cringed at the sight of both the anger and the hurt he saw them bring to her flashing eyes.

"I never once asked for or got any help from him," Rebekah said through clenched teeth, "or any special treatment from anyone else in getting where I am today." She jerked her arm free.

A peal of thunder and a fat drop of rain on her cheek drew her attention to the gray clouds sluggishly roiling across the sky.

"Oh, great! It looks like a storm is coming up. As if you weren't enough to spoil an otherwise nice day. You needn't stop by to see me or call me for the next few days, Lt. Hill. I'll be taking depositions, gearing up for the Giamatti trial, preparing briefs, speaking to--oh!"

The impact on her right shoulder from behind spun her around. Hill seized her left arm to steady her as an obviously preoccupied man took several steps past them down the stairs before stopping.

He turned to look back at Rebekah and both froze for an instant.

"Kirby King!" the lady D.A. hissed.

As trained, Hill instinctively memorized the black man's broad nose, full lips, and hair that was cut so close to his head as to almost make it appear clean-shaven. Hill noted that the man was short; probably no taller than 5'7." But the thick, muscular neck that was almost too big for his shirt collar, coupled with the chest, arms, and legs of a weight-lifter or boxer made him look more ominous.

"You two know each other?" Hill asked Rebekah.

"I'd say we do. This is Kirby King, Jack. Mr. King's was the first case I handled in the D. A.'s office here-- and I won, getting him convicted of assault with intent to kill a few years ago."

"Railroaded me is what she means," King snapped with a booming voice that seemed too deep for a man so small in stature. "And don't think I've forgot, neither."

"That sounds a lot like a threat, pal," Hill growled menacingly. "What are you doing here, anyway?"

"Not that it's any of your damn business, mister, but I just got my final release from my parole officer."

King continued to stare balefully at Rebekah a moment longer, turned abruptly and stalked away down the steps to the street as she and Hill watched him.

"Nice fellah," the detective said sarcastically. Then he turned his attention back to the woman, while making a mental note to further check out this King character.

"So," he said, grinning boyishly, "what time can I pick you up for lunch tomorrow?"

"Don't try to push me into a corner, Jack," she snapped, obviously still angry.

She spun on her heels and began to leave, only to be stopped short when Hill grabbed her arm and jerked her roughly back around.

"And don't you ever walk away from me like that!" he warned. She saw the menacing look in his intense eyes, but was un-intimidated by it. She'd seen it before.

"You're hurting me, Jack," she told him, but her words didn't seem to register.

With a sound like a hissing wildcat, Rebekah pulled free from Hill's grip and, never looking back, stomped down the steps. A second peal of thunder rolled overhead, and the spattering of rain increased as the detective watched her go. As quickly as it had erupted, his anger now faded, and he shrugged.

"Women," he muttered.

CHAPTER THREE

The storm rolling in across Lake St. Clair had intensified into winds like fists and a downpour of heavy rain as Rebekah Nixon pulled her new Buick Super 61 into the dry and welcoming parking garage next door to the Lee Crest Apartments at 8711 2nd Avenue.

She lived on its seventh floor. As she carefully pulled her motor car into a parking space between a '34 Ford Coupe and a '32 Packard 1104 Roadster, the Assistant D.A. sighed with relief. The last thing she needed to ruin a not-unusual and productive twelve-hour work day was damage to her father's 'housewarming' gift for returning to Detroit.

At this hour, the parking garage was nearly full, leaving her to park some distance from the apartment's entrance.

A more upscale place would have come with her own personal parking space. But "upscale" and "Assistant D.A.'s salary" didn't go together. The gift of the car had been more than she'd wanted from her father; she adamantly refused to let him pay the difference in the rent to put her in more luxurious surroundings.

A heavy peal of thunder reverberated in the garage as she turned the Buick's lights out and opened its door.

Nixon fumbled for a moment with the many keys on her key ring as she also juggled her purse and her briefcase, then slipped the appropriate key into the lock. The task was made even more difficult by the almost complete lack of lighting in the garage.

She was totally off guard when the man slammed against her back, throwing her up against the Buick as his left arm whipped around her neck.

He jerked her backwards and slightly off of her feet.

She gagged. One of her shoes fell off.

Her keys clattered to the concrete floor.

A powerful, gloved hand clamped over her mouth, stifling her screams.

Hot and wet, he pressed his left cheek against her right cheek. Her eyes were wide with terror and wet with tears.

"Don't struggle, bitch," he hissed in her ear, "and we'll both enjoy this."

Frantic, Rebekah struggled against his smothering grip. As his fingers momentarily slipped down from her mouth, she managed to maintain her composure enough to inhale the air to gasp, "Don't do this...please."

The lights flickered in the parking garage.

Her assailant violently jerked her back and up again, taking two steps back from the Buick, strangling any additional word from her by pressing his left arm more tightly around her throat.

A peal of thunder reverberated in the garage as he dropped his right hand and began to run it up the back of her suit jacket. The thug jerked her blouse free from the waistband of her skirt.

Rebekah's struggles intensified as she tried to snatch his arm from her throat with her hands even as she wildly flailed her legs in a vain attempt to kick him. She fought to suck enough air through her nostrils to prevent fainting.

She felt his right hand, holding something flat and colder than her flesh; begin to crawl up her back beneath her blouse.

It was the blade of a knife.

She kicked again. Thunder grumbled.

"Quit struggling," he warned.

The blade slipped under the catch of her bra. She kicked harder, a scream dying in her throat. The blade jerked up and back, cutting her bra strap and a slit in the back of her blouse. Instinctively, her hands cupped her breasts to keep her bra from falling down beneath her blouse. She began to sob. Her body sagged as all the fight in her seemed to disappear.

But then she flung her right leg as far out in front of her as possible and kicked back hard. The thug grunted in pain, dropping his knife. His left arm fell away from her throat and he doubled over, clutching his shin.

The lights blinked out in the parking lot, plunging the garage into near total darkness.

Sobbing, Rebekah ran, hobbled slightly by her missing shoe. She kicked off its mate.

Thunder crashed. Then, at first limping, then gaining speed with each moment, her assailant ran after her.

Rebekah raced toward the exit from the parking garage, and as she ran she opened her mouth to scream for help.

The thug tackled her before she reached the exit, knocking her face first, onto the cement floor.

Straddling her back, he sank his right hand into her hair. He lifted up her head and slammed her face into the concrete floor. Stars danced in front of the woman's eyes. Lightning crashed, partially illuminating the garage.

He jerked her head up and back, then slammed her face into the concrete again. Her body went limp under him. He jerked Rebekah's head up and back and slammed her face yet a third time into the floor. Its gray surface was spattered with overlapping splashes of red.

Blood bubbled in her nostrils; her nose was broken. Her left eye was swollen nearly shut, blood filling the socket and spilling down her face; her right cheek was bruised purple, and her lower lip was split and bleeding.

Rough hands tore at her skirt, and she felt the full weight of the man fall atop her.

Gasping for breath, her attacker whispered in her ear, "*Now...only one... of us....will enjoy...this.*"

"No," she pled weakly, choking on vomit and her own blood. "You don't have to do this…please."

Mercifully, shock had rendered Rebekah Nixon insensate by the time her animalistic attacker finished his dirty business and rose up off her.

Still lying face down on the floor, she couldn't see as he pulled a snub-nosed .38 Smith and Wesson from his jacket pocket.

She probably never felt either of the two slugs he coldly fired into the back of her head.

Certainly never heard the sadistic giggle that issued from her killer's mouth as he calmly strode out of the parking garage and into the night.

CHAPTER FOUR

The anticipated misery was palpable as the two men slowly walked down the sterile corridor of the county morgue.

Supporting his massive bulk with the help of a cane in his beefy right hand, Justice Malcolm Nixon walked shoulder to shoulder with Lt. Hill; the old man's head hung low above his chest.

The seventy-two year old retired State Supreme Court Justice wore his trademark black suit with an antiquated, short cape over his shoulders, and a broad-brimmed black hat.

His salt and pepper beard was trimmed to a blunt point four inches below his chin. Despite his age, his eyes were penetrating, bearing the weight of both exceptional wisdom and tragedy.

As they walked, Hill raised his arm to lay it across Nixon's shoulders, but found he could not physically express that intimate a compassion to a man who had amassed an enormous fortune while wielding a political power and knowledge of Michigan law unequalled by any living man in the state. He patted the judge's shoulder instead, and let his arm drop.

"Again, sir, you don't have to do this. She has already been identified."

"Lieutenant, the she you refer to was the love of my life, second only to my dear wife. This is the little girl I held in my arms as a baby, escorted her to her graduation from High School and University, the little girl who cried on my shoulder when she fell off her skates and skinned her knee; who came to me for solace the first time her heart was broken by a boy; whose laughter brought joy to my life, and whose every accomplishment made me burst with pride."

The old man paused in his verbose monologue.

"I'm sorry. I've said too much. Too many years on the bench. Thank you for your concern, detective. But this isn't exactly my first trip down these gloomy halls, although it will most likely be my last. You are correct in that I don't have to do this; I want to do it. In fact, there's nothing in the world you or anybody else could do to stop me."

"Of course. Of course. I didn't mean to imply…"

"I think we're here," Nixon said and stopped in front of a door on his left side.

The police detective opened the door and they both entered a room barely larger than one of the rich man's closets.

The room was lit by one, low-wattage light bulb in the ceiling. The upper half of the wall to their left had been replaced by a large sheet of plate glass. Behind that window, a table stood in the middle of a room almost as small as the one where the detective and the judge were.

That room was well lit. A human body on the table gave its outline to the white sheet that covered it. Behind the table stood a man in a white smock with his hands crossed in front of him.

They always changed into white smocks for a viewing.

"Judge Nixon, we can still leave…"

"Do it, detective," said Nixon with a dismissive wave of his hand, in a voice that allowed no room for dissent. The judge removed his hat.

Hill nodded to the man standing behind the table.

The Medical Examiner bent and gently pulled the sheet back from the unnaturally waxen face of Rebekah Nixon and draped it across her bare shoulders.

Her father looked away, more stricken by the sight than he could have imagined.

"I want you to know, sir," Hill told him, "that I will personally see to it that every effort is made to apprehend the bastard who did this."

"Thank you, son," said the old judge with his back to both Jack and the window.

Nixon turned to face Jack again, and placed a beefy hand on the police detective's shoulder.

"And I will hold you to that promise. Do whatever you have to do to find him. It won't bring my daughter back, but I still want to see that man dead."

He put his hat back on his head.

"I'll do everything possible under the law to make sure that happens," Hill assured him.

"To hell with the law, young man. I want *justice*."

Seeming now to be leaning even more heavily on his cane for support, Judge Nixon moved to leave the morgue.

"I know it isn't much," Jack said as he opened the door for the older man, "but at least the worst is over, sir."

Oh?" asked Nixon. "You're still a relatively young man, detective, and probably somewhat ignorant of all of the unexpected twists and turns life can take. Things can always get worse."

"I know," the aged judge said, lightly tapping the side of his head. "Just last week, my doctor informed me that I have an inoperable tumor in my brain."

+++

"You wanted to see me, Chief?" said Michael Yellowstone as he rapped on the doorjamb of Chief of Detectives John Harper's office. The massive man behind an equally massive desk looked up from his work and waved him inside.

"Come in, Yellowstone, and close the door behind you," Harper said.

"Uh-oh; what did I do now?"

"Nothing," answered Harper. "Nothing yet. That's why I wanted to talk to you. Please, sit down."

Yellowstone dropped easily into a chair opposite the chief, barely noticing the light, popping sound from his abused knees; he'd grown used to it in the years since he'd left Hollywood and stunt work behind him.

Harper sat behind this large desk in the 3rd Precinct Station because his forty years on the force had earned him that rank and the right to do so. The size of the chair behind that desk was dictated by the size of the man who sat in it.

Nevertheless, the twenty years of administrative work and inactivity that had caused once powerful muscles to degenerate into little more than suet had done nothing to diminish his unquestioned authority.

"Just because I'm stuck in this office most of the time doesn't mean I don't see what goes on out in the squad room," Harper said, getting straight to the point.

"And what I see is that you and Lt. Hill don't seem to be warming up to each other. Is that about the size of it?"

Yellowstone squirmed uncomfortably in his chair before responding.

"I wouldn't put it that way, chief."

"Well, how would you put it?"

"We've only been partnered up for a few weeks now," Yellowstone replied. "The lieutenant just needs a little more time to break in his new sidekick, that's all. Nothin' for you to worry about."

"I hope you're right, sidekick. You won't find a better cop than Jack Hill; you can learn a lot from him."

"I 'spect that's right, sir."

"Maybe it would help if you knew a little more about the man; things he won't bother to tell you himself."

"I'm all ears, chief. Like folks back home say: you learn more by listenin' than by talkin'."

"They say that, do they? Then shut up and listen," Harper snapped.

"Yessir."

"Jack Hill came up the hard way, having to scratch and claw for everything he ever got, while still managing to keep his nose clean.

"He wasn't much more than a boy when he got a job on the docks of the Detroit River, loading barges. In case you don't know, that's the kind of back-breaking work that'll leave a man old before his time."

"Breaking horses in Oklahoma wasn't no walk in the park either," Yellowstone declared.

"I suppose not," Harper conceded. "But we're not talking about you now, detective. We're talking about Jack Hill."

"Yessir."

"He was one of the first kids from around here to volunteer when we jumped into the Great War. Fought with distinction in France and Belgium; had a medal pinned on him by 'Blackjack' Pershing himself. Still carries a piece of shrapnel in his leg to this day."

"That says a lot about him," Yellowstone observed.

"Damned straight it does. But you won't hear any of that from him.

When he got home, he joined the force. Started out walking a beat in uniform and got where he is today by slow, hard work.

"He's a good cop, Michael. But he might resent you a little."

"Why's that, chief?"

"Lots of reasons. Your education, for one; Jack barely made it through high school. The fact that you're not from Detroit; you may be a little too 'Hollywood' for his tastes. And because you made detective so fast."

"There's nothing I can do to change any of that, sir."

"I'm not asking you to. I'm just telling you that Jack Hill is a no-nonsense kind of guy, with very traditional values and ways of doing things. Be aware that he's seen it all in his years as a cop, and he has no sympathy for lawbreakers.

"But he's one of the best men I've got. He should be: I trained him myself. I think you could also become one of the best, Michael, given time.

"That's why I put the two of you together. It's why I've given you the Rebekah Nixon case. We can't blow this one; it's too important. So if you and Hill can't work together, I need to know it – and I need to know it damn quick. You got me?"

"Yessir."

"Good. Now get back to work. And just remember: don't ever squat with your spurs on."

"Beg pardon?" Yellowstone asked, puzzled.

"Just showing you I can be homespun too, son. But homespun alone don't get it done." Harper returned his attention to the stack on reports sitting before him on his desk.

"You're dismissed, detective."

CHAPTER FIVE

"Why did I do to deserve this?" Lt. Hill muttered to himself. It was a rhetorical question.

With naked resignation and with the heels of his brogan's resting on the edge of his desk, Hill watched as his new partner, Detective Michael Yellowstone, wound his way through the random chaos of the 3rd Precinct squad room.

Yellowstone wore the same mundane clothing as most of the men in the Precinct…jeans or slacks, a short or long sleeved shirt, leather shoes. Besides a denim jacket, the only distinctive feature about his apparel swung in little arcs at his throat: a string tie with what resembled a circular spider's web fashioned in silver as its slide.

Yellowstone had joined the 3rd Precinct six months earlier, and had been assigned over Jack Hill's objections as his partner only three weeks ago. But it had already proven, at least for Hill, to be something less than a marriage made in heaven.

Yellowstone tipped the rim of an imaginary hat as he passed each of his fellow police officers.

To Hill, that was just one more irritating proof that Yellowstone was still wet behind the ears and, therefore, not worthy to be anyone's partner yet.

The product of a purely blue-collar upbringing, Hill would much rather have had a regular guy with street smarts guarding his back than a guy with too much book smarts.

Almost the only aspect of this new partnership that Hill did enjoy was hearing the racy stories of Hollywood actors, directors, and actresses that Yellowstone gladly told him when things were running a bit slow in the Precinct…which wasn't often.

"Good morning, sunshine," said Yellowstone, smiling as he sat down in his chair; the fronts of their desks had been shoved together to save space: yet another thing Hill found to be irritating.

"What's good about it?" Hill groused, making no effort to drop his legs from a desk cluttered with both finished and unfinished paperwork.

"I want you to know," said Yellowstone, "what a pleasure you make it to come in to work every mornin', just knowin' you'll be waitin' for me with a smile on your face and a song in your heart."

Assuming the cowboy role Hill expected of him, Yellowstone added, "It's sort of like walkin' through a pasture full of cow patties. You walk carefully, while being thankful at the same time you haven't run into the bull that left 'em."

"I think you're pretty to, cowboy." Hill dropped his feet off the desktop and leaned forward.

"Let me ask you something, Hollywood. Powlowski downstairs told me he read in the *Police Gazette* that Clara Bow once serviced the whole UCLA football team. Is that true?"

"Nah," Yellowstone scoffed. "That's just your typical yellow rag journalism." Then he winked.

"It wasn't the *whole* team."

Hill gave out a short, barking laugh. This new partner of his might not be so bad after all.

"Something else I've been meaning to ask you," he said, pointing a finger at Yellowstone. "What's that thing you wear almost every day around your neck?"

Yellowstone smiled as he touched the silver metal circle at his throat.

"It's a string tie. And the silver slide is a metal replica of a *dreamcatcher*. My grandfather made it with his own two hands. It's sort of a family heirloom, and you're right; I do wear it almost every day."

"A dreamcatcher, eh? What's that mean, exactly?"

"According to Indian legend," the Osage detective explained, "its strands will allow good dreams to come through to you – while catching the potential nightmares and keepin' 'em from disturbing your sleep."

"Do you believe that?" Hill asked skeptically.

"Doesn't matter if I do or not; my grandfather and the other old timers did." As he was wont to do when lost in thought, Yellowstone was stroking the polished silver ornament.

"I keep it on me for luck. And to remind me of home and family."

"Well while you were dreaming in bed this morning, I've been poring over the preliminary forensic report on the Rebekah Nixon murder," Hill announced, growing suddenly serious.

"And...?" said Yellowstone, leaning over the top of his desk.

"Nothing. Not a damn clue of any substance," said Hill with an intensity that caught Yellowstone by surprise. "No one else was in the parking garage at the time of the assault and murder. I wish that proved it was planned, but the murderer may have just been lucky.

"The forensic team didn't find her purse, so it could have started as just a robbery, then gone bad."

"But you don't think so," Yellowstone interjected.

"No," Hill growled. "My gut says different. There were no fingerprints, so the murderer must have been wearing gloves. Only Rebekah's...only Miss Nixon's blood was found at the spot where she was raped and shot. We don't know if he intended to kill her all along, or only did so in a rage because she resisted.

"The shoe we found at her car indicates she *did* resist, and at least briefly escaped. The contusions on her face...the deep bruise to her cheek, her broken nose, and split lip..." The hardened detective's voice quivered and broke slightly, to Yellowstone's surprise. A dark cloud seemed to descend over Hill's face, but it just as quickly dissipated.

"The silver slide is a metal replica of a *dreamcatcher.*"

"The damage to her face would indicate the bastard is a sadist as well as a rapist and murderer. It's almost certain she was running to the entrance of the parking garage when the bastard brought her down.

"No strands of hair were recovered that didn't belong to the victim. The murdering maggot who did this was thorough; he put two slugs in her. They've been retrieved, and Ballistics is testing them now. They'll let us know what they find."

"This one seems to be really getting to you, Jack," Yellowstone observed. "Did you know this woman?"

Hill paused for a moment, his eyes narrowing and his teeth biting down on his lower lip.

"Just in my role as a policeman called to testify in some of her cases," he finally said in clipped tones.

"Well then, I think I may make your day, partner. The reason I'm in late is I've been canvassing the residents in and around the apartment building where Miss Nixon lived with some of our uniforms, and I think one of the guys has come up with our first piece of evidence, a possible eyewitness."

"Hot damn!" Hill exclaimed. "What have you got, Yellowstone?"

"An older woman has come forward. She actually lives a block away, but was out walking her dog across the street from the victim's apartment, at about the time we think the murder occurred. This woman didn't witness the crime, but she did see a man walking away from the scene."

Hill shot straight up from his chair to his feet.

"Then what are we waiting for? Where is she?"

"She's in interrogation room number..."

Hill was gone before Yellowstone could finish the sentence.

+++

"Mrs. Tyree, this is Lt. Jack Hill," said Yellowstone with an introductory flourish of his right hand. "Lieutenant, this is Elvira Tyree."

"Mrs. Tyree," said Hill, as he took a seat in a metal folding chair on the opposite side of the plain metal table where the woman sat, her hands folded primly in her lap.

It was an expensive lap. The middle-aged woman was dressed in a stylish and obviously well tailored grey suit, and wore a black, pill-box hat pinned to what was doubtless artificially platinum blonde hair, and white gloves. She also wore thick, black-rimmed glasses. It was obvious that the woman had once been pretty. She was now what men kindly called handsome.

"Thank you so much for coming in today," Hill continued as Yellowstone seated himself next to Mrs. Tyree. "We have a few questions to ask. Your answers could go a long way toward helping us solve this terrible crime, so take your time before answering. We're in no hurry."

Elvira Tyree raised her gloved right hand and pointed her index finger at the window set in half of the wall opposite her.

"That's a one-way mirror, isn't it?" she said, "and someone sitting behind it is watching us and listening through a hidden intercom."

Hill looked at Yellowstone, who shrugged his ignorance with his shoulders.

"Yes, it is, Mrs. Tyree," Hill grudgingly answered. "How did you know that?"

"I read *Black Mask* magazine," she answered with self-satisfaction. "I just love murder mysteries, you know."

"That's nice to hear, ma'am," Yellowstone interjected. "We do that so a third person can verify what's said in here."

"I know, I know. I'm glad to help," said Mrs. Tyree. "I just hate to see something awful like this happen in our neighborhood. I moved there to get away from this kind of horrible thing after my husband died. It's so important what part of town one lives in, you know.

"It was shortly before eight, I think; it was raining fairly hard by the time Gigi and I drew near the Lee Crest. Thank goodness I had a stout umbrella."

"Who's Gigi?" Hill asked.

"My poodle. We were just about to turn back and head for home when I saw a man coming out of the Lee Crest's parking garage."

"Anything unusual about him?"

"Well, yes," she said, eyeing Hill almost suspiciously. "He was *walking* out of the garage …not driving."

"Very observant," Yellowstone said in soothing tones. "Did you get a clear look at him?"

"Not very, I'm afraid. It was dark and rainy, after all. And I was on the opposite side of the street."

"Anything you can tell us will be helpful."

"I'll try." The woman closed her eyes for a moment, as though trying to visualize the scene once again.

"I think he was about medium height; not much taller than me. He wore a hat and coat. I think his hands were in the pockets of his jacket, and he kept his head down as he stepped into the rain."

"So you didn't see his face?"

"Not clearly, no. Just a glimpse during a flash of lightning. But I think he may have been a colored man."

At that, Yellowstone saw Hill grow tense and move about. The lieutenant leaned toward Mrs. Tyree.

"Had you ever seen him hanging around the Lee Crest apartments before, Mrs. Tyree?" pressed Hill.

"No, I don't think so. We don't see many colored people in our neighborhood. That's one reason why I moved there. And that's why I noticed him like I did."

"May I ask a favor of you, ma'am?" said Yellowstone. "Could you take your glasses off for me?"

"For heaven's sake, why?"

"It's just a little test that detectives make, like in the magazines, ma'am."

Reluctantly and with suspicion clearly showing on her face, she removed her glasses.

"Thank you, ma'am. Now, could you look at Lt. Hill and describe him for me?"

"Whatever for?" the woman asked as she squinted at Hill.

"Please? Just pretend I'm the Continental Op."

"Well. He has a little cleft in his chin, and nice eyes."

"What about his hair? And his eyes; what color are they?" "Not long or short. Kind of blond hair, I think, or maybe grey. I can't tell the color of his eyes in this light."

"Thank you, Mrs. Tyree," said Yellowstone. "You may put your glasses back on." Once she did so, he asked, "After the man walked away, did you see the body of the victim lying on the floor of the parking garage?"

'No. No, I didn't, thank God. It was very dark in the garage; the lights had gone out and I didn't even know there had been a crime committed until I heard about it on the radio."

"Do you think you could identify this man who walked out of the garage if you saw him again, Mrs. Tyree?" asked Yellowstone.

"I don't know," she said. "To be honest, colored people all seem to look alike to me."

Yellowstone looked at Hill. Hill seemed to be looking at something Yellowstone couldn't see.

"That's all for now," Yellowstone said to Mrs. Tyree. "We thank you so much for your time. We are indebted to you."

"I can leave now?"

"Please do," said Hill.

"Oh, good! I just hate to miss *Dick Tracy* on the radio!"

+++

With his hands shoved in his pants pockets, Yellowstone watched Hill pace back and forth in the interrogation room for a moment. He could tell his partner was both deep in thought and somewhat agitated. When the moment seemed opportune, he spoke.

"I'm not sure, now, how good a witness she is, Jack. She wears some fairly thick eyeglasses, it was dark in the garage, and she only saw him for a few seconds. And while she doesn't appear to be inordinately bigoted, she did say that all black men look alike."

"She told me all I need to hear to be certain who the culprit is, Hollywood."

Hill proceeded to tell Yellowstone, in truncated form, of his and Rebekah Nixon's tense encounter with Kirby King on the courthouse steps; and of the implied threat the ex-con had made against her.

Yellowstone remained silent after his partner finished his narrative. It seemed clear to him that Hill had left out a few details in the telling, and he wondered why.

"What?" Hill snapped perceiving skepticism in Yellowstone's expression.

"Nothin'," Yellowstone said softly. "That just seems like a mighty small nail to try to hang our hat on, that's all."

"In the big city, we call it motive, Hollywood," the lieutenant snarled. "It'll be enough to get an arrest warrant, and it'll be enough to hang the little bastard from." He was already heading for the door of the interrogation room.

"Trust me; Kirby King is our man!"

CHAPTER SIX

Michael Yellowstone stared out of his window in the back seat of the unmarked, '33 Chevrolet police car as it pulled over to the curb and parked on Michigan Avenue between Washington Boulevard and Fifth Street.

The street was littered with trash, tufts of grass grew in the cracks in the sidewalk, and the two and three-story buildings were dirty and shoddy. The burned out neon letters on the small sign above the front door of their destination hung perpendicular to the wall and read: Livin..stone Apts.

"When his parole officer said King lived in Detroit's cesspool, he wasn't kiddin'," Yellowstone said as he began to open the Chevy's door. "This is one tough part of town. We don't have anythin' like this in Stroud, Oklahoma."

"So what?" snapped Hill. "You don't have indoor plumbing in Stroud, either." He slapped the back of the bench seat in front of him to grab the attention of the two uniformed policemen in the front seat of the unmarked patrol car. "Listen up. I don't want any grandstanding from anyone. That especially means you, Hollywood. No handstands. No back flips. No swinging from a light fixture. This isn't a movie. Got it?"

"Got it," said all three of the other officers.

"But don't forget this man is a convicted felon. He has a history of violence and is probably armed. At the first sign of trouble...don't hesitate to put him down."

Yellowstone flinched slightly.

"You've all got his description," Hill said. "Let's go!"

As the two uniformed policemen and the two detectives in street clothes tumbled out of the car, a handful of people on the sidewalk or in the entrance of shops doubled their speed, turned their heads away, or ducked back into a doorway.

Guns drawn, they were up the stairs, then in and through the front door of the Livingstone and moving quickly but quietly down the hallway of its first floor in ten heartbeats before Hill raised his hand, signaling that they had reached Kirby King's apartment.

Hill rapped his knuckles on the door.

"Police!" he barked. "Open up!"

There was no answer.

Hill pounded harder on the door. "Open up, King!"

Still no answer.

"Screw this!" said Hill and, stepping back and raising his right leg, kicked the door open. It swung back, striking the interior wall of the apartment's living room, then bounced forward. Hill slapped the door out of the way as he stepped into the apartment.

There was little to see: the flophouse "apartment" consisted of but a single room. All eyes were quickly drawn to the rear of the room, where a short black man stood frantically trying to make his way out a grimy window that barely opened halfway.

"Get away from the window, King!" Hill ordered. "It's over!"

His back still to the policemen, Kirby King froze in place and yelled, "Don't shoot! I got no gun!"

"Turn around real slow like, with your hands in the air," snarled Hill. "Now!"

The black man took several steps back from the window sill and then turned to face the policemen, both of his arms raised above his head. His hands were empty.

Hill nodded at Yellowstone, who holstered his pistol and quickly moved behind King. Then Yellowstone jerked the man's arms down and behind his back.

"Going on a little picnic?" snarled Hill as Yellowstone handcuffed King's wrists.

"I'm goin' nowhere," King replied. "And I ain't done nothin'!"

Yellowstone spun the ex-con around to face him.

"If you haven't done anything, then you don't have anything to worry about, Mr. King," he said.

"You go to hell, Mr. Policeman," King snapped. "This is about that bitch, Rebekah Nixon, ain't it?"

Hill took a lightning step to King's side and punched him in the mouth.

Yellowstone yelled, "Hill!" and placed a hand to his partner's chest, pushing him back.

"Back off, cowboy!" Hill yelled; but he made no further move against King.

"I knew this would happen," their prisoner muttered and spit blood. "I knew this would happen."

"I'll bet you did," Hill sneered. "Kirby King, you are under arrest for the murder of Rebekah Hill.

"Take this idiot down to the car," Hill commanded of the two uniformed policemen. "Don't bump his head against any doorjambs by accident. Yellowstone and I are going to take a little look around his digs to see if we can find anything like, say, a smoking gun."

As the two uniformed officers hustled King to and through the bedroom door, Hill began to pull out drawers and their contents from the only dresser in the room. His arms almost mechanical in their repetition, he discarded each useless article behind him on the floor.

"I don't think you really need to tear the place apart, Lieutenant," said Yellowstone from behind him. "After all, this King fellow is still innocent until proven guilty and this stuff is the little he even owns."

"Innocent my ass. Shut up and look."

"What, for maybe something like this?"

Hill spun around to see Yellowstone studying a scrap of paper he'd lifted from a small end table covered with little yellowing rectangles of newsprint.

"This one is about Rebekah Nixon."

Hill snatched the newspaper clipping from Yellowstone's hand. The story about Kirby King's trial was topped by a black and white photograph of a young Rebekah; the cutline read: *Rising Star in D.A.s Office, Rebekah Nixon.*

A red circle had been drawn around her face with a diagonal line drawn through it.

His hands partially full of clippings he'd taken from the end table, Hill said, "All of these clippings relate to King's earlier arrest and conviction. Yeah, he's innocent, all right."

Barely able to contain his rage, Lt. Hill barked, "Don't lose those, Hollywood. Each one is a nail in King's coffin."

Then he, with the help of a somewhat more methodical Yellowstone, finished tearing up King's room.

But they found no gun, smoking or otherwise.

+++

Hill and Yellowstone entered the main lobby of the police station to find a vortex of vultures...Hill's favorite term for Detroit reporters... wearing new holes in their cheap shoes as they paced the floor.

Hill surmised that every major newspaper and most of the radio stations in Detroit had sent one or more such vultures; five carried cameras. He didn't know how they knew, but it was obvious that the hacks had been camped out at the stationhouse since they had caught wind that a suspect had possibly been apprehended for the brutal murder of Rebekah Nixon.

He silently vowed that if and when he found the employee or cop who had leaked the news to the press, a head would roll.

The idea of facing a hailstorm of questions left the detective dark and scowling.

"Oh, look," said Yellowstone. He grinned and waved a hand. "This should be fun."

"Then they're all yours," said Hill, slapping his partner on the left shoulder blade. So saying, he turned on his heels and unceremoniously left the room the same way he had entered it.

The reporters swarmed Yellowstone in a churning mass of flailing elbows, a blizzard of questions, and flashing cameras. The Osage Indian raised his arms in welcoming surrender.

"Slow down," he grinned, "slow down. I'm Detective Michael Yellowstone, and I'll answer each and every one of your questions if you'll just ask them one at a time."

But Yellowstone's smile faded and his face blanched slightly as he caught sight of one particular reporter, the notorious Stacy Lord from Detroit's radio station, WXYZ. The poor technician charged with carrying her enormous and heavy recording equipment reminded the Osage of a mule more than a man.

The reporter was all of twenty-seven years old with striking good looks. Her long, auburn hair was rather wild and unruly and not her only attractive feature; she was slender and small-busted, with long, shapely legs.

Her well-defined cheekbones and full lips only added to her similarity to Diana, the Goddess of the Hunt in Greek lore, and Lord's green eyes seemed to sparkle with mischievous intelligence and driving ambition.

Yellowstone knew that Stacy had made quite a name for herself for hard-hitting and often provocative reporting for the prestigious station WXYZ, the radio station that first broadcast the adventures of *The Lone Ranger.*

He knew all this and more because he and Stacy were lovers. Strictly on the sly, so far. They were still trying each other on for size, as Stacy liked to say.

In the course of their intimate and secret moments together, the detective had even nicknamed her "Firecracker" because of her mercurial personality...and because of her passion as his clandestine lover.

"Jason Wolling. *Detroit News,*" one of the other reporters now said urgently. "Is the report true that a man has been arrested for the murder of Assistant District Attorney Rebekah Nixon?"

"Yes," said Yellowstone. "We have arrested, booked, and fingerprinted a suspect in the murder of the Assistant District Attorney." He didn't add the word "rape." No need to add to these hungry animals' feeding frenzy, he felt.

"What is the suspect's name?" asked a reporter from the *Detroit Free Press.*

"Now, you boys know I can't give that out yet," said Yellowstone. "It's still early in the investigation; too early to risk ruinin' a fella's reputation unnecessarily."

"His name's in the police blotter. He's Kirby King...and he's a black man."

There was an audible gasp as all eyes turned to Stacy Lord pointing a microphone at Yellowstone. "Isn't that right, detective?"

"Now, listen, guys," said Yellowstone, all trace of casual friendship gone from his face and his voice. "We don't need to start another race riot like they had down in Tulsa a few years back."

Then the conclave of reporters exploded apart like a drop of water on a hot grill, each eager to file his story.

"Crap," Yellowstone cursed under his breath.

"Will the D.A.'s office rescue itself from the investigation?" asked Stacy Lord as most of her competitors ran through a broken field of furniture and their fellow reporters struggling for the exit. "After all, she was one of their own."

A whimsical smile had returned to Yellowstone's face as he placed his hands on his hips and spread his legs to anchor his feet on the floor.

"I don't think so, miss...miss...?" he asked, pretending to forget her name. "With a breaking story like this, why aren't you hot on the heels of those other yahoos?"

"Because I already broadcast that story, a half hour ago," Stacy answered and winked.

CHAPTER SEVEN

"Coffee, boys," said Detective Sam Turner as he slid into the dimly lit, close and somewhat hot interrogation room carrying three paper cups of coffee on a makeshift tray made from the bottom of a cardboard box.

"Thanks, Sam," Yellowstone said without looking up from the open folder he carried as he paced back and forth. "Just put it on the table."

"Your wish is my command, Hollywood," said Turner as he set down the box before handing a cup to Hill. Turner noticed half-moons of sweat under the armpits of Hill's shirt.

Both sullen and with heads lowered, Lt. Hill and Kirby King were seated on two of four metal chairs at a small, metal table in a room otherwise devoid of furnishings or even a window. Turner sat down next to Hill.

"Now, as I was sayin'," Yellowstone resumed, still reading from the folder, "Your prison record, Mr. King, says, and I quote, 'Because of the effects of his imprisonment, he can be both volatile and violent'. The warden characterizes you as being 'an incorrigible troublemaker'."

"I don't kiss nobody's ass," said Kirby in a voice low, deep, and consciously controlled. His close-cropped hair glistened with sweat. "Not inside the Joint or out. So what?"

"So that's one more reason to think you're our man," Hill said. "Why'd you do it, boy? Why'd you kill Rebekah Nixon?"

King said nothing.

Hill suddenly slammed the table with the palm of his hand. Yellowstone saw King flinch almost imperceptibly but otherwise show no reaction.

"I know all about you, King," said Hill as Det. Turner pushed his chair back and stood up. He slowly walked over to stand behind King, his eyes never leaving the ex-con.

"You never left the Motor City until we sent you to the pen," continued Hill. "Yeah, I know all about you, King. You can't hide anything from us."

"Petty thefts, mostly," added Yellowstone, still reading from the file. "Took a couple of motorcars that weren't yours for joy rides when you were a teenager."

"You wanted to get things the easy way, didn't you, boy?" Turner said.

"I was young and stupid," said Kirby. "That don't make me no killer. I kept my nose clean ever since I got out. I ain't done nothin' wrong to nobody."

"Then why," demanded Turner, "did you try to run when we came to your apartment?"

"'Cause I learned to stay away from you bastard cops like the plague a long time ago. Nothin' good ever comes from it."

He looked up at Hill and Turner, and then at Yellowstone with a hatred born of long experience.

"C'mon, King," Hill pressed. "We know you did it."

"I told you, I didn't do nothin'. I ain't sorry the bitch is dead, but I never laid a hand on her."

"You did more than lay a hand on her, you twisted little freak," Hill barked, his fists clenching. "You raped her before you shot her!"

King jumped as if he had been jolted by a livewire. "What? No. No. I'd have gladly killed her, but not that." His eyes grew clouded. "Never that."

In response, Det. Turner savagely slapped King's right ear with the palm of his hand, eliciting a yell of pain.

"What the hell are you doin', Turner?" Yellowstone demanded.

"Yeah," intoned Hill without inflection. "What are you doin', Det. Turner?"

"Sorry, Hollywood," Turner said, and winked at Hill. "I guess I got a little carried away."

Lt. Hill extricated a seemingly new cigarette lighter from his right pants pocket and then patted his shirt pocket.

"Looks like I'm out of cigarettes, Yellowstone," he groused. "Would you mind going downstairs to the vending machine and spotting me afresh pack of Luckys?"

Suspiciously examining Turner, the Osage closed his folder and laid it on the table. "It's a bad habit you should kick, partner."

"Right. Just not today, okay?"

Yellowstone's left hand rose out of habit to stroke the dreamcatcher slide of his string tie. "Sure thing, buddy. I'll be right back."

So saying, he reluctantly turned on his heels and left the room.

Downstairs, Yellowstone put the coins in the vending machine's slot and bent at the waist as he searched the various little windows for Lucky Strike cigarettes.

The hands that suddenly and unexpectedly clapped around his eyes from behind were warm and soft.

"Quess who?" the voice without a visible body giggled.

Shaking himself free of the hands, Yellowstone spun around.

"It's my little firecracker! What are you doin' here?"

"You," said Stacy Lord, and, looking around and seeing they were alone, rose up on her toes and planted a kiss on Yellowstone's lips.

A little embarrassed, he also glanced around the room to make sure it was still empty.

"Seriously, Stacy, what are you doin' here? I thought you left."

"I figured you'd give me some real news, exclusive stuff, after they were gone, so I stuck around, big boy. So, spill! What evidence do you have on Kirby King?"

"I'd love to help, Stacy, but you already know I'm not going to feed you or anyone else any insider info on a case we're working until we're dead certain about the facts."

He pulled the knob above the displayed cigarettes that he wanted, and the desired pack fell into the retrieving bin.

"Aww, come on. That's no way to play nice! And since when did you take up smoking those awful things?" the reporter asked.

"I didn't. These are for a friend."

"Uh-huh, like you have any friends. That's what I used to tell my mother when she caught me smoking behind the garage."

"No kiddin', Stacy, honey. I really don't have time for this right now. We're in the middle of something. Tell you what. I'll make it up to you later. How about a ball game?"

"What kinda ball?"

Yellowstone grinned. "A baseball game. The Tigers are really hot this year."

"So am I, Hollywood, but not for baseball."

"Not...now," Yellowstone grinned, and slapped her on the butt. "Now get out of here."

"That's no way to treat a lady," she pouted, then smiled wickedly. "Lucky for you, cowboy...I'm no lady."

And so saying, Stacy bounced out of the room.

+++

Naked anger on his bronze face, Yellowstone stood in the door to the interrogation room, the package of cigarettes forgotten in his hand.

Kirby King was on the floor, doubled up and moaning in obvious pain. Detective Turner was standing over him; he wore a pair of brass knuckles on his clenched right hand.

King looked up at Yellowstone but said nothing. One of his eyes was beginning to swell shut, and he was bleeding from his mouth.

"What the hell's goin' on here?" Yellowstone demanded to know.

"He fell," Turner said smugly, a sneer curling one corner of his mouth up as he began to remove the knuckles from his hand.

"Where I come from," Yellowstone continued, restrained anger in every line of his face, "a man who likes to throw his weight around can expect to eventually be introduced to his own self to the business end of a two-by-four."

Sam Turner stopped removing the brass knuckles.

"Are you threatening me, cowboy?" he snarled.

"Nope. I'm making a promise, Det. Turner. You lay a hand on that boy again... *you'll* be the next one in handcuffs."

Turner took a step towards Yellowstone. Hill stepped between the two men.

"Stop it, both of you," Hill barked. "This won't get us anywhere. Yellowstone, I can make promises too. You won't see anything like this again. Right, Sam?"

"Whatever you say, Jack."

"Good. Then the matter's settled, and just in time too," said Yellowstone. "You'd better clean him up right quick. I just passed King's lawyer in the hall demanding to see his client."

"My what?" King muttered through his swollen lips.

CHAPTER EIGHT

"How was this man injured?" said Virgil Lowery, the hint of a soft Southern accent doing nothing to mask the fact that his was a demand more than a question.

Yellowstone's first impression of the forty-something black man standing in the doorway of the interrogation room was that he was a person of quiet dignity. He had the air of an educated man, along with a sprinkling of gray at his temples, and dressed nicely in an inexpensive but well-kept, pin-stripped suit topped by a stylish Fedora.

Such was not Hill's first impression. He'd encountered Lowery before, and knew him to be one of the shrewdest, toughest lawyers in Detroit.

"He fell," said Det. Turner, the smirk back on his face as he finally deigned to answer Lowery's query. "And just who the hell are you?"

Lowery took a step forward but was restrained by his slightly younger, shorter, but equally well dressed assistant, also a black man.

"I am Virgil Lowery," he said, and removed his hat. "I'm a lawyer hired by the Detroit branch of the National Association for the Advancement of Colored People, the NAACP, to represent Mr. Kirby King. This is my assistant, Mr. Marcus True."

"Mr. Lowery specializes in representing the poor and indigent of all colors," said True.

"That's mighty white of him," sneered Turner.

Neither Lowery nor True chose to react to this slur.

"I repeat my question," Lowery said instead. "What happened here?"

"I told you; he fell," Turner replied.

"I was speaking to my client," Lowery said coldly.

King, who had been sitting with his head sunk between his shoulders, now looked up at his lawyer, then at the cops surrounding him.

"...I fell," he said softly.

"I see. May we sit down?" asked Lowery.

Hill stood up from his chair at the desk opposite King and waved an invitation with his hand for Lowery to take his seat. Lowery did so, with his assistant sitting next to him. Both lawyers laid their hats on the metal table.

With his eyes never leaving his client, Lowery said: "Mr. King, I have found it useful to give a bit of information about myself when meeting new clients.

"I was born in Kentucky. My mother was freeborn, but my father spent the first five years of his life as a slave.

"He bore the sign of it all his life. One day a particularly vicious overseer had decided to display his prowess with the whip by using it to snap off the lobe of Daddy's left ear."

Yellowstone winced slightly at this. He noted that Lt. Hill seemed lost in his own thoughts, while Det. Turner's face bore an expression of sheer boredom.

"I was the first Negro to graduate from law school in the state of Michigan," Lowery continued with his narrative.

"The day I received my diploma, my daddy said to me, 'Now *you* hold the whip, boy'."

Det. Turner made a growling sound.

"But my whip is the law," Lowery went on, ignoring the detective, "and I use it well. As of now…I'll be using it for you."

Lowery leaned back slightly, only now looking again at the detectives.

"Now, I ask that you gentlemen leave so that I can speak alone with my client."

"Come on, fellas," said Yellowstone. "He's well within his rights in making that request."

The Osage detective opened the door. Reluctantly, Hill and Turner left the room with him following, closing the door behind him.

"Mr. King, let's get down to brass tacks, as they say," said Lowery at the sound of the door closing. "Did you rape the Assistant District Attorney, Rebekah Nixon?"

"No," said King, rubbing his split lip with the back of a muscular hand.

"Did you kill Rebekah Nixon?"

"I haven't done nothin' wrong," said King. "I swear to God, nothin'."

"I hope that's true, son" Lowery stated bluntly. "Because the press, the police and the public have already decided you're guilty."

King said nothing in reply.

+++

"Sit down, gentlemen," said Captain John Harper with the authority of a man who broached no dissent. "You to, Detective Turner."

"How are you, Chief Harper?" asked Yellowstone and Turner, almost in unison.

Hill said, "John."

Captain Harper did not respond.

Virgil Lowery was already seated, with his hands patiently crossed in his lap, on one of the two, cracked, ancient, brown leather sofas that stood to the right and left sides of Harper's desk. Nothing about him acknowledged the presence of the three detectives as they found a place to plant themselves.

"Let's make it short and sweet, gentlemen," said Lowery. "I'm sure we all have more important demands on our day than to waste much time on this matter. After talking to my client, Mr. Kirby King, and looking over the police report, I want Mr. King released...immediately."

"Over his dead body," snarled Hill without looking at the lawyer. He removed a cigarette from his shirt pocket, and began searching for his lighter in his pants pocket.

"No more of that, Lt. Hill," said Harper. "Please excuse his remark, Mr. Lowery. He's already feeling the...stress...of a very high profile investigation that is still ongoing at this time. Could you put a little more meat on your request?"

Unfolding his hands, Lowery now took a moment to scrutinize Hill, Yellowstone, and Turner, one at a time, in an office where the tension could not have been cut by a knife.

"I accept your apology, Chief Harper. Other than what seems to be a possible but is actually a farfetched motive, you have not one shred of evidence against Mr. King. May I remind you, you have found no gun, you have no eyewitness to the murder and no evidence to place King anywhere near the scene of the crime. Until such time as you do...and you won't... Mr. King walks."

"Are you forgetting the witness who saw him leaving the scene?" Hill asked as he lit a Lucky Strike.

"I believe that 'witness' is a white woman named Mrs. Elvira Tyree. A woman who thinks she saw a black man near the scene...at maybe the right time. In the dark. In the rain. For a brief second or two. A woman who wears thick glasses.

"Your witness is a joke, but I'm not inclined to laugh. Captain, we both know that's so flimsy you couldn't hang a silk scarf on it on a windless day without it tearing."

"Maybe not," Yellowstone said. All eyes turned to the Osage.

"With your permission, chief, it wouldn't take long to arrange for a line-up. Then we can see if Mrs. Tyree can finger King for sure."

"I have no objection to that," Virgil Lowery said confidently. "So long as I'm allowed to be present, of course."

"Make it happen, detective," Chief Harper ordered.

✦✦✦

One hour later, the five men were escorted into the small observation booth adjoining the line-up room. Mrs. Tyree was already there, standing next to a young, uniformed policeman. Turning away from the one-way mirror at the sound of their entry, she smiled and nodded in acknowledgment of their presence.

The lights were dimmed in the observation booth as six men dressed to match Mrs. Tyree's general description of the suspect she had seen filed into the well lit room on the other side of the window to stand uneasily facing the mirror. Behind them was a wall marked with lines and numbers indicating various heights. Four of the men were colored, one was Hispanic, and one was Caucasian. One of the six was Kirby King.

"Mrs. Tyree, please take your time," said Captain Harper, "and look at the six men you see before you very closely."

He lightly rapped his knuckles on the glass window that they all faced. "Remember, this is a one-way mirror; these men can neither see you nor hear you. In fact, they don't know you are in this room, don't know your name, and don't even know you are here in the 3rd Precinct Station.

"You are completely safe. Take your time, because a man's life and reputation are on the line right now."

The silence in the room was broken only by the low sound of their breathing as Mrs. Tyree studied each face and body meticulously, slowly, occasionally clucking her tongue.

Hill took a last drag from the nub of his cigarette and let the butt fall to the floor. He ground its remaining glow out with his left foot.

Yellowstone looked at his wristwatch.

Turner methodically cleaned out his left ear with the pinky finger of his left hand.

"Mrs. Tyree...?" Harper said, encouraging her decision.

"That's the man; number three," she finally said with certainty as she pointed a white gloved finger at Kirby King. "He's the one I saw leaving the parking garage."

As one, everyone in the room smiled except Lowery.

"Or maybe number five," Mrs. Tyree added before turning away from the one-way glass. "I don't know. It could be him."

As quickly as their smiles had spread, every smile in the room died. Mrs. Tyree turned to look at each of the policemen, one at a time.

"I'm sorry," she said. "I thought I could do this. But they just all look so much alike."

Yellowstone had the sinking feelings that Mrs. Tyree was talking more about skin color than about the six men standing uneasily in the line-up.

"And that's that," said Lowery.

"Officer, show Mrs. Tyree out," said Captain Harper, "and be sure she arrives home safely."

As the door closed behind the woman and the policeman, a dour Lowery said:

"During our earlier interview together, I hadn't noticed that Mr. King and I are twins."

"This doesn't mean that our case against King is falling apart, Lowery." said Hill. "King is unable to account for his whereabouts at the time of the murder, claiming to have been out walking alone. There is no one who can corroborate this. So King is still a suspect."

"The last time I checked my rather substantial library of law books... Det. Hill, is it?...it is not a crime to be unable to account for where you are every minute of every day.

"Gentleman, I'm afraid my schedule is tight today. So I must excuse myself, now, again reminding you that Mr. King's apartment has been searched and no gun was found. I repeat, you have no evidence, forensic or even circumstantial, to hold my client and I expect to see him in my office later today, a free man."

So saying, Lowery stepped to the door, opened it, and was gone.

"That arrogant son of a...." Hill began, only to have his last word cut off by Captain Harper.

"He's right, Jack," the Captain of Detectives said, "The night of your arrest of Kirby King, Detective Hill, he freely admitted he had been looking over the old newspaper clippings you found, as he had done on more than one occasion, and that he had tried to run away only because he 'feared the police'.

"I must admit, this doesn't look good for our case against him right now. The evidence against him, at *best*, is circumstantial; nothing *was* found in his apartment. There is no gun, and our eyewitness would never stand up under cross-examination."

"I hadn't noticed that Mr. King and I are twins."

"But, Captain..." Hill began again.

"I'm not saying this is over. But until you and Yellowstone bring me something more substantial, I have no choice but to turn King loose."

As the captain left the interrogation room, Hill cursed under this breath.

"Don't take it so hard, Jack," said Yellowstone and laid a reassuring hand on Hill's shoulder. "As they say back home, 'there never was a horse that couldn't be rode nor never a cowboy who couldn't be throwed'."

"Did anyone back home ever tell you to shut your cowboy face up?"

"Well, now..." began Yellowstone.

"I didn't think so," said Hill.

+++

The young black woman in a flowered summer dress stood on the sidewalk in front of the three-storied 3rd Precinct Station when its front door swung open.

A squad car waited behind her at the curb.

She pointed and yelled, "Racists!"

Hill, with a Lucky Strike hanging from the corner of his mouth, Yellowstone, and Kirby King, with his head lowered, stood in the entrance on the landing of a short flight of steps falling to the sidewalk. King looked up.

"Uh-oh," Yellowstone said. He knew that the temperate breeze that ruffled his black hair and the cloudless, cerulean-blue sky was about to degenerate into a storm. Unconsciously, his left hand went to the slide of his string tie.

"Damn," Hill growled and snatched the half-consumed cigarette out of his mouth and tossed it to the cement landing.

A middle-aged black man standing next to the woman who first yelled began shaking a sign that read: *FREE KING* to the chant of "police brutality!"

The vortex of journalistic vultures that had diminished to four bored and restless reporters lounging around the entrance to the 3rd Precinct Station leapt to their feet; Stacy Lord was the first to jump up. By long reflex, her technician carrying her heavy recording equipment jumped as well.

Several more Negroes joined the bitter chanting of "racists!" and "police brutality!"

Smiling tightly, Kirby King raised his unshackled arms over his head.

"Look!" one of the newspaper reporters yelled, and, at seeing King's wrists bare of handcuffs, added, "he's free!"

Raising his bulky camera, the reporter snapped a picture as the clutch of reporters began to swarm toward the policemen and King.

"Hurry!" barked Hill over the noise without looking at Yellowstone. "I'll try to distract them for a second. You hustle King to the squad car."

Hill raised his own arms as King's fell.

"People, people, people!" he yelled. "Settle down, and I'll answer your questions one at a time!"

Yellowstone, with his right hand firmly gripping King's left bicep, began to descend the stairs.

"Are you releasing Kirby King?" Stacy Lord shouted at Hill, trying to jab her microphone as close to the detective as possible.

Hill lowered his arms. "Yes..." he began.

The black chants turned to cheers.

"Yes," Hill said more loudly. "Mr. King is being released."

The black bystanders cheered again and parted to let Yellowstone and King pass.

"I assure you that our investigation into the murder of one of Detroit's best and brightest will be relentless, and we will not rest until her killer is brought to justice," Hill asserted, though by now the reporters had switched their attention away from him and toward the squad car.

Hill watched Yellowstone holding the door to the squad car open as King scooted onto its back bench seat. Yellowstone closed the door and trotted around the back of the car seconds before the crush of reporters descended upon it.

Seeing that speaking further was pointless, Lt. Hill clamped his mouth shut. He knew that in the moment at least, the murder was less important to the press than was the murderer; and the thought sickened him.

As Yellowstone pulled the squad car slowly away from the curb, Hill found himself looking directly at Kirby King, whose face was pressed against the car window, staring back at him where he stood above the crowd on the station steps.

His expression as cold and implacable as Arctic ice, Hill raised his right hand and pointed at King with his index finger. The detective's thumb stuck up, but now he dropped it, pantomiming the firing of a pistol as he jerked the hand up and back.

The other reporters had begun to disperse, eager to file their stories. But Stacy Lord had lingered behind, and she witnessed the gesture.

Both she and Kirby King knew: if fingers fired bullets...King would now be a dead man.

CHAPTER NINE

Kirby King always expected the worst, and he had seldom been disappointed.

It seemed to him that he'd lived his entire life under a dark cloud. Being the prime suspect in a murder investigation was simply the latest in a string of calamities, he thought, as he walked the dirty Michigan Avenue sidewalk close to Washington Boulevard.

The ex-con was carrying a small paper sack of groceries he'd bought at the corner grocery store. A very small sack; he could afford nothing more.

It was the first time he'd made such an extensive trip since his release from police custody. King had spent most of the last two, relatively quiet days holed up in his room at the Livingstone Apartments hoping the public furor focused on him by his arrest would die down.

No one had confronted or even noticed him on his trip to the grocery. He was gloomily hopeful the outrage would soon completely evaporate into thin air.

As he trudged up the front steps and into the foyer of the apartment building, King saw the weary, heavily-bearded face of the apartment manager, who was sitting near the stairwell reading a copy of the *Michigan Citizen*. The man looked up and followed King with a queer look in his beady little eyes.

King chose to ignore him…he was no stranger to queer looks inside and outside of the slammer. He ascended the faded and worn carpeting that covered the stairs to his room oblivious to the subtle stink of urine, stale beer, dirty diapers, and food fried in rancid grease that had become so much a part of his life that it was beneath his notice.

It took only a moment to fish his key out of his pants pocket while juggling his bag of groceries, to unlock the door to his apartment, and shove it open.

He froze as he crossed the threshold.

Two men, both of them white, both of them strangers to him, were waiting for him inside.

A convict develops a keen awareness of the look, the feel, the "smell" of a cop and neither of these men had it.

Yet one of them had already pulled a pistol out of a jacket pocket and was swinging it up to draw a bead on King.

There was neither time nor, he knew, point in trying to talk to the gunman, so Kirby simply reflexively slung his sack of groceries at the man.

A shot was fired errantly, sending tiny splinters flying from the doorjamb near King's left ear.

His heart pounding in his chest, King turned and ran through the hallway. The slap of his leather soles on the tiled hall floor was echoed by the sound of the two would-be assassins behind him.

Another shot was fired.

King stumbled down the stairs. The apartment manager dropped his newspaper and threw himself behind his chair, bullets flying around him and King as the two gunmen give chase.

As he ran, King screamed, "Somebody help me!" but was not surprised when no one responded.

Even as he screamed and yelled and ran through the entrance of the apartment building, he also thought *so that's why the old bastard gave me the stink eye on the way in. He set me up!*

Chest aching from the exertion and already panting, King bolted down the steps of the apartment building, racing for his life from the two white men.

As he reached the bottom of the steps, he grabbed the newel of the balustrade and swung himself to his right and down to the landing under the stairs that opened onto its basement, and jumped behind a battery of stinking, overflowing trash cans.

The two white men also turned to their right at the bottom of the stairs, and, without slowing their pace, began trotting down the sidewalk, glancing to their left and right sides.On cat's feet, King rose from behind the trash cans, stepped onto the sidewalk, and ran gingerly, afraid his attackers would hear him.

He swung left into the mouth of the first alley he came to, only taking a second to glance to his right. He saw no white men, no black men, no men. No one.

He ran to the intersection of the next street, and swung out of the alley right out onto the street's sidewalk, now slowing to a rapid walk. He then turned into the mouth of the next available alley, and repeated his diversionary tactic again, and again, until he was certain he had lost his pursuers in the maze of turns.

Covered with sweat and shaking with fear, Kirby pressed himself flat against the wall of the last alley he'd entered to catch his breath and slow his heart.

He put his hands on his knees, and, leaning forward at the waist, took three painfully slow and deep breaths before raising his head.

In the dim light cast by a street light, King saw a flier pasted to the left side of his head on a brick wall.

It caught his attention instantly as he realized his face was reproduced in the center of the poster.

Despite the sweating caused by his exertion and the warmth of the summer night, King's blood froze in his veins as he read the bold type above and below his photograph on the flier.

It said that a bounty of $1 million would be paid for Kirby King.

Dead.

No questions asked.

+++

Sean Carpenter barely heard the drone of his small radio on the end table next to his easy chair.

His left hand, holding a reward poster, shook slightly.

With his right hand, Carpenter adjusted the metal-rimmed glasses on his nose just beneath the permanently inverted "U" of flesh between his eyebrows.

There was a part of him that found the $1 million bounty on the head of the black man on the flier more than outrageous.

The very thought of a reward for murdering another human being was abhorrent to him.

But then, so were the numbers he had so meticulously written down in the ledger book he held open on his lap.

As he had feared and expected, the figures showed his income for the month would not quite cover all the bills staring him in the face. The tiny salary he earned as a sales clerk in a gun shop barely sufficed in the best of times; and the best of times now seemed so far behind him that he barely remembered them at all.

Now, with the additional financial burden of his youngest daughter's mounting medical expenses, his budget was stretched beyond the breaking point.

He closed the ledger book and leaned back in his chair, resigned to the fate of financial ruin. He'd have to tell his wife the truth about their situation; the lies he'd been soothing her with for the past several weeks would no longer hold. That cut deepest of all: the knowledge that he would have to admit his failings as the head of his own house.

Wanting to push such thoughts out of his mind, he focused on the words spilling out of the radio.

Stacy Lord was reporting what details she had regarding the failed attempt on Kirby King's life by "persons unknown."

"King," she said, "is a suspect in the murder of Assistant District Attorney Rebekah Nixon, a case now more than three days old.

"King was released by the police due to insufficient evidence. Ironically, according to my sources, that same police force is now holding him in protective custody in an undisclosed location, following an apparent attempt on his life.

"Which brings us to a new and bizarre twist in this story. Hundreds of wanted posters have begun appearing throughout the city. These fliers are offering a staggering $1 million reward for the death of Kirby King.

"Whether the posters are genuine or part of some gruesome and macabre joke is not yet known. But the result is the same regardless; hence, presumably prompting the alleged attempt on King's life.

"The poster states that in order to collect this reward, the claimant must deliver Kirby King's head…yes, you heard me right, ladies and gentlemen, his *head* …to a secure location across the river in Canada.

"A police spokesman tells me they have been unable thus far to uncover the identity of the person or persons responsible for this flier.

"Since word of the reward has already begun to spread throughout the country, the police also fear that hordes of armed bounty hunters will soon descend on our city.

"In other news…"

Sean Carpenter clicked off the radio.

He looked down at the forlorn ledger in his lap, then at the wanted poster in his left hand, and finally over at the modest gun cabinet set against one wall. Its contents were meager: one shotgun, one rifle. He'd never shot anything in his life except the occasional quail when he used to go hunting with his father, before the old man passed away.

But the desperate sales clerk felt certain that for a million dollars…even he could kill a killer.

+++

The symbols of their rancid hatred were locked in the basement closet.

Their white, pointed, conical masks where folded carefully in the closet shelf above a row of white sheets draped on wire clothes hangers.

Ceremonial accessories denoting rank in the Invisible Empire also hung over a few of the carefully ironed and creased sheets, and the cheap sacramental objects used in their arcane ceremonies littered the closet floor.

The closet was a sacred place to them. It was in the basement of a rundown tenement that was the secret headquarters of a cell of a section of the Detroit Realm of the Ku Klux Klan, once among the largest and most powerful of the Realms in the nation.

The Detroit Realm and the entire movement were now barely a mockery of the once powerful secret society originally formed to reestablish White Supremacy in America. It was a movement continuing to choke and die on its own bile. But none of the men in the basement believed it was dying, and none wore ceremonial sheets or masks this morning; this wasn't a regularly scheduled meeting.

Five men stood together in the dank room, nervous and expectant. Some of them smoked cigarettes, some laughed occasionally, while a sixth man stood apart by design.

"My brother Klansmen," said that sixth man, Craig Conway, the Gray Goblin of the cell. He waved the metal claw that had taken the place of his amputated right hand and the newspaper in it to indicate a card table in the middle of the basement. "Please find a chair."

Without delay or question, the five men sat awkwardly down on chairs positioned around the well-worn card table. They were almost laughably mundane in appearance; all would have gone unnoticed in any crowd. All were Protestant Christians...one was a pastor...all were Caucasian, and all were of the lower-middle class. None looked like the knights on white steeds that they all pretended to emulate.

As they sat, Conway slapped the rolled up newspaper against his thigh.

Only five core members of the KKK section had been called by their Goblin. The basement bore none of the ceremonial decorations of a clan meeting.

The card table was surrounded only by a furnace, un-insulated cement walls, and the boxed or free-standing junk stored by the renters in the tenement above them. Each of the five men had been hand-picked by Conway for being one of those who burned brightest with the festering hatred ignited and fed by their distorted brand of Christianity and misplaced patriotism.

They gave their undivided attention to the sixth man, a man who physically did not command respect or fear in other men, nor seemed capable of naturally rising to a position of authority. It was his unmatched hatred of Jews and Blacks and Catholics that had elevated him to his exalted post.

The twenty-eight year old Conway had thinning, mouse brown hair and eyes, and a face easily forgotten. Nevertheless, he was the Gray Goblin of the smallest section of the Ku Klux Klan in Detroit, his greatest and perhaps only source of pride.

The three other bands of Klansmen in the city largely ignored him and his, but Conway didn't care, for he had nothing but contempt for them. It was the Klan as a whole he cherished, and he feared it was dying on the vine in Detroit.

Desperate times demanded desperate measures.

Conway began to wave his copy of the *Detroit News* newspaper held in his two-pronged claw in the air.

"You have all read the story about Kirby King and the $1 million bounty on his head?"

Each of five nodding heads indicated they had indeed read the story.

"It is as if God himself has spoken to us and given us a mission. Tonight, my friends, I am happy to say the Holy, Sanctified Klan of Detroit takes justified delight in the idea of being able to kill a murdering Negro and getting paid for it."

The door of the basement was unexpectedly flung open.

As one, all five men at the card table leapt to their feet as Conway pivoted on his heels to face the intruder.

Conway screeched, "This is a private meeting! Who the hell are you?"

A man, half hidden by the shadows in the stairwell leading to the basement, calmly stood in the doorway. "Gentlemen," he said, "you having nothing to fear from me...

"Unless you are afraid of collecting $1 million and the head of Kirby King."

+++

Bored beyond belief, Tony Matson set his black, leather bag down and stepped up on the platform of a glass and chrome machine that promised to tell him his weight and predict his future for a penny.

He looked in the little mirror above the dial that measured a person's weight. He took off his hat and ran his right hand through his thin, slightly oily hair. His half-smoked Camel cigarette flicked as his mouth drew up into a smile; he thought himself to be a fine looking specimen.

Tony put his hat back on and scrounged around in his pants pocket for change. He dropped a penny into the machine's slot.

Some destination announced through a loud speaker echoed through the terminal, but he ignored it. Then a little cardboard card popped out of another slot as the scale beneath the mirror registered 172 pounds. He frowned, thinking that was a bit much for a body made of steel rods held together by iron nuts and bolts, of which he was very proud. He tossed the card away without bothering to read his fortune.

He stepped off of the machine and picked up his bag.

Behind and all around him, Cleveland's huge Central Depot train station was teeming with men, women and children coming to or departing from the city.

Big crowds were not to his liking. Tony simply could not tolerate being touched, so even the few steps to the newsstand on his right side made him feel like he was tiptoeing through a minefield.

At the newsstand, which offered a wide selection of newspapers from around the country, he bought a copy of the *Detroit Abend Post* to take his mind off the crowd while waiting for his boarding call on the next train to Pittsburgh. He finally spotted a mostly empty bench, and made for it.

Once seated, Matson opened the newspaper. His eyes were immediately drawn to the headline and story about Kirby King and the million dollar bounty placed on the alleged murderer's head.

He chuckled to himself. *Someone down there loves me*, he thought.

In certain select circles, Anthony Matson was better known as "Tony the Torpedo," or simply "the Torpedo."

It was a nickname he had more than earned as a hit man for the Mob. He was strictly freelance, owing allegiance to no single family or town. The job and the money were what mattered most to him, and he traveled wherever the two called him.

He was a killer, plain and simple.

Matson was very, very good at what he did; probably because he enjoyed his job so much. Everybody knew it; that's why there was always a demand for his services.

That's why he was on his way to Pittsburgh…or had been.

Now he'd been handed a golden opportunity to leave the life behind him once and for all. For, much as he liked it, he was smart enough to know that everybody's string of luck runs out eventually.

But with one last hit…and the million dollar payout that came with it… he could retire to Brazil and lead a life of luxury and decadence.

(And if the old, familiar urges traveled there with him…well, there were bound to be Brazilians who needed killing.)

Well worth the risk, he felt sure, to make a return visit to Detroit and the bounty waiting there to be grabbed by the right man. A man like him.

He picked up his bag, plotted a course through the press of human flesh around him and headed for the ticket window to exchange his ticket.

The Torpedo smiled coldly to himself as he waited in line. The first order of business when he reached Detroit…would be to find a place where he could buy an extra-large *hat box*.

CHAPTER TEN

Michael Yellowstone chanted, "Batta, batta, batta....sa-wiiiing!"

"Schoolboy" Rowe connected and the ball sailed past the leftfielder for the St. Louis Browns to strike and bounce off the wall.

Yellowstone and the crowd rose as one, cheering and throwing their arms, hats, popcorn, and even beer above them into the cloudless blue sky over Navin Field.

The Osage Indian glanced at the empty seat next to him as he sat down, then looked down and up the aisle closest to him. His face brightened and he stood up for a moment as he saw Stacy Lord in a light, flowered, summer dress with her hair up in a ponytail that bounced behind her as she descended the stairs to that aisle.

When she caught sight of him as well, she waved, smiled broadly, and began to take two steps at a time. When she reached Yellowstone's row of seats, she crabbed sideways to reach him as quickly as possible.

"Michael!" she called.

"Over here, baby!" Yellowstone responded, waving an invitation with his free hand for her to sit in the empty stadium chair beside him. "Late as usual, I see!"

"Who's playing?" she asked as she sat down. "Can I have one of those?" she added, without waiting for an answer to her first question, pointing to the paper cup full of beer in his right hand.

"You betcha. What took you so long this time?"

"Occupational hazard, just like for you, honey. We're both on call twenty-four hours a day, seven days a week, remember?"

"Don't I know it," grinned Yellowstone. "If I hadn't just come off of a sixty-hour week myself, I wouldn't be here right now. How about for you?"

"Just came from a Black Mass where a bunch of Satanists sacrificed a baby on a blood stained altar down at City Hall. Now, you tell me about the Nixon case."

"Very funny. You know I can't talk about an ongoing investigation. Now ask me something you don't know that I can answer, Firecracker. And watch this next guy; he's terrific."

As he spoke, Mickey Cochrane, #2 of the Tigers, strode up to the home plate.

"Can't blame a lady for trying."

"I'll try to remember that, sweetie, next time I see one."

Stacy placed two fingers on her puckered lips, then pressed those fingers against Yellowstone's mouth.

"I love you too, darling."

Hank Greenbery, #6 for the Tigers, was now walking up to the plate and took some practice swings with his bat.

"I'm gonna grab a hot dog," Yellowstone said, motioning to a passing vendor. "How 'bout you?"

"No, thanks."

"C'mon, dollface. You really need to put a little more meat on those bones."

"I like the meat that's already there just fine, cowboy. So do you. Besides, I expect you to buy me a *real* meal later…at a place with real chairs and drinks that come in real glasses."

"Yer a pretty high maintenance gal," Yellowstone jested.

"And worth every penny, my friend," Stacy shot back.

"I don't take guff from anyone," she told him. "I learned that at my mother's knee back in Boston. She was a suffragette, you know."

"Really? And yet you turned out to be such a wallflower."

"Make all the fun you want, big boy. The fact remains that women are capable of doing anything a man can do…when they're given the chance."

"So you're old school and old money…but with newfangled ideas," Yellowstone observed. "So tell me: what do you have in common with *me*?"

"We both like horses," she said tartly, "and riding. That's how we met, remember? That morning in the park?"

"How could I forget? You almost sent me flying off the bridle path."

"That's the 20th century for you, cowboy. If you move too slow…you'll get run over."

"Is that how you look at your job, too?" he asked, growing a bit more serious. "If someone gets in the way of where you want to go, you just steamroll over them?"

"Isn't that what a man would do?"

"Some, I guess."

"I understand Rebekah Nixon was like that," Stacy said, slyly sliding her eyes to the side to observe her beau's reaction.

"Maybe," he said, noncommittally.

"Maybe that's what got her killed."

Yellowstone tensed. "And maybe now I know the real reason you hang around with me."

"Whatever do you mean, darling?" she said innocently.

"You know damn good and well what I mean, sister," he snapped back. "Maybe all I am to you is another source of information."

"You know better than that, Michael," she replied, a wounded look on her classic face.

"What I know is that you'll do whatever it takes to get ahead," he said gruffly. "What I don't know is where that leaves you and me."

"Buy me another beer, sweetheart," she said, puckering her lips and making a smooching sound, "and maybe you'll find out!"

CHAPTER ELEVEN

"It's hot in here," said King, leaning against a water stain on the papered wall.

Sullen and nervous, he ran a hand over the sheen of sweat on his usually nearly bald head; in the past few hellish days that he'd been unable to shave it; a faint horseshoe of hair had grown from ear to ear.

"Oh, dear, I'm so sorry. Let me run get yah a nice cool sip o' champagne," said one of three policemen, all wearing shoulder holsters and sitting at a card table in the center of the room. The cop did not look up from the promising fan of cards in his hands. The other two men snickered around the cigarettes in their mouths.

One of the two policemen, trying but failing to be funny, added, "What did yah expect on a July night, Jack Frost?"

"What you *deserve,* King, is a bullet in the head," said Jack Hill, sitting on a couch behind an open newspaper. "Maybe that'd cool you down."

Through what had seemed like an eternity to Lt. Hill in the rundown hovel on the edge of Detroit that was serving as a safe house for King, he had made no attempt to hide his scorn for the ex-con.

"He's just pullin' your leg, Kirby," said Yellowstone who stood by the worn drapes covering the only window in the small room. "Why don't you give him some slack, Jack. Like they say back home, 'if it don't seem like it's worth the effort, it probably ain't.'"

"You're right, One Take," said Hill, folding his newspaper. "Kirby, I'm sorry. Why don't you pull back those curtains, and open the window? Maybe you'll catch a breeze…or a bullet that'll put you on ice permanently."

"Lt. Hill's just a little on edge, from the heat," said Yellowstone, sending a reproachful look to his partner. "Say, Kirby, I've been wondering. Did you know Rebekah Nixon *before* she tried your case?"

"No. We didn't exactly travel in the same circles," said King sullenly, unbuttoning a shirt button at his throat and staring straight ahead.

"Hey!" barked Hill. "Maybe you shouldn't be using that tone of voice with the only one of us in this room who doesn't want to smash in that dirty mug of yours, King. If I had my way, brother…"

The window shattered; the drapes billowed with glass shards.

Yellowstone jumped back as a brick rolled edge over edge to the foot of one of the three cops jumping up from their chairs around the card table.

The Osage detective quickly stepped back to the drapes and pulled an edge back, cautiously glancing out through the window.

"It's the Klan!" he exclaimed, pulling his weapon from its holster. "Armed to the teeth."

"How many, cowboy?" barked Hill as he shuffled through broken glass to King's side and grabbed the black's right bicep in an iron grip. The three other cops stood by the card table with service revolvers drawn, waiting for Hill's orders.

"Four or five, tops, in full sheets and dunce caps." Yellowstone paused. "Looks like they're all running around to the front of the house now."

"Well, what do you mugs think you're here for?" said Hill. "Get your asses out there and take care of this! I'll keep watch on our houseguest here."

"I'm going too," said Yellowstone, and all four men were through the dwelling's front door in a heartbeat, slamming it behind them. Seconds later, gunshots could be heard piercing the night.

Hill grabbed King by the front of his lightweight jacket and jerked him up to his feet.

"Let me go!" snarled the felon.

"I'll let you go, all right," Hill said, his eyes blazing with murderous intent. "Go straight to hell!"

Hill shoved King hard against a wall and drew his gun, pressing it against the ex-con's ribs.

"It's time you knew something about me, King," he hissed. "I'm a vengeful son-of-a-bitch. I know you killed Rebekah Nixon, and I'm the one who's going to make sure you pay for it, you murderin' black bastard!

"*I* tipped off the Klan as to the location of this safe house. And now, while they distract Yellowstone and the others, I'm the one who's gonna put a bullet through your stinkin' head… while you were attempting to overpower me and seize my weapon. I had no choice but to defend myself."

The door swung open abruptly as Michael Yellowstone rushed back inside.

"Jack!" he snapped, "What…?" but he didn't wait for an answer. The Osage had reached Hill and yanked him away from King before his partner could even respond.

Without hesitation, King turned on his heels.

He jumped through the mouth of the window ringed with shards of broken glass, momentarily dragging the drapes through the gaping wound after him.

Kirby landed like a cat on one knee and the palm of one hand on the turf below the window.

In the intake of a breath, King had leapt to his feet and run around the corner of the house, disappearing into the hot, black night.

"Goddammit, cowboy!" Hill snarled as he leaned through the broken window and peered into the darkness. There was no sign of King; the moment of opportunity had been lost. "You let him get away!"

Hill stepped back from the window, angry. But something about his words did not ring true with the Osage.

"What happened out front?" Hill snapped.

"Not much," Yellowstone replied, eyeing him intently. "Once bullets started flying, those morons in bedsheets took off like scalded cats. I don't think they'll stop runnin' till they reach Alabama."

The Osage failed to see the relief on his partner's face; with the Klansmen in the wind, there would be no chance they could finger Hill for his complicity in this botched murder scheme.

Still, Yellowstone let out a deep sigh.

"Why did you have your gun drawn on King, Jack?" he asked grimly. "He was unarmed."

"To stop him from doing just what he did: escape! Listen, I knew you were wet behind the ears when they made you my partner, but I didn't expect anything as bumfuddled as this, Yellowstone! You just pulled off the most bone-headed stunt I've ever seen in all my years on the force."

He shook his head in disbelief and turned his back on Yellowstone, holstering his revolver.

"Dammit," he hissed, but with less intensity.

He turned back to an emotionless Yellowstone, who hadn't moved a muscle.

"Dammit," he said again, but this time with resignation. "Listen, Hollywood; against my better judgment, I'm gonna give you a break this one time, but never again. I'm not going to report that your stupidity allowed King to get away.

"But if you ever go off half-cocked like that again…I'll bury you."

Yellowstone's eyes did not leave Hill, nor did his face express his suspicion as he smiled and said:

"Well, like they say back home…"

But the intensity of Hill's baleful gaze stopped his words.

+++

Twenty-four hours had not erased Yellowstone's growing suspicion or Hill's smoldering anger as both of the detectives stood in front of a small table in a side room of the precinct. Sleep had eluded both men for the most part, and the long hours of unproductively poring over their notes about the rape and murder of Rebekah Nixon had left the mark of exhaustion on both of their haggard faces.

The bewildering chaos of knives of every imaginable length and use, including serrated steak knives, three machetes, and a butter knife completely hid the top of the table.

Yellowstone scratched the top of his head.

"A butter knife?" he muttered. "A *butter* knife! In God's name, what are we dealing with, Jack?"

Hill picked up the butter knife, ran a finger over its smooth, blunt blade.

"We are dealing with a rapidly escalating and grim situation," said the detective, "in which the city of Detroit, full of average, everyday Joes for the most part, is turning into an irrational, ill-equipped, money-hungry mob, Hollywood. These knives have been confiscated from more than two dozen citizens and out-of-towners, in just the last few days. People who are likely to end up killing innocent bystanders and each other before they ever even catch a glimpse of Kirby King."

"The number of these amateur 'bounty-hunters' is increasing exponentially even as we speak, and eating up the manpower we need to actually bring King in."

Yellowstone shook his head from side to side, and he took the butter knife from Hill and laid it back on the table.

"Jack, we've gone over this a hundred times. We keep looking for evidence, but there is still nothing concrete that points specifically to King."

"You're a mule-headed idiot," snarled Hill as the two men turned and left the room, walking back to their desks.

"Like they say back in Stroud, Jack, don't judge people by their relatives. And mine were *good* mules. Now, we've both gone over what we have, or, actually, what we don't have, a hundred times. There is something in particular that still puzzles me, that maybe you can help me with."

"You're wearing me out, cowboy. What is it now?"

"When Miss Nixon's body was found, there was no sign of her purse; that was to be expected.

"But when I interviewed her co-workers, they said she was also carrying a briefcase when she left her office that night, same as on most nights. Seems she made a habit of bringing work home with her."

"Yeah, so?"

"So where's the briefcase?" Yellowstone asked. "There was no sign of it at the crime scene."

"It doesn't take Sherlock Holmes to figure that one out," Hill huffed. "The perp probably took everything he could carry with him. When he found no valuables in the briefcase, he dumped it along with her purse, after he emptied it.

"Hell, it's even possible some bum came along before the first police unit arrived on the scene, and made off with it."

"Maybe," Yellowstone agreed. "That might explain why our near-sighted 'eye-witness' didn't mention seeing the man leaving the garage carrying anything." He shook his head.

"But it still bothers me that we also didn't find a gun when we nailed King."

"Trust me, cowboy, it's as easy for a crook to lose a gun as it is for him to get one."

"True. But I presume Miss Nixon had money in her purse…yet King had less than fifty cents in his pocket when we booked him. He hadn't had much time to spend a lot of money."

Hill snorted derisively. "Just how wet behind the ears *are* you,

Hollywood? A lowlife like Kirby King can blow as much money on booze and broads in a single night as you make in a month!"

Yellowstone stretched his arms above his head, balled his fists, and yawned.

"You're probably right, partner. It's gettin' late, and I'm beat. Maybe I'll think better after a good night's sleep. I'm goin' home to get some shut-eye."

"Don't make promises you can't keep, cowboy," said Hill with a weariness in his own voice that couldn't be hidden.

"And don't let the door hit you in the butt on your way out."

+++

The quarter-moon hung in a cloudless sky splattered with dim stars. The street in front of the 3rd Precinct was empty and dark except for the yellow halos of light from occasional street lamps.

A lone man sat on a bus stop bench across the street from the police station and under one of those lamps, his face hidden behind the pages of the *Detroit Saturday Night* newspaper. Michael Yellowstone ignored him as he wearily descended the steps to the sidewalk.

The click-clack of his shoes on the sidewalk and the distant noise of traffic in the city were the only sounds to break an otherwise eerie silence.

On the bench, the man's face was obscured by the newspaper; by the upturned collar of a light jacket; and by the brim of a cap pulled low over his forehead. As he saw Yellowstone shove his hands into his pants pockets and swing left down the sidewalk, the man rose, dropped his newspaper, instantly forgotten, on the bench, and crossed the street.

He began to follow Yellowstone at a discreet distance, making sure that the sound of his footfalls on the concrete sidewalk did not reach the detective's ears.

Yellowstone rounded the corner of a building.

The man in the jacket and cap quickened his pace, rounding the same corner.

When he did, he found the barrel of Yellowstone's service revolver pointed at his face.

"D-don't shoot," stammered the stalker, raising his hands.

"Well, I'll be damned," Yellowstone whistled as he lowered his revolver. "Kirby King!"

The detective holstered his gun.

"I don't know if I should punch you in the mug," said Yellowstone, "or sing 'Amazing Grace'. Why'd you run away last night?"

He began to follow Yellowstone at a discreet distance...

"I ran because I don't believe I can trust anyone anymore, Mr. Yellowstone, except maybe you…even after what that cop buddy of yours, Hill, almost done to me. I think maybe him and the rest of 'em want to collect the reward their own selves. So I laid low till I could see you alone." The ex-con hesitated before speaking further.

"Someone else tried to kill me a couple hours ago," King now told the detective. "Came close, too. Close enough to make me realize I might need help if I'm gonna stay alive. You stopped that cop with the crazy eyes from killin' me last night, Mr. Yellowstone, and…"

"So you say."

"The point is: you helped me then…so I thought you might help me now. That ain't an easy thing for me to do, either: askin' for help, I mean."

Yellowstone glanced around him as he placed both hands on King's muscular shoulders.

"I sure as hell want to hear what you think Hill did to you, but the first thing is to get off the street. You're a right popular fellah these days, you know."

As the two men walked down the sidewalk to Yellowstone's waiting '34 Ford Roadster, King told him of Hill's plan to have the Klan serve as a diversion while Hill killed the ex-con he was supposed to be protecting.

As they stopped at his vehicle and Yellowstone unlocked its door, he shook his head from side to side and sighed.

"That sounds pretty far-fetched to me, mister. Why in tarnation should I believe you for one minute instead of my own partner? Lt. Hill told me you were trying to escape, and I saw you jump out the window!"

"Only because I was afraid he was gonna kill me, boss," said King earnestly. "Why would I lie to the only man in Detroit who doesn't seem to want me dead?"

Yellowstone turned the key in the ignition; the car roared to life, and pulled away from the curb.

"What makes you think I'd be willing to help you?" Yellowstone asked. "You're still my number one suspect in a cold-blooded murder."

"Because you're not sure I did it," King stated flatly. "And until you are…I figure I'm safe with you. And I figure you won't stop turning over rocks till you find what you're lookin' for."

Yellowstone grunted. "And what if you've got me figured wrong?"

"Then I'm a dead man for sure," King replied in a voice deep but virtually devoid of emotion.

"Still…why did you come to me, old son, instead of goin' to a friend or someone in your family for help?"

"The only friends I had on the outside pretty much abandoned me when I was sent upstate, boss…and all my family is dead."

Yellowstone said nothing. But he knew King had just lied to him.

From having studied his file, the detective knew King had a sister who had visited him in prison on a few occasions and who lived in Detroit. *What else is the man lying about*, the detective pondered as he took a right turn and headed toward home.

Arriving at his simple frame house, Yellowstone pulled his Roadster into the garage, from where he and King could enter the dwelling unseen by prying eyes. Once inside, he directed the ex-con to the living room sofa.

"You can bunk there while I figure out our next move."

"Thank you, Mr. Yellowstone."

Yellowstone could see King's body visibly loosen as he sank down into the seat cushion. The detective decided to do a little probing.

"You know, Kirby, if you were to confess to the murder of Rebekah Nixon, the possibility exists that the bounty on your head would just disappear."

"I never had much schoolin', but I ain't stupid, Mr. Detective," King responded indignantly.

"I confess to murderin' a white girl…and they'd fry me in the electric chair before God could get the news."

The ex-con raised his head, and his eyes bored into Yellowstone's. "And how many times I gotta tell you: I didn't kill the bitch!"

"Well, somebody did," Yellowstone said flatly. 'I tell you now, boy, I mean to find that man. And if I discover *you're* the man…I'll gladly strap you into the chair myself. You understand?"

"I understand the deck's been stacked against me from the get-go," King replied, glaring at the detective, "same as it is against everybody like me. But you wouldn't know what it's like being a black man."

"Cry me a river, convict," Yellowstone snapped back. "Try bein' an Indian like me. At least the white man left enough of you alive to kick up a complaint. Ain't enough of us red men still breathin' to make a splash in a mud puddle."

King made no reply save an exhalation of exasperation. Swinging his legs up onto the sofa, he rolled over onto his side so his back was presented to the detective.

Yellowstone continued to stare at his unexpected houseguest. He had been deliberately trying to provoke the ex-con and thought he'd done a damn fine job of it.

Yet King had not responded to that provocation with any act of physical violence, or even a verbal threat.

The Osage smiled grimly. Their little exchange may have told him something very important about King's nature and character. But then again, maybe not.

After all, Yellowstone was a trained police officer, facing him head-on; not a slightly built woman taken by surprise from behind.

CHAPTER TWELVE

The sun had risen little more than three hours earlier on the goon guarding the massive front door to Judge Malcolm Nixon's mansion located in the beautiful residential area called Saint Clair Flats. The guard looked like a well-beaten slab of beef with a shoulder holster.

"The judge ain't available right now," he said without blinking.

"If you'll check Judge Nixon's dance card," said Lt. Hill, "you'll see Michael Yellowstone and Jack Hill of the Detroit PD have been penciled in for just about now."

"And how do I know," answered the guard, "youze two are Yellowstone and Hill? For all I know, you could be the Katzenjammer Kids."

The detectives both presented their badges, palmed. The slab looked both of the police badges over carefully before looking up again at the two officers.

"Judge has been expecting you," he said as he took out a key and unlocked the front entrance to the house. "First door on the left."

"We're just wasting time, One Take," Hill said as they approached the door to what he assumed was Nixon's den.

"Right now, Jack," Yellowstone answered as they stopped in front of the door to the den, "time is about all we've got. I know you've already spoken with the judge before, but I have a few questions of my own I'd like to ask."

He knocked on the door. The invitation to enter was somewhat muffled.

Yellowstone opened the door on a den luxuriant beyond his experience, and saw a fat old man dressed in a black suit slumped in one of several large, overstuffed chairs placed around an unlit fireplace. He was nursing a glass of what Yellowstone guessed was Scotch, even though it was early in the day. There were dark bags under his eyes and above his sallow cheeks.

"Come in, gentlemen," said Nixon. "Please be seated. I've been expecting you. In fact, I'm somewhat surprised you weren't here days ago. Because I'm somewhat difficult to locate at the moment, I sent *you* the invitation to visit."

"I tried to call, sir," said Yellowstone as he sat down. "Your telephone has been disconnected."

Nixon looked at Hill.

"Surely Lt. Hill has told you why my phone has been disconnected?"

"No, sir; I've told no one," said Hill as he sat down near the judge. "I didn't think you'd want that information to be general knowledge."

"You were mistaken, son," said Nixon, squirming for a moment in his chair. He took a sip of the Scotch. "Det. Yellowstone has every right to be privy, considering his involvement in my daughter's murder investigation." He turned those hollow eyes toward Yellowstone.

"What Lt. Hill and I are talking about, Det. Yellowstone, is the fact that I'm dying of terminal cancer."

The Osage's expression clearly showed his surprise. "I'm sorry, sir."

The judge waved away Yellowstone's condolences. "I'm old. I've had a full life, and now it's done. No need to make more of it than it is." He took another sip of his drink.

"I assume you have questions: ask them."

Yellowstone glanced first at his partner. The expression on Hill's face clearly showed his desire to let this drop; though why he would feel that way perplexed the Osage. He was, after all, just doing his job; so he plowed ahead.

"I won't beat around the bush, Judge Nixon. Are you responsible for placing the bounty on Kirby King's head?"

To his puzzlement, Nixon smiled slightly.

"What if I am?"

"Beg pardon?"

"If I admitted responsibility, what would you do, young man?"

"I'd arrest you, sir," Yellowstone replied, quickly regaining his composure. "You'd be charged with solicitation of murder."

"Exactly," Nixon concurred. "You know the law. But given that, I would be foolish indeed to admit to any such thing, wouldn't I?"

"That's not an answer to my question, sir," Yellowstone said.

"It's the only answer you'll get from me."

Yellowstone exhaled loudly in exasperation. "I understand how you must feel, sir. If it had been my daughter…"

"But it wasn't," Nixon snapped, cutting him off in mid-sentence. "It was *my* daughter." With slightly trembling hand, the retired judge reached for a decanter and refilled his glass; perhaps hoping liquor could kill more than one sort of pain.

"I feel partly responsible for what happened to Rebekah," he told the detectives. "It was because of me that she wanted to enter the legal profession.

"If she'd had the influence of a mother's touch growing up, maybe she'd have stayed on a more womanly path: gotten married and given me grandchildren instead of wallowing in the mud with low-life criminals." He took a deep swallow of the expensive Scotch.

"But she was always a willful child; always insisting on having things her own way."

"Like her father?" Yellowstone commented.

The old man merely shrugged.

"And you still haven't answered my question about the bounty on Kirby King, judge."

The retired justice drew himself as erect as he could manage. "Do you realize the steps that would have to be taken to instigate such a bounty?

"A man would have to have layers of subordinates beneath him, each charged with a different task. None would know about the others, and no more than one would know the identity of the man at the top.

"One to print the posters, another to distribute them. Still another to arrange for the delivery of proof of death. An agent in Canada in a secured location to accept delivery of same. One to make the payment. All these you would need, and probably more."

"And you'd need a million dollars," Yellowstone added.

"Obviously."

"All those resources, all that influence, all that money: you've got it all," Yellowstone pointed out. "Plus the acumen to know that Michigan still has an old law on the books that makes bounty hunting legal."

"Believe me, dear boy, you're not the first to latch on to the absurd notion that I'm the man who posted the bounty on King's head.

"Why do you think I disconnected my phone? Posted a guard at my door? It was to shield me from all the half-wits seeking what they think is easy money.

"Is it too much for a sick old man to ask: to be allowed to grieve and die in peace and privacy?"

"No, sir, it's not," Lt. Hill said softly. He turned his gaze toward his partner. "We should go now."

"Not yet," Yellowstone demurred, his eyes never leaving Nixon.

"No offense, judge," he said, "but like any good shyster, you've managed to talk and talk and talk without ever saying what I wanted to hear. So I'll ask you again, straight out:

"Are you responsible for the bounty on that man's head?"

"All right, son," Nixon said gruffly. "Then I'll say it straight out: I had nothing to do with the bounty." He stared down at the amber liquid in his glass, then back up. His face bore a look of repressed rage.

"But if I *had* posted such a reward, there's nothing you or anybody else could say that would compel me to rescind the offer.

"Kirby King's the lowest form of animal imaginable. Whatever the manner of his death…it will be more merciful than he deserves."

An uncomfortable silence fell over the room, broken finally by the shuffle of Lt. Hill rising from his seat.

"I think we're finished here," he said.

"I have one more question for the judge," Yellowstone declared.

"No you don't, cowboy."

"It's all right, lieutenant," Nixon said. "Ask your question, detective."

"Do you know if your daughter was seeing anyone? Socially, I mean. Romantically."

"What kind of question is that?" Hill demanded.

"A pretty standard one, actually," Yellowstone replied. "Just trying to fill in some of the blanks, that's all."

A phlegmy sound that may have been a chuckle gurgled up from the infirm judge's throat.

"He's only trying to do his job, lieutenant; I understand that. I wish Rebekah *did* have a love life, detective. But she was too consumed by work to think of romance.

"That was probably my fault, too. She was always trying so hard to impress me with her accomplishments: to make me proud.

"As if I wasn't already proud of her."

"Did you ever tell her that?" Yellowstone asked.

"That's enough!" Hill practically shouted. "We're leaving now."

Nixon said nothing, merely sipped at his drink.

"Thank you for your time and patience, Judge Nixon," Hill said in a placating voice. "And again, please accept our condolences."

The corpulent old man was again reaching for his decanter as Hill grabbed Yellowstone by the arm and dragged him out of the den.

"He's the one who put the price on King's head, all right," the Osage detective asserted once they had left the house. "Just as sure as God made little green apples."

"Of course he is," Hill concurred. "So what? He's just making sure his daughter's murderer gets what's coming to him."

"I thought that's what the legal system was for."

"Only when it works right."

"You think this is any better, Jack? Our city's about to turn into a bloody shootin' gallery."

"You mean *my* city, don't you? It's a dog eat dog world, my friend. Get used to it." Hill abruptly turned to face his partner.

"And what was with the personal questions about the lady's love life? And asking her own father, no less. You were way out of line, Yellowstone. Way out of line."

Hill grabbed for his pack of Lucky Strikes and popped one of the cigarettes into his mouth. As he then patted his pockets in search of a light, he said, "The old-timer was right about something else, too. If his daughter had stayed home and made babies like women are supposed to do…she'd still be alive."

"You really think that's true?" Yellowstone asked, gazing hard at the lieutenant.

"I know it is," Hill growled. He snatched the unlit cigarette from between his lips and threw it to the ground before climbing into the passenger side of their waiting car.

As Yellowstone rounded the rear end of the car, he could feel the hair on the back of his neck rising. As he gently stroked the replica dreamcatcher at his throat, he wondered what else his partner knew that he wasn't sharing.

+++

That night, Michael Yellowstone returned to an empty house. The only evidence that Kirby King had been there came in the form of a note he had left atop the kitchen table, addressed to the detective.

Though simply written and marred by misspellings, the message was clear and concise.

King expressed his gratitude for Yellowstone's kindness and asked that the detective continue his efforts to find Rebekah Nixon's killer. But the note also spoke of his feelings of the walls closing in on him and of his intention to try to find evidence of his innocence on his own.

Yellowstone's left hand crumpled the note, while he slammed his right fist sharply against the Formica table top.

For a man who claimed a desire to cling to life, Kirby King certainly seemed to have a death wish.

CHAPTER THIRTEEN

The street was seedy and on the wrong side of the tracks; one that Kirby King had traveled in the past. It was nearly midnight, and few people, mostly drunks and prostitutes too old to work the better parts of Detroit, were on the sidewalks. Motorcars were as scarce as hen's teeth. King knew that among the cheap hash joints, liquor stores and pawn shops, only Josephine's Bar and Grill would be open. Made no difference; the man he sought conducted his business on the street.

King had met Amos Dunn in the pen, where the antsy little black man had continued to conduct the drug peddling trade that had landed him in the joint in the first place.

King had felt sorry for the little guy; he wasn't exactly sure why. More than once he'd saved Dunn from a beating, helped him survive long enough to see his way out of that hellhole.

Now he hoped the pusher could return the favor.

Dunn had been leaning against a telephone pole, but pushed away anxiously when he saw King approaching him.

Then King lifted the brim of his cap high enough to reveal his face, and a smile lifted the corners of the pusher's mouth.

"My man!" Dunn exclaimed as he grabbed Kirby's hand and pulled him close enough to hug. "Long time, no see!"

As he drew back, Kirby sadly noted that Dunn was acting even more hopped up than usual; beads of sweat dotted a face blacker than King's and his eyes were little more than pinpricks.

It seemed apparent the pusher had begun to use his own product.

"But what the hell are you doin' out on the street like this?" Dunn now asked him, casting his gaze about nervously. "You should be getting' outta this town, man. Way out."

"You know the trouble I'm in?" King asked.

"Man, *ever*'body knows," Dunn declared. Clutching at King's coat sleeve, he drew him closer to the telephone pole. Tacked to the pole was one of the wanted posters.

"What you got yourself into, boy?"

"More trouble than I've ever known before, Amos."

"I feel yah, brother. So, you gettin' outta town, or what?"

"I thought about it, yeah. But from what I hear, my picture's showin' up all over the country. I might not be safe nowhere."

"Then you need to find a hole, brother; crawl into it and pull the dirt in after ya."

King shivered slightly, as if from a cold breeze. "No," he said firmly. "No hole for me."

"Whatcha gonna do, then?"

"I figure the only thing I *can* do, Amos, is find somebody else to pin that lady D.A.'s murder on."

"That'd do it, all right," the pusher agreed, then frowned. "But I gotta tell ya, man: word on the street is that you *are* the killer!"

"I'm tryin' to figure out a way to prove otherwise, Amos. You think you can help me out?"

"How?"

"Just keep your ear to the ground; that's all I'm askin.' See what you can find out for me."

"I ain't the kind o' guy most people tell secrets to," Dunn said apologetically. "You know that. But I'll do the best I can, man. I owe you that much, at least."

"Thanks, Amos," King said, laying a hand on the pusher's sloping shoulder. "I'll check in with you every few days."

Dunn nodded, then reached into a pants pocket and extracted a couple of crumpled dollar bills.

"I expect you could use a little walkin' around money," he said.

"No," King objected, holding up one hand. "I can't take money from you."

"Sure you can, brother," Dunn said, shoving the bills into King's shirt pocket.

"I just wish I could give you more," the pusher sniffed. "But times are tough, y'know?"

"Yeah. I know."

King gave the drug dealer another hug before turning and walking away.

Hands in the pockets of his pants, head down, the ex-con allowed his mind to become lost in its own swirling thoughts.

It was a lapse that nearly cost him his life.

He was roughly pulled back to reality by the blast of a shotgun that sent buckshot and splinters from a power pole whistling past his ear.

King hunched his shoulders and scurried away from the pole.

Amos Dunn screamed and ran in the opposite direction.

Shaking like a leaf and sweating like a steam engine, Sean Carpenter slid back into his car and sent it leaping forward in pursuit of King.

The cash-strapped and increasingly desperate sales clerk had been purposefully patrolling the seamier parts of the city every night since he had decided to claim the bounty on Kirby King's head. He'd lied to his wife Amanda, telling her he had taken a second job, so as to deter any further questions about his nightly excursions.

Until the instant he had pulled the trigger on his shotgun, he had not been sure he could go through with it. The excitement of actually spotting his intended prey, the pounding propulsion of adrenaline through his veins, had momentarily dispelled any such doubts.

As Carpenter sped after his fleeing target, he saw that King was heading toward the dark opening of an alleyway. He accelerated, then yanked the steering wheel hard to the right, jumping the curb with a teeth-rattling jolt.

Almost too late, he realized the gap toward which the accused murderer was headed was not so much a true alley as it was simply a narrow walkway between adjacent buildings. Far too narrow, he saw, to accommodate the width of his car.

He slammed on the brakes, flinging open his door and grabbing his shotgun in a virtually single move. He was only halfway out of the car when he triggered a second blast.

Flakes of shattered brick sprayed King as he ducked deeper into the walkway. Off-balance as he was, Carpenter was nearly thrown off his feet by the recoil of the weapon bucking against his shoulder.

Regaining his equilibrium, he pumped a fresh shell into the chamber and raced forward. He threw himself against the wall to one side of the walkway, his hands shaking and his face blanched with fear.

Licking his lips, he slowly inched his head around the corner. He could make out the dark shapes of discarded debris littering the ground, but he saw no movement. The far mouth of the alley opened onto another avenue dimly lit by a street lamp. Kirby King was nowhere to be seen.

"Damn!" Carpenter hissed, and let his shotgun fall to his side.

His knees suddenly buckled and he fell heavily to the sidewalk. Sharp contractions caused his belly to spasm; he clutched his stomach with both hands.

Hot liquid and the little he had eaten that day spewed from his mouth and sprayed the pavement.

Carpenter knew this was not a reaction caused by any physical illness, nor even by the fear that still squeezed his innards like a vise.

Rather, it was from the realization that he had just attempted to murder another human being. Twice.

He, who had never before broken the law; who had always tried to follow all the rules in the mistaken belief that that was what you did to get ahead in life.

Retrieving his shotgun and pushing himself back up to his feet, Carpenter stumbled down the sidewalk to his waiting motorcar.

He fell back into the driver's seat and threw the shotgun in the passenger's seat next to a large knife and the poster featuring Kirby King's face. In the chaos of his emotional upheaval, the struggling clerk began to beat his forehead against the steering wheel.

Yet even through this self-inflicted pain, what he mainly felt was the helplessness he experienced every time he looked at his precious baby girl as she inexorably faded away. He would continue to hunt down King. And he also knew that…given the opportunity…he would pull the trigger again.

CHAPTER FOURTEEN

"I don't believe this," Lt. Hill muttered, yawning and shoving the pile of papers in front of him on his desk away. The low, almost yellow light in the squad room of the 3rd Precinct added a look of weariness to his already haggard face. In addition to the stacks of papers, the ash tray on his desk was overflowing with cigarette butts, and the inside of his ceramic coffee mug was stained as brown as a diseased lung.

"Nothing, nothing, nothing; not one shred of new evidence. I feel like we've wasted the entire day, Hollywood."

Michael Yellowstone's head popped up from one of his own stacks of papers on his desk.

"*I* spent most of the day digging through trash bins, so I hear yah, partner. Even I'm at the point of believin' that what we do have points to no one *but* King."

"You must have known," said Hill, "that the grunts had already gone through all of the trash in a four block radius of the parking garage three times."

"Yeah, I knew. Just write it off to desperation. We still haven't found the murder weapon…not in King's apartment, not anywhere…so where is the gun that killed Rebekah Nixon? So I've been retracing the most likely path between the scene of the crime and King's apartment, searching every nook, cranny and, yes, dumpster. No luck."

"Remember," said Hill, "there was a little time elapsed before we searched King's apartment, enough time for him to have ditched the gun any number of places."

"I know. Still, this kind of grunt work is necessary. And knowing where the gun *isn't* at least slightly narrows down the list of places where it might be. Right now, I know one thing for damn sure. The best place that I could be is in bed."

Yellowstone stretched his arms above his head and yawned.

"I'm beat. I'm going home."

"I mean to do the same," Hill said. "See you tomorrow, cowboy."

Yellowstone smelled the faint aroma of food cooking even before he unlocked the front door to his small house. By the time he quietly pushed the door open, he had his revolver in hand.

Kirby King stood in front of the stove in the small kitchen just off of the living room. The wonderful smell of bacon, eggs, toast, and coffee was strong now, and Yellowstone felt his mouth begin to water.

"Don't shoot till *after* you've tasted my cookin', boss," King said without turning.

Yellowstone exhaled and holstered his weapon. "You got good ears, Kirby."

"I spent five years in a joint where you can wind up dead from lettin' people sneak up behind you."

The ex-con turned away from the stove, an iron skillet full of scrambled eggs in one hand, a metal spatula in the other. With the spatula he pointed toward the dining table, where two places had already been set.

"How'd you get in here?" Yellowstone asked as he draped his jacket over the back of a chair and took a seat.

"Do you really want to know?" King replied, scooping some of the eggs onto a plate in front of the detective.

"Prob'ly not. Better question: why'd you come back?"

King paused for a moment before pushing the remaining eggs onto a second plate and turning back to replace the skillet on the stove.

"I got no place else ta go," he said simply.

He placed two more platters...one holding toast, the other bacon...on the table before filling Yellowstone's cup with hot, black coffee.

"Figure fixin' supper was the least I could do by way of repayin' ya for what ya done for me," he explained. "Ain't much, but it'll fill ya up."

Yellowstone had already sampled the eggs and bacon, and smiled tightly. "Tastes better than I usually manage. O' course, a nice, thick steak woulda been even better."

"You want steak, you better do some grocery shoppin', boss," King observed. "This here was all you had in the place by way of foodstuff."

"Yeah, I'll do that," Yellowstone drawled. "Right after I solve a murder." He motioned with a jerk of his square chin.

"Why don't you turn on the radio next to you?" he said. "On the counter there. I like to listen to music while I'm eatin'."

Kirby turned on the small, inexpensive radio. Some woman was just finishing singing a torch song. Yellowstone grimmaced slightly at the sound of the next voice that came over the air waves. It was that of Stacy Lord.

"Support for Kirby King," the lady reporter said, "the man first arrested and then released in the case of the murder of Assistant District Attorney Rebekah Nixon, is unexpectedly beginning to grow.

"In particular, leaders of the Negro community are strongly protesting not just the bounty being offered for King's death but the police department's failure to either find the person who offered it or to protect King from attack. Or better yet, to solve the crime.

"The entire sordid affair is the subject of mounting national attention that is not good for our city. Clashes between blacks and whites are escalating in Detroit as the city swarms with amateur bounty hunters. Innocent people, especially Negroes, are being injured in growing numbers."

King turned off the radio. For long moments, neither man said a word.

"That other cop," the ex-con said at last. "I heard him call you 'cowboy.' Why's that?"

"'Cause that's what I was, once upon a time."

"For real?"

"Real as it gets," Yellowstone said, slathering butter on a slice of toast. "I worked on a ranch in Oklahoma, breakin' horses.

"The boss man put me in charge of gettin' a trainload of cayuses out to Los Angeles; the picture people needed a lot o' horseflesh for the Westerns they were startin' to crank out.

"I kinda took a likin' to Hollywoodland, and when the rest of the crew headed back home I stayed behind. Because I could handle a horse and a gun, I got some work in the pictures.

"But my big break came when I struck up a friendship with Tom Mix," he said, referring to one of the biggest of the Western movie stars. "You know who he is?"

"Course I do," King replied around a mouthful of bacon. "We didn't have much, but every Saturday my paw would take me and…" He hesitated, as if fearing he had said too much. "And we'd go to the flickers."

Yellowstone eyed the ex-con closely, suspecting he had intended to say "me and my sister." He wondered again why King seemed intent on pretending she didn't exist.

"I'd met Tom once or twice before, when I was just a kid" the detective went on. "My daddy knew him back when he was a lawman over ta Dewey, back home.

"I was honest enough with myself to know I didn't have the makin's of a matinee idol, but thanks to Tom's recommendation, I kept getting plenty of work as a stunt man."

"So how'd you end up here?"

"I'd always had an interest in the law, too. I knew that sooner or later I'd either get too old or too stove up to work in the movin' pictures, so I used part of my wages to pay for college.

"It was a director I knew, a fella who came from Michigan originally, who suggested I come here and put that education to use."

"I never got past the sixth grade, myself," King confessed. "But I fell in love with cars when I was a teenager. Learned every thing I could about 'em, inside and out."

"When you weren't busy stealin' 'em?" Yellowstone said.

King scowled. "I could fix one with my eyes closed. That's why I worked mostly in the machine shop in prison.

"Worked some in the kitchen, too. That's where I learned to cook a little bit." He then went back to eating. It was the most the detective had heard him speak since they had met.

Yellowstone scooped up more scrambled eggs.

"So what fool thing did you do last night?" he asked.

"I nearly got killed," King replied.

The spoonful of eggs stopped halfway up to Yellowstone's mouth.

"Some fellah with a shotgun," Kirby added.

Yellowstone put the spoon back on his plate.

"Has it occurred to you that every time you go out on the streets, someone tries to kill you?"

"So?"

"So don't it strike you as kinda *stupid* to keep doin' it?"

King dropped his spoon. "I ain't stupid," he said hotly. "I just can't stand doin' nothin'. And I don't like havin' four walls around me for too long."

"Beats havin' the six sides of a coffin around you forever."

"Says you."

"So you're gonna just keep on puttin' yourself out there?"

"Till I find a way to clear myself, yeah."

The man seemed to be going to extreme lengths to prove his innocence, Yellowstone thought. Maybe that meant he *was* innocent.

Or maybe it just meant he was working on a scheme to throw suspicion onto someone else. And Yellowstone knew he had no legal way of stopping the ex-con; for the moment at least, he was free to do as he pleased.

But either way, he needed to be watched closely.

"All right, Kirby," the Osage detective said, pushing his empty plate away. "Then I guess I'll mosey along with you while you're makin' your rounds."

"I don't recall invitin' you along, Mr. Detective."

"And I don't recall askin' your permission." Yellowstone rose to his feet.

"What we need is information," he declared. "So we'll begin by talkin' to a cop's best source for gossip."

"Who might that be?"

"Who else?" Yellowstone said, smiling. "Hookers."

+++

For a man in the know, it wasn't hard to find a streetwalker in Detroit, especially late at night.

Three of them clustered together under a street lamp as Yellowstone and Kirby King approached on foot. Seeing the potential customers, the ladies did their best to preen.

Their best wasn't nearly good enough; and the harsh halo of light cast down upon them by the lamp overhead did them no favors either.

Two of the soiled doves were colored girls: one tall and willowy, the other short and going to fat. The third was a white woman: the wild, rat's nest of red hair atop her head made her look like a caricature of the Little Orphan Annie character from the funny papers.

"Hey, handsome," she said to Yellowstone, "you lookin' for a good time?"

The detective responded by flipping the collar of his jacket to expose his badge. All the women tensed, prepared to run.

"Take it easy, ladies," the detective said soothingly. "We just want to talk, that's all."

Relaxing slightly, the taller of the black girls bent over slightly, checking out Yellowstone's companion.

"Is that you, Kirby?" she asked.

"Uhh…hey there, Nanette," he replied uncomfortably, then looked over to see Yellowstone grinning at him.

"What?" he said defensively. "A fellah gets lonesome sometimes, y'know!"

"Uh-huh." Yellowstone turned his attention back to the hookers. "Listen, ladies; let us get down to our business and then you can get back to yours."

"Whatchoo want?" asked the short black dove, just a hint of Latina in her voice.

"Just some information. I want to know what the word on the street is about whoever killed the lady D.A. last week."

"That's easy," said "Annie," pointing an accusing finger at King. "Everybody says *he* did it!"

Kirby hung his head as Yellowstone glared at him, then turned back to the three women.

"Anybody have *proof* he did it? Anybody *see* him do it, or hear him brag about doing it?"

The three women of the night exchanged questioning glances with each other, shrugging.

"Well, no," Nanette admitted. "But who *else* woulda done it?"

"That's a good question," Yellowstone replied, handing Nanette a business card with his name and work number on it.

"You girls hear anything that sounds like an answer, you give me a call, ya hear?"

"No offense, handsome," said Annie," "but why should we?"

Yellowstone smiled charmingly. "Because you're all such good, conscientious citizens…and because if you do, the next time vice sends a paddy wagon around…I might be able to get 'em to look the other way."

Nanette quickly snatched the card from his hand and shoved it down the plunging bodice of her too-tight dress.

"We'll keep a close eye out for you, baby," she said, looking at Kirby.

"Thanks, Nanette," he mumbled as he turned to walk away. "I 'preciate it."

Yellowstone tipped his hat to the soiled doves, then trotted to catch up to King.

"By the time we're through passin' out business cards," he told the ex-con, "we'll have painted eyes looking out for info from one end of this burg to the other.

"Though that may not be such a good thing for you, old son," he said, growing more serious. "So far, everything I've learned just makes you look *more* guilty."

King wasn't listening to him. His attention was fixed on a pick-up truck that had just passed them, going the opposite direction. Four men were standing up in its bed, staring intently at the pair on the sidewalk.

One of the men leaned down and forward to say something to a fifth man, who was driving the truck. The vehicle squealed to a halt.

Unknown to Kirby, the men in the truck were members of yet another band of the city's contingent of the Ku Klux Klan. Word had spread among the Klansmen about how the Gray Goblin and his motley crew had so ignominiously bungled their attempt to get to King, and all the other individual cells of the hate group were now more determined than ever to collect the bounty on the black man's head.

Not that this internecine rivalry mattered; when all five men came spilling out of the truck, Kirby knew full well their intent.

"Run, boss!" he yelled, taking off like a shot.

Yellowstone followed King's gaze, saw the five armed men and set off at a gallop after the ex-con.

Realizing they had been spotted, the Klansmen let out a whooping holler they thought sounded like a Rebel yell and gave chase.

Arms flailing, feet pumping, Yellowstone began to gain ground on King, whose shorter legs were working even harder.

The detective's eyes were focused straight ahead; thus he was unaware of an up-thrust crack in the pavement ahead of him until the toe of his right shoe caught it, tripped him and sent him slamming flat to the sidewalk.

Not realizing what had happened, King kept running, until a hurried look back over his right shoulder brought him skidding to a halt.

With the breath momentarily knocked out of him, Yellowstone was still struggling to regain his footing. Seeing the pursuing vigilantes closing in on the detective, King hesitated.

He raced back to the fallen detective, grabbing him by the back of his collar and roughly pulling him upright.

"Go!" he shouted, shoving Yellowstone forward and then setting out after him.

A pistol shot cracked from not far behind them. The bullet flew wide of its intended target, but it lent wings to their feet. Literally running for their lives, they gradually put more distance between themselves and the Klansmen.

They were a full block ahead of their pursuit when they rounded the corner of a building under construction and chanced stopping to catch their breaths.

Sucking air into his lungs, Yellowstone glanced up and saw a large scaffold hanging 30 feet above their heads, near the partially finished roof.

Next to the scaffold was a large pallet of bricks, suspended from a rope and pulley. The other end of that rope was tied off at street level, near where the two men now stood.

Yellowstone could tell by the slapping sound of leather on concrete that the pursuing Klansmen were very close now.

"Grab this rope," he yelled at a baffled King, while snatching a Barlow knife from his pocket, "and hold on for dear life!" Without knowing why, the ex-con did as he was ordered.

Yellowstone also grabbed the rope with only one hand…cutting the strand with the knife clenched in the other.

The overhead pallet of bricks instantly plummetted down toward the pavement below. Both men were jerked off their feet and sent hurtling skyward at dizzying speed.

The brick pallet's weight rapidly pulled the severed rope…and the two men grasping it… up to the scaffolding. King had closed both eyes tightly as they ascended, opening them only after Yellowstone swung them onto the scaffold and ordered him to lie flat.

Startled by the commotion, an unseen cat hissed, howled and ran down the nearest alley, raising a minor ruckus by tipping over a small can of garbage.

Moments later, the five armed men stopped in the mouth of the alley.

"I thought I heard something," said one of them, as all five gasped for breath.

"It was just a cat," said another of the Klansmen.

They all looked down to the darkened end of the alley.

The Klansmen saw it was a dead end.

They saw no men.

"Where the hell did they go?" asked one of the thugs.

A second Klansman scratched his head as he lowered his pistol.

Both men were sent hurtling skyward at dizzying speed.

"Beat's me," he said. "This ain't possible!"

"Maybe we just thought they turned in here," said a third thug.

"Where else could they have gone!" snarled the first Klansman.

"Well, it's obvious they ain't here," another member of the crew chimed in.

Above the Klansmen, Yellowstone and Kirby held their breaths. Unnoticed by King, the detective's right hand had snaked under his jacket, gripping the butt of his revolver.

The heat and excitement of the chase and the sounds of the ersatz bounty hunters' argument rose to a climax and then began to dissipate. One by one, the disappointed Klansmen turned from the mouth of the alley, still muttering curses, and headed back to their truck.

When he was certain that they were gone, Yellowstone cautiously raised his head to face Kirby.

"I can't believe it," he whispered.

"Me neither, boss," answered King. "I thought we were sure enough dead."

As Kirby's head sank back down to the floor of the scaffold, Yellowstone studied him more closely, puzzled by the ex-con's actions. He had come back to help the fallen detective, even though he could have kept running and left Yellowstone to the mob's tender mercies.

He was almost beginning to like the little man, and that disturbed him also, fearing such feelings might begin to cloud his judgment. He was still unsure whether he could trust the felon or not; it was possible he had saved the detective for no other reason than to win him over, to continue to receive his help.

Yellowstone knew he had to keep one sobering fact in mind: he had still uncovered no evidence that King had not killed Rebekah Nixon.

CHAPTER FIFTEEN

Bleary eyed, only half awake due to the sleepless night before, Michael Yellowstone was the first one into the squad room the next morning. He had left Kirby King asleep on his couch, and shut-eye for the jerk who had denied him sleep rankled him. To add insult to injury, a telephone rang somewhere among the maze of desks in the squad room as he shook the final scoop of coffee into the communal coffee pot.

The second ring found Yellowstone standing in the middle of the stand of desks scratching his head and trying to figure out which telephone to answer.

On the seventh ring, the Osage detective snatched up the handset on the telephone on his own desk.

"Yeah?" he said curtly.

"Hello? This is Stacy Lord of radio station WXYZ. Has detective Michael Yellowstone made it in yet this morning?" Clearly, due to the raspiness in his throat, she had not recognized his voice.

"Who wants to know?" he barked into the receiver.

"Uh, I just said this is Stacy Lord."

"Never heard of her."

"I'm the star reporter of WXYZ."

"Never heard of it. I read newspapers."

"Listen, dimbulb, if he isn't there, may I leave a message?"

"Sure. How do you spell message?"

There was a pregnant moment of silence from the handset.

"When you get a moment, *Mr. Yellowstone*, tell yourself that I'm concerned."

"About what?"

"About whether my...zealous reporting on the Kirby King case may have caused the detective to think less of me."

"Would it bother you if it had?"

"You know it would, Michael."

"I'll tell him, Miss Lord," Yellowstone said softly.

"And I'm sure that Detective Yellowstone will want to assure you that the two of you are still on for dinner and a movie at the earliest opportunity."

"I'm glad to hear that."

Yellowstone started to hang up the handset, but hesitated when he realized Stacy was still talking.

"I had another reason for calling you, Hollywood," she said. "I have a tip for you; actually, more like a rumor to report.

"Word has reached me that some of the younger and more aggressive men in the Negro community plan to start patrolling the streets at night... with the intent of protecting Kirby King."

Yellowstone sighed heavily.

"Forget their intent," he said. "The result will most likely be more bloodshed."

"With you caught in the middle," the reporter said.

"Mostly," he replied. For a long beat, he heard nothing further from the other end of the line. "Was there something else, Stacy?"

"I hope." She paused again. "I've given you some information that could be helpful, cowboy."

"You're right. Thank you."

"I was hoping for a little more in return."

"Oh?" A smile began to turn up the corners of his mouth.

"Maybe you could pass on a little inside dope to me?" she asked. "An exclusive scoop on the King story right about now would sure make my bosses happy."

And the smile disappeared.

"No," he said brusquely.

"Oh, come on," she wheedled. "Throw a working girl a bone, will ya?"

Yellowstone saw Jack Hill entering the squad room and heading his way. "I gotta go, Stacy," he said softly.

"Be careful, Michael. I…"

He set the receiver down in its cradle.

Again he was left to wonder: was the fiery and ambitious reporter only interested in him because she wanted a news source inside the police department?

A nagging voice in his head, a voice he couldn't seem to still permanently, had told him more than once that there could be no other reason for a beautiful, uptown girl like Stacy Lord to take up with a poor, homely cowboy like him.

This gnawing bit of self-doubt angered him as much as his firecracker of a girlfriend did.

"Who's calling at this ungodly hour?" asked Lt. Hill as he pulled his chair back from his desk. "And what are you doing here this early?"

"Couldn't sleep, Jack," said Yellowstone. "And that was Stacy Lord, the reporter from WXYZ."

"What did that witch want?"

"What you'd expect: a scoop," Yellowstone replied, fighting to ignore Hill's characterization of Stacy.

Hill snorted.

"But she gave me a scoop instead," the Osage told him. "If it's true, we could soon be adding roving bands of young black men to the mix: self-appointed bodyguards for Kirby King.

"We've already got a fire burnin' out there. This could be like tryin' to put it out with gasoline."

"Don't worry about it, Hollywood," said Hill as he struck a match and brought it up to the Lucky Strike dangling from his lips. "That sounds like the best news I've heard in days."

"What?"

"You betcha. It would save the taxpayers some dough and the department a boatload of work if all these malcontents take each other out." The lieutenant exhaled a small cloud of smoke.

"I just hope they take King down at the same time."

✦✦✦

A few hours later, Yellowstone and Hill were driving to interview yet another person claiming to have information regarding Kirby King and the murder of Rebekah Nixon…a lead that would doubtless prove to be as bogus as all the others they'd received and were required to check out.

Yellowstone was distracted by doubts about his own judgment. He was keeping multiple secrets from his partner: about his relationship with Stacy Lord; about King's whereabouts. And about the fact that he was actually aiding this known felon.

Life had looked much simpler when he'd viewed it from the back of a horse.

To divert his thoughts and clear his head, he reached over and turned on the car radio. A deep male voice came through the speakers.

"The opinions expressed by Stacy Lord do not necessarily reflect the views of station WXYZ or its management."

"Oh, lord," groaned Yellowstone. He reached for the dial to change stations, but Hill slapped his hand away.

"Leave it be, cowboy," he said. "It's always good to know what the enemy's thinking."

"If you know nothing about the recent murder of one of our finest young city attorneys," Stacy's familiar voice began, "you've either been living in a cave …or you're a member of the Detroit police force."

Lt. Hill chuckled at this, but there was no humor in his voice.

"Maybe the police *are* working this case. We just don't know, because they refuse to speak on the record about their progress in the investigation. Or their lack of same.

"But while they fiddle, our beautiful city is in increasing danger of going up in flames. Amateur bounty hunters…acting alone or in packs like wolves…are threatening to turn the streets of Detroit into rivers of blood.

"And if this Motor City Manhunt for a depraved killer is simply too much for the boys of the DPD to handle…we may soon all find ourselves at the mercy of vigilante justice."

"Okay," said Lt. Hill, now shutting off the radio himself. "That's about enough of that."

"Amen, brother," Yellowstone said, agreeing wholeheartedly.

Yet inside, he was beginning to worry that Stacy's words could soon become a self-fulfilling prophecy.

CHAPTER SIXTEEN

Michael Yellowstone was back on the street that night, with his other "partner."

Not wanting to be seen in his car with Kirby King, Yellowstone had risked a bus ride into the heart of the city before setting out with the felon on foot. There were a lot more shadows for a body to dive into for cover, he reasoned, than there were for an automobile.

"I still don't get it," the detective was saying. "Just what is it you think you can accomplish alone that the entire police force can't?"

"That's just it, boss," King replied. "Except for you, that entire police force you're so proud of ain't doin' *nothin'*. Why should they? As far as they're concerned, they already know who killed that woman…*me*.

"Be honest, Mr. Detective…has the law questioned anybody else besides me?"

"I wouldn't tell you if we had."

"Right."

"I will tell you, though, that the few tips we've received pointing to anyone other than you have all turned out to be groundless."

"I reckon the same is true of any tips pointin' ta me."

"Why would you say that?"

"Because if it wasn't, I'd already be a corpse in a holdin' cell."

"You don't know that, boy."

"No? Remember what your friends did to me in interrogation? You tell me: if any cop other than you saw me about to be gunned down by a bounty hunter…would he try to save me?"

Yellowstone's non-response was all the response King needed.

When the detective did finally speak again, his voice had a decided edge to it.

"Don't forget, Kirby; you haven't found anything to help your cause either."

"That's why I gotta keep lookin'."

"And it's why I'm cuttin' you so much slack. But don't ever forget: if what we find convinces me once and for all that you did it…I'll put you down without battin' an eye. Don't think I won't."

"I don't doubt it for a minute, boss; but I'll take my chances. Here we are."

King had stopped and was looking up at the traditional three balls display sign that identified the establishment they were facing as being a pawn shop.

"What are we doin' here?" Yellowstone asked him.

"Thought I'd talk to the fella what runs this place. He used to be plugged in to most everything that went down on the streets."

"You told me you didn't have any friends."

"I don't know that I'd call Claven a friend, exactly. But we know each other, and he might feel like he owes me."

"Why's that?"

"Before they sent me down the river, I helped him out once. Took an old junk car he had and restored it near good as new: no charge.

"He sold the car and used the money to help pay for an operation his poor ol' maw needed. I'm hopin' he'll still think kindly of me."

Yellowstone shook his head. The more he came to know of this man Kirby King, the more confused he became.

+++

Claven Dupont was a middle-aged black man who liked to picture himself as a man of fashion. In truth, his rather garish and often mismatched clothing ensembles and the multiple ostentatious rings on his fingers proved him to be just the opposite.

Still, the delusion allowed him to ignore the fact that he conducted business from behind a mesh wire grill and counted among his clientele some of the city's more questionable types.

It was for this reason that Yellowstone hung back when they entered the pawn shop. Given the part of town they were in, and the nature of this particular enterprise, he had no doubt some of the merchandise on display was stolen.

He had no interest in such at the moment; but if the veteran pawnbroker caught even the faintest whiff of "cop" about him, he would probably clam up and become worthless as a source of information.

"Claven?" King said in his deep but quiet voice as he approached the shop owner. "You 'member me?"

Dupont's initial glance showed boredom more than anything else. Then his eyes widened in recognition. A wide smile revealed two gold teeth; one of them had a tiny diamond implanted in it.

"Kirby? As I live and breathe…Kirby King!"

He thrust both arms forward through the semi-circular opening in the grill behind which he sat, grabbing King's right hand and pumping it up and down vigorously.

"Do I remember you?" he said. "I think of you every time I go to visit mama!"

"Is she still doin' okay?"

"Feisty as ever. She'll outlive us all."

"That's good."

The smile on Dupont's face grew strained. "But I know things ain't been going so good for you, Kirby."

"No. Not so good."

"So what can I do for you?"

"I know you hear things, Claven. I was hopin' maybe you'd heard something that might get me out from under some of it."

The pawnbroker shook his head sadly. "Not a thing, Kirby. All anybody wants to talk about is that damned reward." He again smiled slightly, this time ruefully.

"Hell, bookmakers have even started taking bets on the day and time you'll be killed, boy."

King shrugged. "Well, I'm doin' the best I can to make sure nobody wins that bet." He took Dupont's hand again.

"You keep your eyes and ears open for me, okay? If somethin' comes up, I know you can find a way to get word to me, and I'll come runnin'."

"I'll do the best I can, Kirby."

"Thank you, Claven. Tell your momma I said 'hi'."

Yellowstone had exited the pawn ship moments earlier, and was waiting outside when King departed.

"What now?" he asked the ex-con.

"I don't know," King replied, the sound of defeat evident in his voice.

"Why don't we just head on home then?" the detective suggested. "Sometimes a good night's sleep'll clear the head."

As they walked toward the nearest bus stop, their path took them past a bar whose neon sign cast its light over them. King stopped, staring up at it.

"An ice cold beer sure would taste good, boss," he said wistfully. "I ain't had one in years."

"I know what you mean," Yellowstone said. "But it wouldn't be safe to go into a public place like this. You gotta know that."

"Yeah," Kirby conceded, running his hand over lips suddenly gone dry. "Wouldn't be safe."

They resumed walking, but as they were passing the entrance to the gin joint, its front door banged open and a patron waltzed out, staggering more than slightly.

Not blind drunk, but definitely vision impaired, the man in his cups stumbled forward and collided with King.

"Beg pardon," he said with slurred speech, a silly grin on his lips. He squinted at King, and what he now saw nearly sobered him.

"Oh…my…God," he moaned.

Spinning on his heels, the drunk raced back to the door leading into the bar. Before it closed behind him, Yellowstone and King could hear him shrieking at the top of his lungs.

"It's him! The fella on'a wanted poster!"

"We'd best make tracks," Yellowstone said.

"If that means run…I agree!"

As they began to round the first corner they came to, Yellowstone paused just long enough to look back at the bar. At least a dozen men had come spilling out of the place. Several were pointing toward the detective.

Even as he ran alongside King, Yellowstone's eyes and mind were casting all about for means of escape. His vision zoomed to a five-story tall building across the street. Near one wall of it, he saw a short stack of long boards, a pair of sawhorses and a garbage can; all probably left behind by workmen.

Grabbing Kirby by one arm, Yellowstone rushed to the site. As the ex-con watched in anxious confusion, the detective grabbed the two sawhorses, dragging them so they stood under the building's fire escape.

He placed them side-by-side, then laid one of the longer boards across the top of them. With one end of the board then thrust down flush to the ground and the other end projecting upward at an angle, this contrivance now looked like a crude imitation of a playground teeter-totter.

"What are you doin'?" King asked.

"Just follow my lead," Yellowstone barked. He pulled King over and directed him to stand on the lowered end of the board.

Yellowstone snatched the garbage can and turned it upright, emptying it of its contents. After placing the empty can upside down on the sidewalk in front of the upper end of the board on his improvised teeter-totter, he climbed atop the can.

"When I jump onto this end of the board," he told the incredulous King, "you're gonna fly up, grab the bottom rungs of the fire escape ladder and haul it down for us."

"I'm gonna *what*?" was all Kirby had time to exclaim, before Yellowstone's weight hit the opposite end of the board and indeed did send the ex-con flying upward and forward.

King grunted in pain as he slammed into the unyielding metal of the fire escape. But he managed to hang on and use his momentum to lower the ladder to ground level.

Yellowstone took the time to dismantle their makeshift catapult, then clambered up onto the escape.

He and King didn't slow for a moment as they made their way up to and over the edge of the building's roof.

After both had taken a minute to get their wind back, King pushed himself up and chanced taking a peek down over the edge of the roof's ledge.

"Oh, hell!" he gasped.

"What is it?"

"This trick ain't gonna work this time, Mr. Stunt Man. They must've spotted us. Half the mob's tryin' to get on the fire escape, and the other half's lookin' for a way through the front door. They're gonna be swarmin' all over us."

Yellowstone grunted and pushed himself to his feet. After looking about briefly, he tore a length of board off an abandoned pigeon coop. He quickly shoved one end of it up under the knob of the door leading from the building's interior to its rooftop, tightly wedging the lower end at an angle against the tarred roof surface.

"That won't hold for long," King said. "We're dead men."

"Only if we stay on this roof," Yellowstone replied.

"Huh?"

The Osage detective was already off and running, moving quickly from one side of the roof to another. Finally, apparently seeing what he was looking for, he waved for King to join him.

When the ex-con did so, Yellowstone pointed to the roof of the next building. Between the two was an alleyway some eight to ten feet in width.

"We have to jump over to that roof," he declared rather nonchalantly.

"Are you crazy?" King demanded.

"It's either that or stay here and wait for the good time boys to arrive," Yellowstone told him. "Your choice. Me...I'm jumpin'!"

So saying, Yellowstone backpedaled several feet, then sprinted forward. Without hesitation, he launched himself off the edge of the roof.

He sailed over the gap and hit the adjacent rooftop with room to spare. He absorbed the impact of the landing by rolling forward on one shoulder with practiced ease. Bounding to his feet, he motioned for King to follow.

Kirby just stared at him with slack-jawed amazement. Behind him, he thought he could faintly hear the voices of men making their way up from street level.

Left with no choice, he scurried back even farther than Yellowstone had, determined to give himself the best running start possible.

Short legs churning, he raced forward. His feet kept pumping even after there was nothing solid beneath them. When he cleared the gap between the buildings…barely…and landed on the neighboring rooftop, he staggered and pitched forward awkwardly.

Yellowstone gave him no time to savor his success, grabbing him by the back of his light jacket and hauling him to his feet.

"Come on," the detective urged. "We gotta do that at least two more times!"

"What? No!"

"We're still too close to that mob, Kirby. We gotta put more distance between us before it'll be safe to go back to ground. Now come on!"

King grimly nodded. This time the two men ran side by side, launching themselves simultaneously toward the next roof.

Yellowstone again landed easily and gracefully. Kirby, however, caught the toes of his left foot on the roof's ledge as he came down, causing him to land even more heavily than the first time.

"Get up," Yellowstone urged, helping him to rise. "One more jump should do it."

"I can't!" Kirby gasped.

"Sure you can."

"No. Go on without me."

"Forget it. C'mon…we go together again."

Gritting his teeth, King nodded. Yellowstone returned the gesture before taking off on the run across the roof. He could hear King just a pace or two behind him.

Again, Yellowstone cleared the gap with relative ease. And again, King came up short.

His feet barely hit the edge of the next roof's ledge and immediately slipped off. His body plunged straight down as he desperately lunged forward with both hands. Only one found purchase.

Clinging to the safety of the ledge by his fingertips, King stared down into the dark abyss yawning fatally below him. The strength in his fingers failed, and he began to plummet.

His descent stopped with a jarring jerk. He looked up to see Yellowstone hanging over the ledge of the building, both his hands wrapped around King's forearm.

"Put your feet against the wall and push up," the detective called down to him.

The ex-con obeyed without question. Yellowstone released the grip of one hand only long enough to take hold of Kirby's other arm. With a valiant surge he pulled the shorter man up and onto the firm surface of the rooftop.

This time, both of them remained prone, fighting to bring their breathing under control.

"Thanks, boss," King managed to gasp at last.

"Y'know, Kirby, you don't have to keep callin' me 'boss'," Yellowstone told him. "You're not in the pen anymore."

"Old habits, Mr. Detective. They die hard." King swiveled his head toward the Osage and smiled weakly.

"Just like us, huh?"

CHAPTER SEVENTEEN

Yellowstone and King managed to make their way back to the detective's home without further incidence, but both were drained and spent by their earlier exertions.

King was slouched on the sofa that also now served as his bed, his elbows resting on his knees. He ran both hands over the top of his smooth head, raising his face to look at Yellowstone slumped across from him in his easy chair.

"Has it occurred to you," the ex-con asked, "that if you had just let me fall off that roof… this would all be over now?"

"Not for me it wouldn't," Yellowstone stated flatly.

King nodded somberly.

"I'm feelin' kinda wore out, boss."

"Not surprised. You and me both look like we was rode hard and put up wet."

"I don't know what that means," Kirby admitted, smiling lamely. "But I know I gotta hit the rack."

"Go right ahead."

Kicking off his shoes but otherwise not bothering to undress, King reclined on the sofa. In less than a minute, his shallow breathing was proof that he had already fallen asleep.

Such deep slumber probably wouldn't last long, Yellowstone suspected as he sat watch over the man with whom he had forged this most unlikely of alliances.

Every night since he'd come into this home, Kirby had spent much of it tossing and turning, stirring restlessly in the night. Plagued perhaps by fear or guilt; or possibly merely haunted by past and present horrors.

The detective pushed up out of his chair. His daytime job responsibilities added to his nighttime endeavors had left him somewhat sleep-deprived himself. The soft comfort of his mattress was calling siren-like to him.

He shook his head as he looked down and saw that Kirby had dropped his lightweight jacket on the floor, where it had doubtless been forgotten by him.

When the detective bent and picked it up, his fingers fell on a small, hard, rectangular object. Curious, he reached into the jacket's inside pocket and pulled out a crumpled piece of paper.

Opening it up, he saw an address written upon it in King's rather crude script. He recognized it as matching the locale of Claven Dupont's pawnshop.

But there was something else in the pocket, nestled in one of its lower corners. The detective's fingers closed around it and pulled it out of its resting place.

Yellowstone's eyes narrowed and grew cold as he opened his hand and examined the object resting in his palm.

It was a cigarette lighter. Apparently fairly new and obviously very expensive. On one side of its polished silver case, a set of initials had been ornately engraved.

R.N.

Before draping the ex-con's jacket over the back of the sofa, Yellowstone returned the balled up piece of paper back into its pocket.

But the lighter…

The lighter went into one of his own pockets.

+++

Yellowstone didn't feel the least bit out of place the next day, amidst the pandemonium that was the District Attorney's office.

It reminded him of the precinct house.

He lifted a small notebook from his inner coat pocket, flipped it open to a list of names representing the people from this office that he had, either singly or in company with Lt. Hill, already interviewed regarding the death of Rebekah Nixon.

There were still a couple of names he hadn't crossed off.

He made his way through the sea of moving bodies toward a specific desk. Behind it, furiously tapping away at a typewriter was an attractive young woman: probably early thirties, well-proportioned, her light brown hair resting against her scalp in short ringlets.

At his approach, she turned from the typewriter, greeting him with the warm smile she reserved for new and intriguing acquaintances.

"Miss Steinbaum? Rosie Steinbaum?" Yellowstone said, flashing his badge.

He noticed the welcoming smile on her lips fading somewhat.

"Oh," she sighed with disappointment. "Another detective. I've already talked to some of you about Rebekah."

"But you haven't talked to me," he replied, flashing what he hoped was a winning smile of his own.

"That's true," she said. The smile returned more fully to her mouth as she began to absently twirl a ringlet of hair with one finger in the way that women often did. "Ask away, officer," she chirped, motioning him invitingly to a chair.

"Let's start with the obvious, Rosie. To your knowledge, had Miss Nixon received any threats in the days or even weeks before her murder?"

"You mean like from somebody she helped send to prison?" The woman chuckled lightly.

"That usually only happens in the picture shows, detective. Not very often in real life.

"And as far as I know, Rebekah hadn't received any threats from that man Kirby King... or anybody else...ever."

Yellowstone nodded, scribbling something in his notebook with the stub of a pencil. Then he leaned toward the woman.

"Of course, we both know who the most likely suspects are in any murder case, don't we, Rosie?"

Her elbows on the desktop, chin resting in both hands, she gave him a conspiratorial grin.

"Sure," she said. "Somebody the victim knew."

"That's right. Rebekah Nixon: she was young, attractive, successful... single."

"You're asking about boyfriends."

"That's what I'm doin'."

"God love her," Rosie sighed. "She was so intense, I'm not sure she could have ever *had* a private life, assuming she wanted one. Most men couldn't have handled her."

"But not *all* men?"

Rosie's face grew serious.

"I worked with Rebekah, detective. I like to think I was her friend. But there were parts of herself, of her life, that she hardly ever let anybody else see."

"But you caught glimpses, didn't you?"

"This is just between you and me, right?"

"Absolutely," Yellowstone concurred. He flipped his notebook closed and returned it to his pocket.

"It's nothing definite, mind you," Rosie said. "More like a feeling, really."

"Growin' up around my dear ol' momma gave me a healthy respect for a woman's instincts," the detective assured her, coaxing more from her.

"I think Rebekah may have been seeing someone," she told him. "And I don't think it was always smooth sailing, either."

"Did she ever tell you that?"

"Not in so many words, no. And I never asked; Rebekah didn't like to be pressed. And if there was a guy, I have no idea who it was. Sorry."

"Don't be," he replied. "You've been a big help."

"You probably should talk to Gladys Cooper. She was Rebekah's personal assistant. She might know something more."

Yellowstone pulled out his notebook and referenced it. "Yeah. I have her on my list. Could you point her out to me?"

"I'm afraid she's not in today. Some sort of family emergency, I think."

"I'll speak to her another time, then," Yellowstone said, rising to his feet. "Thank you for your help, Rosie."

"Any time," she replied, the warm smile back on her lips, flashing an invitation he chose to ignore as he turned to leave.

"Detective?" she called after him softly.

"Yes?"

"Please find whoever did this."

"I aim to," he replied firmly.

✦✦✦

The tiny bell suspended over the front portal of Claven Dupont's pawn-shop tinkled as the door swung inward.

The proprietor, perched as usual behind the relative safety of his wire grill, like a brightly plumed bird in a cage of its own making, looked up from the racing form he had been studiously perusing…and the blood flowing to his brain turned to dust.

Death in the form of a man had just entered his shop.

Dupont had only a passing acquaintance with Tony "Torpedo" Matson, but what he knew and what he'd heard of the mad man was more than enough to make his limbs go numb with fear.

"Hey, Tony," he said, in a voice that came out as more of a squeak.

"Claven."

Matson said nothing more, pulling a cigarette from its pack and taking his time to light it. Dupont's eyes began to dance around in his head nervously.

"Last I heard," he spoke to break the cloying silence, "you were in Chicago. What brings you back to Detroit?"

Matson blew smoke that drifted into Dupont's eyes and made him blink, then smiled coldly.

"I had a million reasons to come back."

The light of realization dawned over Dupont's face, and his fear grew even more palpable.

"You're here for Kirby King," the pawnbroker said in a hushed tone.

"Yes."

"How'd you even hear about that?"

"Everybody's heard about it, Claven. It's not surprising, really.

"I mean, some darkie ups and rapes and murders a pretty little green-eyed white girl…there are going to be repercussions."

"I guess. I don't know about such things."

Matson's right arm shot forward, through the opening in the grillwork that separated him from the pawnbroker. He grabbed a handful of the front of Dupont's purple satin shirt and yanked him forward savagely.

Dupont cried out in pain as the side of his face slammed against the metal grill. Matson kept him pulled up flush to the mesh.

"Don't ever lie to me again," the hit man growled. The wild and murderous expression on his face spoke plainly of the consequences of doing so.

"Sure, Tony, sure," Dupont practically blubbered. "I didn't mean nothing."

"That's better. Now, let's start over. I've been asking around since I got back in town, Claven. People tell me you're one of the closest things to a friend King's got."

"No, Tony. Not friends." Dupont yelped as Matson pulled harder on his shirt; the pawnbroker felt the metal web of the grill digging into the flesh of his cheek.

"Close enough," the hit man said, moving in nearer to the pawnbroker's sweaty face. "He's been to see you, hasn't he?" His fingers twisted the slick material of Dupont's shirt.

"Think real hard before you answer that, Claven."

Dupont's body sagged at the knees.

"Yeah," he said at last. "He's been here."

"And you know how to get a message to him, don't you?"

Dupont hesitated a fraction of a second too long. Matson pushed him back then pulled him forward slamming him against the counter grill even harder.

"Don't you?" Matson was practically screaming now, and the pawnbroker knew he was on the razor's edge between living and dying.

"Yeah, Tony," he admitted, tears welling up in his eyes; their wetness attempting unsuccessfully to wash away the stain of betrayal and shame. "I know how to contact him."

"Good," Matson crooned. "That's just what I wanted to hear. You're going to send a message to our Mr. King." The gangster was smiling now, but if anything it simply made him look even more insanely dangerous.

"And I'm going to tell you what message to send."

CHAPTER EIGHTEEN

The sight that greeted his eyes as he approached the 3rd Precinct Station didn't surprise Yellowstone.

Indeed, he'd quickly come to expect to see small clusters of demonstrators gathering on the sidewalk outside the building. One group, mostly whites, was shouting and waving placards demanding that killers not be allowed to walk free on the streets of their city.

Separated from them by only a few precarious feet was a slightly larger group, composed largely of blacks but with a few white faces sprinkled within. One of its members was waving a hand-lettered placard that especially caught the detective's eye:

"You're here for Kirby King."

JUSTICE FOR *BOTH* VICTIMS

Yellowstone did a quick head count. The number of people participating in the demonstrations was slowly growing: mostly on the colored side.

As he slid around the periphery of the small throng as inconspicuously as possible, he noted that Virgil Lowery was standing at the forefront of the black demonstrators. That wasn't surprising, either; King's attorney had been his client's most vocal defender from day one.

What occurred next had become equally commonplace. The Osage detective smiled and shook his head as he saw Stacy Lord thrusting her way through the crowd to reach Lowery. The poor technician charged with carrying her enormous and heavy recording equipment valiantly kept up with her, switching on the device as Lord stabbed a microphone toward Lowery's face.

The attorney didn't hesitate to speak to the radio commentator. It was as if the two of them fed off each other, Yellowstone thought. Lowery used the radio to defend Kirby King in the crucial court of public opinion... chumming the pool from which potential jurors would be drawn...while Lord exploited that same public's fascination with all things related to this case in order to elevate her own profile.

Yellowstone sighed heavily. He was still crazy about the girl, he admitted to himself...but there were times lately when he didn't much like her.

Not wishing to be seen by her, lest she try to draw him into today's version of this repetitive dog-and-pony show, Yellowstone further averted his eyes and scurried into the building.

He paused long enough at the front desk to ask the sergeant on duty there about his kid who was hoping to earn a tryout with the Tigers (on the police force, as in the Army, it was wise to cultivate a good relationship with sergeants) before bounding up the stairway to the second floor, taking it two steps at a time.

It seemed to be business as usual in the detectives' squad room: barely contained chaos. Yellowstone's eyes swiveled rapidly from side to side, seeking sign of his partner.

Lt. Hill was perched at one of the windows facing the street, one leg and part of his rump resting on its sill. As the Osage detective approached, he saw the veteran detective fish a pack of matches out of his shirt pocket and light up a cigarette: probably at least his fifth of the young day.

As Yellowstone came to stand beside him, he noted that Hill was staring down at the demonstrators clustered below. Hill exhaled a small cloud of smoke, waving the hand holding the cigarette downward.

"You know, cowboy," Hill said, his voice sounding rather pensive, "there was a time…and not too long ago, either…when the Chief would have just marched a few uniforms down there and broke up that bunch of loudmouths by busting a few heads."

"Is that what you think we should do, Jack?" Yellowstone asked.

"Don't get your Hollywood panties in a bunch, partner," Hill snapped, his flaring eyes reflecting his exasperation.

"I'm just saying that's the way things *used* to be, that's all. But times change. Those days are long gone." He took another drag on his Lucky Strike, exhaled slowly.

"We'll never see anything like that happening in America ever again."

CHAPTER NINETEEN

Once again, a pleasing aroma wafted into Yellowstone's nostrils as he entered his little house that evening.

"What's on th' menu for tonight?" he asked as he walked into his small but efficient kitchen area.

"Nothing fancy, boss" Kirby King replied, turning away from the stove atop which sat a large pot. "They don't teach fancy in the joint," he explained. "It's just some good old-fashioned beef stew."

"Sounds good to me," said Yellowstone. He meant it, too: compared to the lone hot dog that accounted for his total food consumption for the day thus far, stew seemed like ambrosia.

"But do I smell something else besides stew?" he asked.

"Good nose, detective. I'm baking us a pan of cornbread, too. *That's* a recipe I learned from my grandma." King turned back to the pot, stirring the simmering contents of the pot.

"It'll be a while yet before it's all done, though. Why don't you stretch out and take a nap? I'll wake you when it's ready."

At the very words, Yellowstone felt a weariness descend upon him. Between the demands of his day job and the time he'd spent prowling the streets at night with King, little time had remained for actual sleep.

"Did we get th' roadster back from the garage yet?"

"Yep."

"Good," said the detective as he drifted into the living room. Not bothering to remove anything save his shoes, his denim jacket and his shoulder holster, he threw his long frame down on the sofa.

So exhausted was he that he was asleep within seconds of closing his eyes. It was a deep and dreamless sleep: no disturbing images of dead women…or living ones…could worm their way into his psyche.

When he awoke, however, the peaceful balm dispersed almost immediately.

Something was wrong.

The shadows within the room seemed to be too deep, too long. The silence that greeted him was too pervasive. A glance at the small clock atop his mantel confirmed that he'd been asleep for more than two hours.

Far longer than it took to finish baking a pan of cornbread.

He hurried into the kitchen, finding it empty as he had expected. Pushing aside the curtains over one window, he saw that the driveway was likewise unoccupied.

Kirby had taken his car and again gone off on his own.

'Cursing softly under his breath, the Osage detective turned away from the window. Stepping to the stove, he gingerly touched the pot of stew still sitting atop it. There was yet faint warmth to it, indicating King had not been gone long. The enticing aroma of the thick brown broth still lingered as well. Glancing over at the tiny dining table, Yellowstone saw a pan covered by a dishcloth: the promised cornbread, no doubt.

"What th' hell," he muttered, reaching into the overhead cabinet for a large bowl; a man had to eat.

Kirby King had already gulped down a bowl of the stew, sopping up the remnants of the broth with a thick slice of cornbread, before making off with Yellowstone's automobile.

He'd been less truthful than he'd realized when he earlier told the detective he had no friends. Now, finding himself in desperate need, he had come to realize that he had more of them than he had imagined.

It wasn't surprising that he'd forgotten. Hopeless and dangerous years in prison would drive the very idea of true friendship from any man's heart and mind. In that world, there were only two kinds of people you encountered: people who watched your back and people who wanted to slip a shiv into your back.

And those who watched your back did so only in exchange for mutual protection.

The only "friends" you had in prison were the bars that offered you nominal and brief shelter from the other animals. It left you suspicious of everyone, even when you got out. Every word, every gesture of friendship that was offered to you was met with hesitance and a jaundiced eye. And always with the thought: what does this person want from me? At what price does their friendship come?

That dim view of the world, as much as anything else, had led him to isolate himself in the weeks since he'd been given what now passed for freedom.

But this crisis had begun to show him that he did have at least a few acquaintances that seemed to wish him well and wanted no harm to come to him.

What an odd thing to discover at the same time that thousands more wanted nothing for him but death.

Then there was the cop: Yellowstone. His whole life, King had thought of the police as nothing more than a new breed of overseers, armed with Billy clubs rather than bullwhips. It seemed he'd been beaten by cops more often than he'd been kissed by a woman.

In the joint, he'd passed blood so many times after receiving such a beating at the hands of the guards that he'd almost forgotten the normal color of urine.

Yellowstone seemed different, though; at least on the surface. Maybe it was because he wasn't exactly white himself; Kirby wasn't sure.

Or maybe that was just on the outside. On the inside, maybe he was the same as every other cop. Kirby had no doubt the detective would slap the cuffs on him without hesitation if he felt justified.

Yet he seemed intent on more than just making an arrest, padding his record, looking good in the eyes of his superiors. He wanted to know without doubt the who and the why of the murder he was investigating. Black or white, man or woman, Yellowstone cared only that the cell door be closed on the true killer.

It was that single-minded determination to find and follow the truth that made Kirby feel he could trust the man.

It did bother the ex-con a little, though, to realize that a part of him was also beginning to actually *like* the man. He just wasn't sure if that was a wise thing to do.

Sometimes, having friends wasn't enough. Thus far, tonight's excursion had proven to be as fruitless as all his others. His friends and contacts on the streets were continuing to keep their eyes and ears open, but thus far to no avail. If anyone knew anything, they were keeping it to themselves. Or they were outside the circles of criminal activity to which King and his contacts had access.

Kirby smiled grimly as he pulled his purloined car to the curb. If he'd been a cop, he might consider himself to be guilty, too.

The closest to a lead he'd received tonight was from a small-time bookie, who told him the pawnbroker Claven Dupont wanted to meet with King again.

As he stepped from the car, King cast his eyes about for any untoward signs. Seeing nothing, he walked briskly to the door of the pawnshop.

Dupont jumped slightly at the sound of the tinkling bell above the door that signified someone had entered his establishment. He relaxed only slightly when he realized it was Kirby King; the smile he forced onto his grizzled face reflected pain more than pleasure.

"What's up, Claven?" Kirby asked as he approached the counter behind which Dupont stood. How's your mom?"

"Nothing much up, Kirby," Dupont replied stiffly. "Other than a cop was in here looking for you. I told him I hadn't seen you. And my mother's just fine, thanks to you."

Kirby's eyes narrowed. It wasn't hot inside the shop, yet beads of sweat speckled Dupont's forehead. The pawnbroker licked his lips repeatedly in nervous reflex.

"Then why'd you want to see me, Claven?" Kirby asked. "You didn't need to see me in person to tell me nothing."

"No," Dupont said with a faked chuckle that ended in a cough. "Of course not."

He rubbed the saliva away from the corner of his mouth with the back of his hand. His eyes seemed to be gazing beyond King rather than at him. Kirby began to pull back away from the counter.

"Here's the real reason I asked you to come," Dupont blurted out. He leaned down out of sight behind the counter for just a moment. When he straightened back up, he was cradling a small bundle in both hands.

Dupont gently placed the bundle down on the glass counter top. He pulled back two folds of chamois cloth to reveal a steel blue .45 Smith and Wesson revolver and a box of cartridges.

His curiosity piqued, Kirby stepped back closer to the counter. He stared down silently at the gun, and then looked up quizzically at the pawnbroker.

"It's untraceable, Kirby," Dupont assured him, pushing the revolver toward him. "I got it just for you."

"I can't afford to go buying no gun," Kirby said, his deep voice little more than a whisper.

"No need," Dupont hurried to tell him. "It's free. A gift…from me to you."

"Why would you do that?" King asked, the old suspicions of people's motives arising within him.

"'Cause of my mom, and because you got a target painted on you, boy. A target as big as all Detroit. People you don't even know want you dead." Dupont pushed the revolver even closer toward King.

"You need to be able to defend yourself."

The concern Dupont voiced for Kirby's safety was genuine. Even though he was setting this man up in order to save his own life, he hadn't forgotten the debt he owed King.

With a gun, he felt, Kirby might at least have a fighting chance when Tony "The Torpedo" Matson…or anybody else…came gunning for him.

"Go on, Kirby," he urged. "Take it."

Almost reverently, as if it was a sacred relic, King lifted the revolver in both hands. It was perfectly balanced. He half-cocked the hammer, held the gun close to one ear as he slowly revolved the cylinder, smiling tightly at the smooth clicking sounds. Reflections of light danced off its highly polished barrel like tiny stars.

He was sorely tempted. The constant and seemingly never-ending tension of having to fight to stay alive every minute of every day was even greater and heavier a burden than the one he had borne in prison. It was beginning to wear his nerves down to raw nubs.

Both men were somewhat perplexed when Kirby set the revolver down and pushed it back toward Dupont.

"I thank you, Claven," he said softly, "but I'd best not."

"Huh? Why not?"

"Well, if nothing else, an ex-con walking around with a loaded gun might set the cops off against me even more than they are already."

"Boy, you think the law needs a *reason* to gun you down?" Dupont said earnestly.

"And what about everybody else? Hell, there's so many people want you dead you can't stir 'em with a stick!"

"That's true, Claven," King agreed. "And I do thank you for your concern. I truly do."

But even as he spoke, Kirby was wrapping the revolver back in its protective chamois covering.

"I'll see you around," he said, nodding to the pawnbroker before turning toward the door.

"Kirby?"

"Yeah?"

"I just want you to know I appreciate all you did for me and my momma. Every time I look at her, I think of you and what you done for us."

"It wasn't so much, Claven."

"It was to me. And I surely do hope you come through this mess all right."

"Thank you. So do I."

Dupont silently damned his own human frailty as he placed the rejected .45 back under the counter. Shame caused him to turn and shuffle listlessly to the back room so he could neither see nor hear what he felt sure was about to happen next.

Outside the pawnshop, Kirby King flipped up the collar of his lightweight jacket, tugged down the short bill of his cap to obscure his profile before heading back to his borrowed car.

Across the street diagonally, Tony Matson waited in the concealing shadows of a doorway. He'd been alert since the man now leaving the pawnshop had first arrived.

A lifetime spent on the shadow side of the law had made Matson familiar with all the traits exhibited by a man on the dodge. He'd caught a clear view of this man's face before he could conceal it under the cover of his clothing and the night.

Just to be sure, the mobster pulled a folded sheet of stiff paper from his coat pocket and examined it. It was one of the wanted posters, and the photo emblazoned on it was a perfect match for the face of the man leaving Dupont's pawnshop.

Tony the Torpedo smiled in anticipation.

CHAPTER TWENTY

Tony Matson had not hidden himself quite as completely as he thought.

As Kirby King had flipped up the collar of his coat around his thick neck, he had caught just a hint of movement across the street. He used the cover of the hand he raised to tug on his cap to mask the movement of his eyes as they scanned the spot where he thought he saw the movement. He was almost sure he then saw a man pulling back even farther into the concealment of the darkened doorway.

Kirby forced himself to keep his walk slow and steady as he returned to Yellowstone's roadster and fired up the engine.

Instead of driving straight ahead, though, he pulled a sharp U-turn and headed off in the opposite direction. Keeping one eye on his rear view mirror, he saw what he expected: a second set of headlights pulling into traffic not far behind him.

He made a couple of random turns to assure himself that he was indeed being followed. As he neared the next intersection he began to slow down; as, of course, did the vehicle behind him. Then, just as the light turned red, King jammed his foot hard against the accelerator. With a roar, the purloined roadster shot through the intersection, barely missing being hit by the crossing traffic.

With a snarl and his radio blaring on WXZY, Tony Matson likewise raced through the intersection. A sharp 12" knife lay on the seat beside him. As he did, another automobile had to swerve to avoid him, jumping a curb in the process and slamming to a halt against the side of a building.

Since he'd been made by King, Matson knew there was no point in hanging back. The needle on his speedometer leaped upward as he sought to close the gap between himself and his prey as quickly as possible.

Two blocks ahead, Sean Carpenter stood next to his car, intently studying a map of the city he had spread out on the vehicle's front hood.

On the floor of the passenger's side of his motorcar lay an 8" knife.

Ever a methodical man, he had drawn a series of concentric circles on the map; at their center was the spot where he had taken his literal first shot at Kirby King. Also marked on the map were other locales where others had allegedly seen the wanted man as reported in the Detroit newspapers and on the radio.

Carpenter assumed most of them represented mistakes in identity or outright hoaxes; some such reports had come from as far away as Mississippi. He felt it safe to disregard these out of hand. Even if King had the resources to get out of Detroit, news of the reward posted for him had spread far and wide; no place in the country, perhaps on Earth, would be considerably safer for him than where he was right now. He had to know that.

But enough of the remaining reported sightings fell within the bounds of the circles Carpenter had drawn; with the outermost circle being no farther than five miles from the spot where he had pursued King, for him to take them seriously. He had accordingly decided to restrict his own night search to that area.

His head snapped up as his ears caught the roar of a racing engine. He caught only a quick glimpse at the driver of the sleek roadster that flashed by him at a speed well above the posted limit, but a glimpse was sufficient to tell that it was a black man behind the wheel.

A second vehicle, the one driven by Tony Matson, zoomed past seconds later. A third car had now joined the chase, hot on the tail of the mobster's automobile.

Bunching his map up in one hand, Carpenter hurried to get behind his own wheel. As he slid into the driver's seat, his right hand fell on the butt of his shotgun.

His stomach tightened with the memory of his first failed attempt at King's life. He stroked the darkly stained walnut stock. By replacing the mental image of his intended target with that of his little girl's pale and drawn face, he felt certain he could do what needed to be done.

Tires squealed in protest as he tore away from the curb. He would follow the others for a ways, but then he meant to veer off on his own. Having memorized the layout of all the streets within his circular grid, he thought he knew a route that would bring him out ahead of King's planned route of escape. Tonight, Carpenter meant to earn that reward.

Tony Matson's crazed eyes hardened with rage as he again glared up and into his rear view mirror. It seemed as if a veritable convoy of amateur hit men was beginning to string out behind him.

Best to ignore them, though; he needed all his concentration to stay close to King, whose twists and turns at high speed could well kill the ex-com even before Matson could plant a bullet in his brain.

Not far away, Michael Yellowstone was pounding the pavement on foot, after having taken a bus to the sleazy side of town. He had put on a light jack and his fedora before leaving his house; he thought of little else as part of him was focused on continuing his investigative work; part of him just wanted to find Kirby King and wring that thick bull neck of his.

Spying a pair of tall, willowy hookers loitering beneath a street lamp, he angled over in their direction. He still believed that if he could find the *right* streetwalker this time, he could learn the secrets of the universe. The confessions priests heard on Sunday morning were often for sins the hookers had witnessed on Saturday night.

"Good evening, ladies," he said cordially as he drew closer. The taller of the two was a colored girl, with dark hair that spilled halfway down her back. The other hooker was white, but with equally dark hair, cut in a short, Dutch boy style. Both wore skirts that were indecently short and made more so by slits in the sides that revealed long and rather muscular thighs.

"Heyy, good lookin'," the white hooker purred in the kind of husky voice cultivated by booze and cigarettes. "What can we do for you?"

Before saying another word, the Osage detective simply flipped over the left lapel of his suit coat to reveal his badge. He held up the other, empty hand as he saw both hookers tense, preparing to bolt.

"It's all right, girls," he said soothingly. "I'm not with vice. I just want to talk."

"Talk costs too, sugar," the colored hooker drawled.

"Not that kind of talk," Yellowstone said, feeling slightly flushed. "I want information."

Truthfully or not, both swore to him that they knew nothing that could prove useful. After exhorting them to keep alert and offering the usual promise of leniency if they came through for him, the detective tipped his fedora and bade them a good night.

"Not so fast, handsome," the white hooker said, reaching out and grabbing him by the hand. She slowly ran her other hand up his arm, squeezing his biceps lightly.

"I'd still like to be of service to you," she said, giving him what she hoped was a seductive look. "No charge."

"Maybe some other time, sweetheart," he replied; but he didn't pull away from her. In truth, he found her attentions somewhat flattering. He was well aware of his rather homely features; no matinee idol was he.

"The offer's good any time you like," she assured him as she reached up and brushed the fantail of hair up from his forehead. "If you don't see me here, just ask anyone for Lily. They'll know where to find me."

"I just might do that, Lily," he lied gallantly as he stroked the slide of his string tie.

"Darlin'," the black hooker interjected, addressing her fellow painted sister, "I think you have a run in your stocking."

Lily released Yellowstone's hand and bent to check on her hosiery. As she did, her black sister in arms leaned forward, placing her lips close to the detective's ear.

"Mister," she whispered in a voice grown suddenly deeper, "you *do* know we're *guys*, don't you?"

"What?" Yellowstone practically yelped. On closer inspection, he could now make out the faintest trace of stubble along the edges of the hooker's jaw line, though it was well hidden by carefully applied make-up.

Without thinking, he recoiled from the whispering hooker, in the process stepping off the curb and onto the street.

Doing so almost cost him his life.

Headlights flaring straight into his eyes alerted him to an oncoming vehicle. So fast was the car traveling that it tugged at one corner of Yellowstone's coat and knocked off his hat as he hopped back up on the curb.

"Hey!" he yelled after the retreating car, only to then realize that the vehicle that had nearly plowed him under! "That's *my* car," he whispered.

As he stood by helplessly, four more cars flashed by at dangerous speeds. What appeared to be a teenage boy was hanging out the passenger side window of one car and he now began to blast away at Yellowstone's roadster with a handgun. His aim was shoddy.

Yellowstone spun away from the street, dropping to a crouch and throwing his arms over his head protectively. The two hookers took off running as best they could in high-heeled shoes so precarious that even a real woman would have had difficulty navigating the sidewalk in them. The detective couldn't help noting that their shrieks of terror sounded authentically female.

As the sound of gunshots receded, the detective leaped back to his feet. Standing at the edge of the curb, he began frantically waving one arm in hope of flagging down a passing car that he could commandeer to join in the escalating chase. If anything, this merely prompted motorists to speed up and get past this wildly gesticulating stranger.

Frustrated in his efforts, utterly exasperated, the Osage detective made a daring move. He stepped out onto the street proper, placing himself directly in the path of an oncoming motor truck. He again flipped over his lapel to expose his badge, and extended one hand out toward the approaching vehicle, palm out.

Unfortunately for and unknown by him, this particular truck was being driven by yet another fanatical member of the local chapter of the Ku Klux Klan.

And he had no intention of stopping for anything.

CHAPTER TWENTY ONE

Too late to jump to safety, Michael Yellowstone realized the motor truck barreling down on him was neither going to stop nor swerve.

With the rapidity only possible for light and the human brain, an idea/memory flashed into the detective's mind. It was of a complex and highly dangerous stunt; one he had been working on developing before he left Hollywood, laboring alongside the already legendary stunt man, Yakima Canutt.

As of the time when Yellowstone left the hills of the movie capital for good, though, neither man had actually yet *attempted* this stunt.

With that, unconscious thought took control of Yellowstone and he threw himself over backwards. Barely had his back hit the pavement than the speeding truck ran over him.

Its undercarriage cleared his splayed feet and his nose by the merest fraction of an inch; so close that Yellowstone could smell the faint odor of a drop of leaking oil.

A wiser man would have left it at that; rolled back to the safety of the sidewalk and staggered on rubbery legs to the nearest house of worship to give thanks for escaping with his life.

Caught in the moment, still driven by that primal part of the brain that first prompted man to take the leap down from the sheltering arms of the trees, Yellowstone thrust upward with both hands as the truck completed its pass over him.

His teeth clacked together painfully, his fingers felt as if threatened with being cut off as he latched onto the truck's back bumper with both hands. His body snapped up off the pavement and then slammed back down with bone-jarring force.

As he and Canutt had envisioned it, this stunt was meant to be performed on a stagecoach, over loosely packed soil. Here, the speed was far greater, the surface far harder and rougher.

Yellowstone heard and felt the fabric of his jacket being shredded as he was dragged along the concrete behind the truck, and knew that within seconds the same would be true of the flesh beneath the fabric.

Every bump in the road caused his body to bounce up and then slam back down. One such bump, he hoped, would prove his salvation.

When a particularly pronounced dip in the pavement jerked him several inches up and off the road, he used the momentum to swing his legs even farther up and over the flat and open back end of the truck.

With the power of his well-muscled arms he raised his upper body after his legs, completing the somersault that took him completely into the bed of the truck. He lay there gasping for breath, fighting to control the violent trembling that now shook every part of his body.

Then, strangely, he began to laugh.

God, but that was fun!

Still, as he pushed himself to his knees, hanging onto the sidewalls of the truck bed for support, he made a mental note to give Yakima a call and urge him to never try this stunt himself.

Yellowstone quickly realized he was not alone in the bed of the truck. Two more Klansmen stood at its front, leaning over the roof of the truck's cab. They were using it for stability as they aimed pistols forward, firing wildly ahead at the car, Yellowstone's car, in which Kirby King was fleeing.

At this distance, in a wildly bouncing moving vehicle, the Osage detective knew they had little more chance of hitting their target than you would have hitting the moon with an arrow.

He also knew that they could inadvertently hit something or someone else, however. Even at this hour and in this part of town there were other cars, pedestrians out and about.

The thrill of the hunt, the jolting of the speeding truck, the sounds of its engine and their blazing pistols had kept the two gunmen from realizing that they now shared the back of the vehicle with a third passenger. Rising to his feet, steadying himself to the rhythms of the ride, Yellowstone leaped forward.

He slammed into the back of the Klansman on his right. The man cried out in pain and surprise; his pistol flew out of his hand. He never knew what happened to him, for Yellowstone grabbed his shirt collar and his belt and flung him sideways out of the truck.

Arms and legs flailing, the Klansman barely missed hitting a light post. The bones of his upper left arm snapped like dry kindling as he hit the sidewalk and rolled. He lay where he fell, crying and clutching at his shattered limb.

The second Klansman would not be so easy to dispatch. Alerted by what had befallen his comrade, he turned to level his gun at Yellowstone.

"I'm a police officer," the detective yelled at the gunman, again flashing his badge.

"Who cares?" the Klansman barked.

Yellowstone's left hand flashed out, grabbed his attacker's wrist and twisted his arm even as he snapped off a shot; the errant bullet plowed harmlessly into the bed of the truck.

At that moment the vehicle turned sharply around a corner, sending the two combatants flying off their feet. They landed heavily on the truck's bed; the pistol flew from the Klansman's hand and skittered back and off the open end of the conveyance.

The two men rolled, with the Klansman coming out on top. He threw a short right that clipped Yellowstone on the jaw; drew the fist back to strike again. This time, Yellowstone was able to pull his head to the side; his attacker yowled as his fist this time connected only with the metal truck bed.

Yellowstone pushed up and over so he now held the upper position. Grabbing his opponent by the front of his shirt, he slammed the back of the man's head against the metal flooring once, twice.

The truck took another corner, this time so sharply that it momentarily tilted onto just two wheels. Yellowstone felt his body rise up off the Klansman, then fly sideways to slam against the sidewall of the vehicle.

The Klansman followed after him, circling both hands around the detective's throat. He dragged Yellowstone up and bent his head over the edge of the truck bed. If he couldn't choke the cop to death, he hoped to break his neck.

The Osage detective grabbed his attacker by the arm, attempting to pull the choking hands loose. When this proved fruitless, he tried for the man's exposed eyes; again to no avail.

The speeding truck hit a pothole with a force that sent both men in the back hopping upward several inches. The back of the Osage Indian's head slammed back down on the edge of the metal sidewall with such impact that tiny stars exploded in his eyes.

But the jolt from the pothole strike had also loosened the Klansman's grip on Yellowstone's throat. In the instant they had been airborne, the cop had also managed to lift his right foot up and plant it against his attacker's abdomen.

Yellowstone kicked outward with all his remaining strength. The Klansman's hands slipped away from the detective's neck, as his body was hurled up and back by the kick.

Screeching in terror, he flew out of the truck and into the windshield of a car racing alongside the truck. The driver of this vehicle was yet another vigilante drawn into the wild chase.

The middle-aged machinist behind the wheel of the car was already picturing what a million dollars would look like spread out over the top of his kitchen table.

Instead, the last thing he actually saw was the body of the Klansman crashing through his front windshield. The machinist screamed as shards of glass drilled into his eyes and face. His hands were torn from the steering wheel as the limp body of the Klansman slammed into him.

Driverless, the car veered sharply to the left. Hitting a concrete center median, it flipped. Then flipped two more times before coming to a rest on its rooftop. Horns blared as other drivers fought to avoid the wreckage and each other.

Yellowstone slumped to the floor of the truck bed; lances of fire burned the inside of his throat with each breath he inhaled.

But he couldn't, wouldn't stay down; the driver of the truck still had to be accounted for.

Immediately behind the cab of the truck, on the driver's side, Yellowstone swung his left leg over the wall of its bed, so he was straddling it. Gripping it tightly with his knees, he leaned over and forward, flinging open the door of the careening vehicle.

With nearly the same motion, he grabbed the startled driver by the cloth of his left sleeve and jerked. The doomed Klansman flew from the confines of the cab like a discarded bag of manure.

Banging against the pavement, the Klansman rolled uncontrollably as other vehicles swerved right and left in an effort to miss him.

All but one succeeded.

Tumbling to a halt belly down in the street, the Klansman raised his head just in time for it to meet the front bumper of an oncoming touring car.

Yellowstone took no note of this, for he was now perched atop a truck without a hand at the wheel: one that would doubtless begin to swerve out of control at any second.

With one hand on the still open door and the other atop the roof of the truck's cab, Yellowstone pitched himself out of the bed and into the seat of the vehicle.

He grabbed the steering wheel just as the truck was about to jump the curb and head toward a storefront. Yanking the wheel savagely to the left, he sent the truck into the middle of the street, ignoring the blare of horns on all sides of him.

With the steel charger now firmly under his control, Yellowstone pulled the vehicle to a stop near the closest sidewalk. He leaned forward, resting his forehead on the steering wheel, his chest heaving like a blacksmith's bellows.

"Let's see *you* do that, Yakima," he gasped aloud.

CHAPTER TWENTY TWO

Sean Carpenter smiled tightly.

His calculations had proven correct. The alternate route he had taken had brought him closer to the fleeing felon, if still a block to the south of him.

Carpenter could make out the car in which he assumed Kirby King was attempting to escape. It was still just slightly ahead of him, but Carpenter knew the street upon which he was pursuing was about to take a diagonal turn that would cause it to intersect with the ex-con's path.

The desperate clerk floored his accelerator. If he had timed it as correctly as he thought, he would be able to cut off King's flight and make him a sitting target. He fought to keep his breathing under control, again reached out to stroke the stock of his shotgun.

Kirby King was unaware of the danger approaching from this new front. His attention alternated between looking straight ahead and glancing into his rearview mirror. It told him that while he was maintaining his distance from most of his pursuers, the car closest behind him, the one that had initiated this escalating chase, was gradually drawing closer.

In that car, Tony the Torpedo began to giggle like a deranged schoolboy. His eager fingers tightened on the steering wheel and his right foot bore down even more heavily on the accelerator.

Approaching the next intersection, King saw no sign of imminent crossing traffic and so stomped as hard as he could on his own accelerator. At this speed, and given the slight dip the road took just his side of the intersection, King's purloined car actually took flight for a harrowing moment before slamming back down to the pavement.

Tony Matson smiled even more broadly; he was now no more than two car lengths behind his prey. He would soon bring him to ground.

Failure.

That was the word Sean Carpenter had begun to associate most closely with himself in recent months. Failure as a provider, as a husband, as a father.

Failure as a man.

His calculations for cutting off Kirby King had been almost perfect. But in the deadly game into which he had interjected himself, almost was the difference between life and death.

As Tony Matson's car tore through the intersection, an unexpected beam of light flared on his right. Sean Carpenter, expecting to be blocking the passage of Kirby King's vehicle, instead caromed into the intersection mere seconds too late.

His right front bumper crashed into the right rear end of Tony Matson's car. Matson's senses swam as the collision slammed his head against the frame of his door. A second jolt jerked him violently as his car smashed sideways into a power pole.

Sean Carpenter was thrown upward by the collision. He hands flew off the steering wheel and his neck bent at a dangerously awkward angle as he struck the roof.

His car began to spin like a pinwheel, sending him hurtling into the midst of the remaining pursuit cars that were only now reaching the lethal intersection.

One car hit his in a glancing blow. A second plowed into him more solidly. He was now being tossed about the interior of his vehicle like a life-sized rag doll. He screamed as bone and tendon began to wrench, tear and break.

A third driver slammed on his brakes, only to be rear-ended by yet another vigilante. The impact drove him into Carpenter's battered vehicle.

Accompanied by an outward explosion of glass, Carpenter's body shot clear of his car as he flew through the windshield. He was beyond screaming now, though not beyond feeling the agony of fresh breakage as he skipped across the pavement like a smooth rock across the surface of a placid lake.

He came to rest in a spreading pool of his own blood. One eye was missing; through the tears misting the other he saw flames. One of the other cars involved in the pile-up was afire.

Carpenter moved slightly, nearly passed out as he felt the jagged edges of broken bones erupt through the skin of his arms and legs. His mouth moved soundlessly, the only thing emerging from his throat being a frothy spout of his own blood.

His last thought before dying wasn't of himself. Before he saw nothing ever again, he had a vision of his ever-patient wife Amanda. Of his children, especially the dying one he couldn't save.

Failure.

A block away, Kirby King eased his foot off the accelerator and applied the brakes. Looking back over his right shoulder, he could catch glimpses of the chaos left behind him, illumined by the flickering flames of the vehicle that was on fire.

What no longer appeared were headlights coming after him.

He resumed driving; now holding his speed down to well within the limit. A half-mile on, flashing lights and wailing sirens alerted him to a pair of police cars approaching from the opposite direction.

Kirby hunkered down in the seat, pulled the bill of his cap even lower. Their attention focused on the carnage that lay ahead of them, the cops paid no mind to his car as they flashed by.

At almost the same time, Michael Yellowstone was rolling his commandeered motor truck into the graveyard of fire and mangled men and machines.

His eyes grimly surveyed the scene, confirming that his own stolen car was not one of them on the scene. He presumed this meant King had escaped.

Upon hearing the rapidly approaching sirens, he turned off the road and set out away from the pile-up. None of this was his doing, he reasoned; and he didn't want to be put in the position of having to explain to brother officers just what he was doing there under such circumstances and behind the wheel of a truck that didn't belong to him.

The detective turned onto Woodward Avenue, following it into the Grand Circus Park. In a darkened and deserted section of the park he abandoned the truck, after first thoroughly wiping its steering wheel, door, even the bed of all prints.

As he walked away from the vehicle, he wasn't particularly bothered by his actions of this evening. He believed he'd acted in justifiable self-defense. Policeman or not, he hadn't created this mess. He had only been sucked into it, and felt free to walk away from it. Any doubts or feelings of guilt would come later.

People had died tonight, some at his hands. But they'd brought it on themselves with greed and their own lust for blood.

He'd have been even less concerned if he'd known the men in the motor truck had belonged to the Klan. Yellowstone had witnessed the fruits of the actions of similar monsters back in Oklahoma; he refused to dignify their existence by applying the term "men" to them.

They'd reaped what they'd sown, and were welcome to it.

Not that the toughened detective was feeling no emotion at this moment. He was.

Anger. He felt anger.

And right now most of it was directed at Kirby King.

Carpenter flew through the windshield.

CHAPTER TWENTY THREE

"**J**ust what th' hell were you thinking?" said Yellowstone, his face still flush with anger.

When the Osage detective had finally found his way home, he'd entered to see Kirby King sitting on the sofa, waiting for him. The ex-con's resigned look told Yellowstone the felon was expecting and prepared for a tongue lashing, and knew the detective was about to deliver it.

"I guess it's partly my own fault. Back home, they say don't approach a bull from th' front, a horse from th' rear, or a fool from any direction. There's no bigger fool than th' one I'm talkin' to right now.

"How many times do I have to tell you, you danged owl hoot," Yellowstone continued as he took off his tattered denim jacket and threw it on a chair, "not to be out there on th' streets alone? Every time you are, you're just invitin' your own murder!"

"And if *you're* with me," Kirby finally snapped back, "you're just inviting a *double* murder. You really think any of those 'bounty' hunters would hesitate to kill you to get to me?"

"You stole my car! And I don't think it, I know it." Yellowstone exhaled loudly, pausing to brush his unruly hair back from his forehead. "I was in that little caravan of murders who were trying to put a bullet in your head."

"No," said King. "What happened?"

"Not now, Kirby. Not now. I'm too mad to talk about it right now."

"Right this minute, I'd rather just strangle you with my bare hands. Maybe I'll tell you later. Other people are already dying over this mess," he added, alluding to that fact and wincing at the knowledge that he'd been the instrument of some of those deaths. "It's got to stop."

"It will," Kirby replied insistently, "when I find out who really killed the lady D.A."

"And that's another thing," Yellowstone told him, punching a finger in the air for emphasis. "Just 'cause you and me have broke bread together don't mean I've ruled *you* out as th' most likely suspect, Kirby.

"I find proof you did it and I'll still nail your hide to th' barn door."

"I've never thought different, detective," King said sullenly.

That's where the matter was left as Yellowstone stomped off to his Spartan bedroom. But sleep would come only in fits and starts, made hard to attain because of repeated mental images of bodies bouncing off concrete.

Finally giving up hope of any real sleep, the Osage rose with the sun, feeling only little more rested than when he'd lain down. A warm bath and a shave at least made him feel like a human being again. He left King asleep on the sofa, though the ex-con's twitching form showed he was not sleeping well either.

On a whim, he decided to stop by Jack Hill's apartment not far from the Campus Martius to see if the lieutenant wanted to join him in an early breakfast before reporting in for their shift at the station.

Yellowstone was a bit surprised when his knock on the door of the third floor apartment brought no response. When repeated knocking still yielded nothing, he shrugged and walked away. Maybe, like Yellowstone himself, Lt. Hill was out following leads of his own.

"Are you looking for that nice police officer?" a thin and reedy voice behind him asked.

Yellowstone turned to see an old woman, probably well into her seventh decade, standing in the open doorway of the apartment across the hall from Lt. Hill's. Her bluish white hair was in curlers; a threadbare robe was clutched tightly around her skinny frame.

The detective smiled slightly. Most every apartment building had at least one resident busybody. He had a feeling she was it.

"Yes, ma'am," he replied politely. "I'm his partner."

Visibly relaxing, accepting that this wasn't a stranger or a criminal, the slender woman took a step outside her doorway.

"He's not here," she declared, stating the obvious. "You just missed him. He left early. Even earlier than usual. And I should know. Between the rheumatism and that yowling cat of Mrs. Schoenfeld on the second floor, I never sleep. Like an owl, I am."

"It's all right, ma'am. I'll see him at th' station. Thank you, though." Yellowstone again turned to leave, only to be pulled up short by the woman's tremulous voice.

"One thing before you go, officer."

"Yes, ma'am?"

"I'm not a nosy person," she said, eliciting another smile from the detective, "but I was just wondering; what's become of Mr. Hill's pretty young girlfriend?"

"What do you mean?" the Osage detective asked nonchalantly.

He didn't let on that this was the first he'd heard of Jack being involved with anyone of the opposite sex. Of course, he and Hill had been partnered for only a short time; there were doubtless plenty of things they hadn't told one another. Still, the subject of a girlfriend seemed like one that would have come up early and maybe often.

Unless the relationship was still new: still in that phase where neither of you wanted to share the other with the world yet.

Or unless it was one Hill was trying to keep under wraps, much like the one Yellowstone was having with Stacy Lord. He hadn't shared that with Hill yet.

"This girlfriend," he said, suddenly curious. "What's her name?"

"Oh, I never got her name, officer. A pretty thing. A bit too stern looking, if you know what I mean; but I'm not one to criticize."

"I'm sure you're not."

"They've been together for awhile now," she continued, oblivious to the hint of sarcasm in Yellowstone's comment.

"Occasionally, he brings her here in the evening. Not sure I approve of that, but you know how these modern girls are."

"I'm learning, ma'am."

"It's best you do. But I haven't seen hide nor hair of her in over a week." The matronly woman shook her head sadly. "I hope they haven't broken up. They really make a perfectly lovely couple.

"Not that any relationship's perfect, mind you. I learned that myself, the hard way. Three times."

"Are you saying they've had some troubles?" Yellowstone prompted: not that it took much of such to keep the old biddy spilling all she knew.

"Well, they do argue from time to time. Not that I eavesdrop, mind you. I use wrapping paper thicker than the walls around here."

"What is it they argue about, if you know?"

"What's to know? Maybe she wants babies. Maybe he wants babies. Why does anybody fight?"

"Do they get pretty angry with each other?"

"Not so much, I think. And it never lasts. The next thing you know, they're happy and holding hands again.

"Sometimes, they just spend the evening sitting together out on our building's front stoop. They share one of those tailor made cigarettes Mr. Hill likes too much.

"And sometimes, when they think no one's looking, they'll share a quick kiss, too. It's cute. Like kids, they are."

At this point, Yellowstone was beginning to squirm a little; not comfortable about hearing the details of a love life his partner was obviously desirous of keeping private. Less comfortable for having elicited the information himself.

"Like I said," the old woman concluded, "I really hope they haven't separated."

"I really couldn't say, ma'am," Yellowstone replied by way of ending the conversation. "Have a good day."

He graciously tipped his fedora, bringing a warm smile that cracked across the woman's wrinkled visage. He turned on his heels and quickly retreated down the stairs.

Yellowstone stopped at a nearby diner to fortify himself with a few strips of bacon and a couple of eggs over easy, washing them down with enough cups of strong black coffee to keep him alert for the next few hours.

Upon arriving at the station house, he'd barely exited his parked car before he found himself being approached by a young black man in a gray suit. Yellowstone recognized the man: he'd been with the lawyer, Virgil Lowery, Kirby King's counsel, when Lowery had shown up to confer with his client after King had first been taken into custody.

"Detective Yellowstone?" the young man said, extending a hand, which the detective gripped and shook warily. "My name is Marcus True. I'm Virgil Lowery's executive assistant."

"I remember you, Mr. True," Yellowstone said. "What can I do for you?"

"Direct and to the point," True said, smiling broadly. "I like that in a man."

"Well enough to actually answer him?"

The young attorney laughed softly, and then grew serious. He glanced quickly all around before returning his attention to the detective.

"Mr. Lowery would like you to pass a message on from him to Kirby King."

Yellowstone grew stiffly alert and freshly suspicious. "What makes him think I know how to contact King?"

True waved a hand dismissively, as if clearing the air of the detective's query.

"The important thing is, Mr. Lowery would very much like to have a face-to-face meeting with Mr. King, at nine o'clock tonight."

"And again I ask," Yellowstone said with steely resolve. "What makes you think I can help you? What business is this of mine?"

True thrust both hands in the pockets of his suit coat, rocking back and forth slightly on the heels of shoes that would have taken a significant portion of a week's salary for the detective to buy.

"Obviously we have attempted to act on faulty information, Detective

Yellowstone," True said. "I apologize for intruding on your time."

The attorney again extended a hand, shook that of the Osage detective and then walked rapidly away.

Yellowstone stood watching the departing lawyer a good while before glancing down at his right hand. Nestled in the palm was a small square of paper True had slipped to him when they shook hands. On the paper had been written an address.

After cautiously transferring the piece of paper to his own coat pocket, Yellowstone had barely resumed walking toward the station house when he again stopped in his tracks.

The doors leading into the precinct house fairly flew open as Stacy Lord came hustling out. Gamely attempting to keep pace with her were two radio engineers, including the poor fellow charged with carrying around the reporter's bulky and cumbersome recording equipment.

"Good morning, Miss Lord," Yellowstone greeted her, bracing himself for whatever inappropriate questions she planned to assail him with.

To his astonishment, she blew right past him, barely taking note of his presence.

"No time to talk now, darling," she informed him. She turned around toward him, but continued to move backward away from him.

"Maybe later?" she called in the clipped tone he knew quite well. "Say five o'clock? Cocktails at Luigi's. My treat."

Then she was gone.

Yellowstone scratched the back of his head, chuckling softly as he looked down at his scuffed brown shoes. The same shoes he wore every day, with every suit, for they were the only shoes he owned. He suspected Marcus True and Virgil Lowery wouldn't be caught dead in them. But they served his principal need just fine.

They were comfortable.

There seemed to be an inordinate amount of activity in the station that morning, with enough lawyers wandering the corridors to hold their own Chautauqua Meeting.

In one of those corridors, he almost literally ran into his ostensible partner. Lt. Hill had his nose buried in a file folder and would have gone right by his fellow detective had not Yellowstone put out both hands to stop him.

Hill looked worse than Yellowstone felt. He appeared not to have shaved. He wasn't wearing a jacket and his shirt, sleeves rolled up to his elbows, looked like it had been slept in by somebody else. With darkly circled and sunken eyes, Hill looked like he himself had been a stranger to sleep for quite some time.

"You all right, Jack?" Yellowstone asked solicitously.

"Huh?" As Hill spoke, the movement of his lips caused the now nearly omnipresent cigarette dangling from his mouth to spill ash down the front of that wrinkled shirt.

"You look like somethin' th' cat dragged in," Yellowstone observed dryly.

"You don't exactly look like a daisy yourself," Hill snarled. "Anything new about King on your end?"

"Not really," Yellowstone replied, disappointed to know that this was no lie.

"That's what I wanted to talk to you about, Jack. Every new lead I try to follow seems to take me nowhere."

"By new lead, I hope you don't mean 'new suspect,' Hollywood."

"I mean just what I said," Yellowstone replied curtly. "I want to put this killer behind bars just as much as you do, whoever he is."

"Then find a way to place Kirby King at the scene the night it happened."

"I'd love to. Any fresh ideas on how we can do that?"

Hill shook his head grimly. "I just don't know, partner. Like you observed, there's nothing much fresh about me at the moment."

At that moment, a small herd of men came shuffling out of the processing room, marching past the two detectives. Among them were a handful of lawyers Yellowstone recognized.

"What's up with that?" he asked Hill as the group of men, all those who were not lawyers looking rather glum, passed by them.

"I'm not sure," Hill replied. "Something to do with a multi-car pile-up on Atchison, just north of Grand Boulevard last night. They've been questioning these clowns for the last few hours, but I guess they've decided to let the shysters have them now."

"I hope no one was hurt too badly," the Osage detective commented, feigning ignorance.

"Couldn't say," Hill replied. "My daddy always said automobiles would be the death of all of us someday. Never owned one to the day he died. Hell, he wouldn't even ride in one if he could help it."

"Yeah, my pa was pretty much th' same way," Yellowstone said. "Liked to killed him when he finally had to get rid of our last horse."

"Let's get back to what we were really talking about," Hill directed. "You know we still have a couple of other cases on our desks. You're spending an awful lot of time on this King case. Why is that?"

As they spoke, neither detective noticed the final detainee who was walking past them. If they had, neither would have recognized or known Tony "The Torpedo" Matson for who and what he was.

Nor did he know them. But he'd heard the word "King," and he wanted to hear more. A drinking fountain was set in the wall near where the two detectives were talking, and the gunman bent to sip water as he listened in.

"Those other cases are pretty cut and dried, Frank," Yellowstone was saying. "This thing with Kirby King is still growin', getting meaner and dirtier all th' time.

"I've seen what can happen when this sort of thing gets out of hand, out of control. It's not a pretty sight. Th' sooner we end this, th' better it'll be for everybody."

"I agree," Hill said. "But if we can't end it, I suspect that million dollar bounty will."

"You really think King's murder will end anything?"

"It'll end him raping and killing innocent women, Yellowstone," the lieutenant hissed, those intense eyes widening, almost glowing in their dark sockets. "That's all I care about."

"Maybe I want more," Yellowstone replied calmly.

"What more is there?"

"I don't know; th' sure knowledge that we took down th' *right* man?"

"Have you got any reason to believe getting him and getting Kirby King wouldn't be one and the same?"

"At th' moment, no. But that's our job, isn't it? To root out th' truth and follow wherever it leads us."

"Hell, I can tell you where it'll lead you, partner. Right to King's front door."

"Then so be it. But till then, I'm keeping an open mind."

Lt. Hill snorted, but smiled as he patted Yellowstone on one shoulder. "Just as long as you don't confuse an open mind with an empty one."

Hill stepped around him to head for the squad room and Yellowstone turned to join him. As he did, the Osage Indian bumped right into a man who'd been drinking at the squad room water fountain a moment earlier.

"Please forgive me, sir," Matson said smoothly, an unctuous smile splitting his mouth. "I guess I didn't see you there."

"No, that was certainly my fault," Yellowstone assured him. But as Tony Matson sauntered away down the hall, Yellowstone turned to his partner.

"That fella there," he said, tipping his head toward the retreating figure of the hit man. "You know who he is, Jack?"

"Not by name, no. I think he was one of the men they brought in for questioning after that pile-up. Why?"

"No particular reason. Just curious, that's all."

His eyes continued to drill into Matson's back, though. The man had done nothing wrong, said nothing wrong. But there was something about him that struck a discordant note in the detective's brain. Without realizing it, he was idly rubbing the silver dreamcatcher replica at his throat with his thumb, as he often did when lost in thought.

Yellowstone turned to head into the squad room. What he was feeling was probably due to nothing more than that brought on by a policeman's naturally suspicious nature.

He turned and took another look at the man.

Sometimes, he knew, a suspicious nature was the only thing that kept a cop alive.

CHAPTER TWENTY FOUR

Retired Judge Malcolm Nixon slowly swung his corpulent figure down the steps of the Wayne County Courthouse. One painstaking step at a time was all his size and his infirmity would allow him now, but the pain was worth it. He had some goodbyes to say today.

This weekly trip to the place that for so many years was his true home was a bit wearisome; it was one he looked forward to with such great anticipation that he was even willing to be confronted by the press.

Illogical as it was, breakfast in chambers with his last remaining friend still on the bench, Judge Kendall, accompanied by the latest gossip filtering through the halls of justice made Nixon feel like he was still part of the process.

More and more, it was nearly the only thing that could still make him feel alive. That made it even more important to him now, with Rebekah dead. A twinge of pain reminded him that soon it wouldn't matter. Nothing would.

Halfway down the steps, he stopped to catch his breath and to simply look out over the city. From his inside coat pocket, he pulled one of the thick, expensive Cuban cigars that were one of his other remaining pleasures.

The doctors wanted to take even that away from him. Well, they could all go to hell. What was enjoying a good cigar going to do, kill him?

He chuckled softly at his own joke as he pulled a lighter from his right vest pocket. He rotated the cigar slowly with the fingers of his left hand as he held the flame up to its tip.

Nixon stared down at the lighter for a moment before returning it to his pocket. He'd given one very much like it to his daughter on her last birthday.

Her last birthday.

He grimaced as he saw an automobile come to a squealing halt at the curb below where he stood. So recklessly was it being driven that one tire had actually jumped onto the sidewalk.

The sign painted on its side read: WXYZ Radio. His grimace became a deeper scowl when he saw three people come spilling out of the vehicle. They conferred together in a small huddle before setting off up the courthouse steps at a trot.

He recognized the woman leading this small pack of mongrels.

It was Stacy Lord, with her damnable microphone.

"Judge Nixon," she said breathlessly and without preamble, "can we get your comments on the Kirby King story?"

Nixon indignantly drew himself up to his full height. Coupled with his girth and the fact that he stood a step higher than Lord and her crew, he fairly dwarfed the reporter.

"Miss Lord," he said gravely, "you've attempted an ambush or two before during my career as an active judge. I told you then I want no part of you or any story that you are seeking to concoct. Nothing has changed." With a wave of his arm, he made to brush past them.

"One thing has changed since then, Judge," Stacy declared. "People are dead now."

The old man stopped his descent, his head swung back on his fat neck. To the reporter's trained eye, it seemed Nixon's face had actually brightened a bit at the sound of her words, and that made her cringe slightly.

"But none of them is Kirby King," she concluded. And the light faded from the judge's features.

"What do you mean?" he said slowly.

"I mean that there are rumors that *you* are the man who issued the one million dollar bounty for the head of Kirby King."

"Your allegation is outrageous," snarled Nixon. "Would I not already have been arrested if I were the man?"

"I *mean*," continued Lord, ignoring his comment, "the city morgue is one of the most thriving businesses in Detroit at the moment, Your Honor." She had her target in sight now, and honed in on it. "Some of them didn't have heads.

"I *mean* that dead colored people in particular are showing up with frightening frequency.

"One was a 76-year-old man.

"One wasn't even a Negro. He was an East Indian gentleman who had run a grocery store in his neighborhood for the last 15 years.

"At least three white people have died as a result of the manhunt that reward poster has ignited like a forest fire."

Judge Nixon tried backing away from the reporter but she followed relentlessly after him.

"One of those white men was a down-on-his-luck fellow by the name of Sean Carpenter. A decent fellow, trying his best. He's left behind a wife, three children and the impending bill for his funeral hanging around one of their necks."

Lord thrust the microphone toward the judge as if it was an assassin's blade.

"What would you say to them, Your Honor?"

Nixon recoiled in horror from the question. Then his eyes narrowed and flared. His fleshy face brightened red with anger. With surprising speed, he grabbed the reporter's microphone and pulled it closer.

"What would *you* say, Miss Lord?" he thundered. "You and all the parasites like you who have been feeding off this tragedy?" Stacy tried to withdraw the microphone but he wouldn't release his hold on it.

"You've been acting like the color commentator at a broadcast of the gladiatorial games in ancient Rome. Deny that you've been egging your listeners on, whipping them into frenzy. You can't, can you?"

Nixon leaned in so close to her that Stacy could feel the warmth of his breath, smell the sickness within him.

"What responsibility do *you* take for all that's happened?"

The judge pushed the microphone away with disgust and turned his back on her. As he cautiously made his way down the steps as quickly as he could manage, Lord made a slashing motion across her throat with one hand, signaling her engineer to shut off the recorder.

The engineer said nothing. He stared intently at Stacy, who, in turn, continued to follow Nixon with her eyes as he shambled across the sidewalk to a motorcar and opened its door.

"You escaped the bullet *this time*," she said under her breath. "But I won't miss again."

As he pulled the door of the motorcar closed, Nixon took out a monogrammed handkerchief from his breast pocket, and wiped the sweat from his furrowed brow.

He sighed deeply.

Then he smiled.

CHAPTER TWENTY FIVE

Tony "The Torpedo" Matson calmly drove his battered but still operable car out of the police impound yard.

When he was a few blocks away, he pulled it to the curb. Lying down in the front seat, he reached up under the dashboard, smiling as his fingers fell on the familiar shape of his revolver.

He'd had no chance to get away from the crush of other cars involved in the pile-up of the previous night before the police had arrived on the scene, but he had managed to conceal his .38 from any prying eyes.

Matson slipped the revolver into his coat pocket and withdrew the wallet he'd lifted from the clueless detective he'd deliberately bumped into back at the police station.

As suspected, the wallet contained Michael Yellowstone's driver's license, including his address. Matson memorized this information, removed thirty dollars in cash from the wallet, and then tossed it out the window.

From the conversation the hit man had overheard, he suspected it would be well worth his time to keep a close eye on this detective.

His car backfired as he pulled away from the curb, and Tony the Torpedo decided his first order of business would be to obtain a new set of wheels, legally or otherwise.

Michael Yellowstone himself arrived home that evening in a foul mood, thinking that things had been bad enough even before he lost his wallet. On a cop's salary, such losses were not to be taken lightly. Nor had the rest of the day proven to be particularly productive. He and Hill had spent most of it at their desks, filling out paperwork associated with some of their other cases. He'd blown off cocktails with Stacy, an offense for which he knew he'd catch nine kinds of hell later; but at the moment, he just didn't much care.

He took some solace in at least finding Kirby King there when he entered the house, rather than out roaming the streets again. Yellowstone considered withholding telling King about the message from Virgil Lowery, but decided it wasn't his place to do so. After supper, he told King all about his brief encounter with Marcus True that afternoon, handing him the slip of paper with the address of the proposed rendezvous site.

"I'm gonna speak my piece and then shut up," the Osage detective said afterwards. "I don't think this is a good idea, Kirby."

"Why's that?"

"It's just flat out too dangerous. You keep puttin' yourself out on th' street and sooner or later your string of luck is gonna run out. It's that simple."

"But I gotta do something."

Yellowstone reached over to the end table next to his easy chair, lifting up the telephone that sat there.

"You want to talk to Lowery, just give him a call."

"He didn't tell you he wanted me to call him."

"Fine. Then let me go to this meeting in your place."

"That won't work either, and you know it. He won't say anything to a white cop."

"I just don't think you're safe outside these walls," Yellowstone persisted.

"I'm tired of walls, boss," Kirby replied. He ran one hand over his smooth head, staring intently down at the floor. "That's all I had for a long, long time.

"In case you forgot, I just spent five years looking at not much of anything but walls. Walls around the prison. Walls of an eight by ten cell. Bouncing off the walls of the hole.

"Even after I got out, even before all this, I'd wake up sometimes in the middle of the night for no reason: just feeling like the walls of my apartment was coming together. Like they was gonna crush me.

"I'd just lay there sweating bullets. I couldn't hardly breathe 'cause it felt like I had an anvil sitting right on my chest.

"I got to break outta those walls, detective. I just got to."

Yellowstone studied King closely, but said nothing in reply. There was nothing he could say, and as they say back home, he thought: *silence is sometimes the best answer*.

"Maybe Mr. Lowery's done turned up something that'll prove I didn't do this thing they say I did," King continued, talking more to himself than to the detective.

"Or at least something that'll get those damned bounty hunters off my back." He finally looked up and over at Yellowstone. He had an almost pleading look in his dark brown eyes.

"I got to do this," he said firmly. "And I'll be careful. I promise."

Yellowstone leaned back in his chair and sighed. "I don't suppose you'd at least let me go with you?"

"I appreciate the offer, Mr. Yellowstone. Truly I do. But I think I'd best go alone."

"Fine," Yellowstone conceded, then pointed a finger at King. "I have no legal way to stop you. But my car stays here with me!"

It was nine o'clock on the dot when Kirby King strode up to the address he'd been given. The building, which appeared to have once been a three-story office complex, was darkened and seemingly abandoned. But its front door opened easily at King's tug.

He stopped just inside the door, looking and listening for anything that might hint at betrayal. Some thirty feet ahead of him, across the small lobby, he could see a rectangle of light spilling from an open doorway.

"Mr. Lowery?" he called out.

"Right this way, Kirby," a voice replied, as the backlit figure of a man in silhouette appeared in that open doorway.

Taking it on faith that this was Virgil Lowery, King carefully approached the doorway, sticking just his head around one side to peek inside.

He relaxed when he recognized the welcoming face of Lowery, and moved on into the room. Several desks still ran down either side of the office, though the dust accumulated atop each spoke to their long disuse. A single window was set in one wall of the room.

King tensed again slightly when he realized Lowery was not alone behind his desk; two other men stood behind him. One of them King recognized as being Lowery's assistant, but the other was a total stranger to him.

"Come in, Kirby, come in," Lowery beckoned, smiling and waving one hand. "You remember my colleague Marcus True, don't you?"

"Mr. True," King said respectfully, nodding his head.

"And this gentleman is Ned Lincoln," Lowery said, indicating the other man. "He's here to represent the NAACP's interests.

"It's good to see you, Kirby," Lowery continued, partially rising and extending a hand which King gladly took. He sat back down. "That's the main thing I wanted tonight; to just see you in the flesh and know you were all right. With all the meanness and the murders going on in this town, I've worried sick about you."

"I appreciate that, Mr. Lowery," King said softly, but his lips formed a frown. "But is that all? You got no other reason for calling me down here?"

Now it was Lowery's turn to frown. "Not much more than that, no; I'm afraid not, Kirby. Oh, on the purely legal front, you're fine, just fine. The police have no more on you now than they did the night they first hauled you in.

"It's the bounty that poses the real threat."

"Well, can't you get rid of that thing?"

"We're trying our best. Believe me we are. I've filed every legal motion I can think of, but so far with no luck. There's a very old law on Michigan's books that states that bounty hunting is not only legal, but encouraged. A bounty hunter isn't even required to have a license. No state Congress has every overturned that law.

"It's an open secret that Judge Malcolm Nixon, the victim's father, is the one offering the reward. But he won't admit to it publicly and I can't convince any of his fellow judges to issue an injunction against an unnamed party. Probably wouldn't help if I could."

"Then what are we gonna do?" Kirby asked plaintively. "Just let 'em kill me?"

"No, no," Lowery assured him. "Of course not. We haven't exhausted all our options yet. In th' meantime…where have you been staying since last I saw you, Kirby?"

For reasons he couldn't explain even to himself, King felt alarms go off inside his head. "Here and there," was all he said, shrugging his bulky shoulders.

"That's what I was afraid of," Lowery said, solemnly nodding his head.

"That's another reason I wanted to talk to you, son. We're prepared to offer you a safe house in which to stay so you can be just that…safe…until we can bring this all to an end."

"There won't be any need for that, Mr. Lowery," Marcus True declared, speaking for the first time.

"What do you mean, Marcus?" Lowery asked, turning toward his assistant and looking at him in puzzlement. "Why not?"

"Because King's not going to be leaving this building…alive."

Before another word could be uttered, Marcus True pulled a pistol from the waistband of his trousers. To Lowery's amazement, Ned Lincoln was now also holding a revolver.

"What's the meaning of this?" Lowery demanded indignantly.

"Looks pretty obvious to me," Kirby King growled. "There's killing about to be done."

"Killing?" Virgil Lowery still failed to comprehend what was happening before his very eyes. "I don't understand."

"Then you're not as smart as the grease monkey there is, Virgil," True sneered. "Ned and I mean to kill this lowlife and collect that reward."

"You can't be serious!" Lowery gasped.

"Why not?" Lincoln chimed in. "We're in a win/win situation here. Once the news of King's demise leaks out and spreads, everyone will assume it was a white man who killed him. He'll become a symbol of racial inequality. He'll become a martyr to our cause, a rallying point for blacks from the cotton fields of Alabama to the halls of Congress in Washington."

"While Ned here and I enjoy the good life in Canada," True finished for his co-conspirator. "Like he said: win/win."

"Yeah?" Kirby said. "And what do *I* win?"

"A bullet in the head," True declared coldly. "Which is all trash like you deserve."

"Are you insane?" Lowery exclaimed, rising from behind his desk. "Are you so blinded by ambition and greed that you'd turn on one of your own?"

"He's not one of ours," Lincoln insisted. "He's nothing but an ex-con hoodlum. Probably a rapist and a murderer as well, just like the law says."

"So your answer is to become a murderer yourself?" Lowery scolded, taking a step toward the gunman on his left side. "No, sir," the attorney said harshly. "I won't have it."

Lincoln and True exchanged puzzled glances briefly before smiles came to both their faces. As if on cue, they raised their guns to aim them at Virgil Lowery's chest.

"Two martyrs to the cause are even better than one," Lincoln said, pulling back the hammer of his revolver.

CHAPTER TWENTY SIX

Chaos erupted as, seemingly, did the room's one window. Glass from its shattered pane sprayed into the confined space of the office. Both gunmen instinctively covered their faces to protect their eyes from spears of flying glass.

Only Kirby King saw and recognized the cause, seeing Michael Yellowstone flying through the window headfirst like a human cannonball.

Virgil Lowery stood frozen in place until Kirby jumped over his desk, grabbed the back of his coat collar, and jerked hard. The lawyer flew off his feet and was dragged by his client behind the protective cover of his desk.

Yellowstone struck the floor with the forearms he had held as shields before his own face and went into a roll that carried him behind yet another desk.

He came out of the final roll up onto his knees, his service revolver held out before him in both hands. True and Lincoln had come out of their stunned daze and were attempting to draw a bead on him.

Yellowstone didn't flinch as they began to fire, ignoring the splinter of wood that flew up off the desktop and past his face.

With practiced precision he snapped off three quick shots of his own. Two went wide of their mark, but the third slapped into Ned Lincoln's right shoulder, causing him to twist and fall to the floor.

Giving voice to an incoherent yell, Marcus True fired toward Yellowstone as rapidly as his finger could pull the trigger. With lead flying wildly all around him, Yellowstone dropped back down behind the desk.

When the shooting finally ceased, the detective popped back up, pistol at the ready. Ned Lincoln was back on his feet; with his left hand gripping his wounded and useless right arm, he was staggering toward the door that led out of the office.

Marcus True was right behind him. He hadn't tried to reload his own now empty pistol, but had scooped Lincoln's up off the floor and was laying down a covering fire for their escape.

The Osage detective again dropped behind the desk, but now rolled to one end of it and began firing from floor level. He saw splinters fly from the doorframe but also saw True lurch as if one of the slugs may have at least clipped his hip.

Rolling back behind the desk and pushing himself to a sitting position, the detective with practiced smoothness flipped open his gun's cylinder, ejecting the spent shells and reloading with some of the fresh bullets he carried in his coat pocket.

No more shots had been fired in his direction, but he still moved cautiously to peer over the top of the desk. Seeing nothing, he dropped back down, and then sprinted from behind the office furniture.

Flattening himself against the wall to the right of the open doorway, he slowly counted to ten. He next ducked and scampered through the opening, leaping out of its revealing light and into the shadows of the lobby. Still no shots were fired at him.

Suspecting the bumbling assassins were gone, he nonetheless kept his revolver at the ready as he made for the building's front entrance.

Flinging the door open, he dropped to one knee on the sidewalk outside, gun extended at shoulder height.

Nothing except for the fading thunder of a car's engine and a pair of taillights growing dimmer as a vehicle raced away from the scene. Probably on its way to Canada.

Re-entering the office building, Yellowstone returned his pistol to its shoulder holster. As he stepped back into the office scene of the gun battle, he saw Kirby King assisting Virgil Lowery back up to his feet.

"Are you two all right?" the detective asked.

"We're good," King replied. "Thanks to you. How about you? You all right?"

"I've been worse," Yellowstone replied truthfully. He placed the palms of his hands on the small of his back, arched it as far as he could, eliciting a grimace and a groan.

"Nnnngh," he grunted. "But it's stunts like this that make me glad I left Hollywood."

"I can't believe it," Lowery muttered, clearly still in shock. "I can't believe they'd turn on their own like that."

"I can," Kirby declared, shaking his head. "I've seen it before."

"Yeah," Yellowstone concurred, hiking one leg up to perch on the edge of a desktop. "I'd say those two have achieved th' true equality you advocate, Mr. Lowery."

Lowery stared at him blankly, failing to comprehend.

"They're just as money hungry and bloodthirsty as any white man."

The attorney was still too dazed to react at all, but King smiled tightly at his grim joke.

"Come on," Yellowstone said, gently taking Lowery by the arm and leading him toward the doorway. "Let's get you home, counselor."

"I'm so sorry, Kirby," Lowery said.

"It wasn't your doing, Mr. Lowery," King replied. "And you did your best to help me. I appreciate it."

Finally starting to regain his wits, Lowery straightened and pulled away from Yellowstone.

"The offer I made before this madness broke out still stands," he told King. "Come with me and I'll have you set up in a safe house, a *real* safe house, before the night's done."

King stared thoughtfully at the attorney, as if silently studying his face. Then his gaze shifted to the detective.

Marcus True fired toward Yellowstone as rapidly as he could.

"What about you, Mr. Yellowstone?" he asked. "What do you think I should do?"

"Kirby," Lowery said. "I don't think…"

"I'm talking to the man now," King said, his deep voice rising not in volume but in urgency.

"What do you think I should do, Mr. Yellowstone?"

"Honestly?" Yellowstone replied. "I don't know, Kirby. Remember, you're a free man. I have no legal way to detain you. Whatever you think is best for you."

"If I stay with you," the fugitive said, "will you keep trying to help me like you been doing?"

"I'll keep trying to do my job," the detective replied. "Beyond that I won't make you any false promises."

"You still think I done this thing; killed that woman, I mean?"

"I still think that's possible, yes," Yellowstone answered truthfully. He noted that King had again avoided any mention of the other part of the crime of which he was accused.

"But anyone other than th' law tries to take you down, he'll have to go through me to do it. You have my word."

King peered deep into the eyes that were nearly as dark as his own. Turning toward Virgil Lowery, he extended his right hand.

"I want to thank you for your help, Mr. Lowery. And I hope you'll keep on trying."

"I will, Kirby. You have *my* word."

"And I know it's a good word," King replied. He released Lowery's hand and went to stand next to Yellowstone.

"But for me, I think I'm gonna stick with the boss here. To the end."

"That's good," said Yellowstone. "Like they say back home, the easiest way to eat crow is while it's still warm."

"You know either one of those 'ends' could cost you your life, son," Lowery said sadly.

"I know," King replied, straightening and throwing back his shoulders.

"But it's my life to give."

CHAPTER TWENTY SEVEN

Yellowstone had never been happier to be back inside the small frame house he called his home.

Kirby King was seated on the sofa that also served as his temporary bed. His elbows rested on his knees; his hands were clasped together as if in prayer. His head was bowed, his eyes avoiding watching the detective pacing the floor in front of him.

"I told you," Yellowstone said. "I told you before you left here it was a bad idea."

"I know you did," King replied testily.

"If I hadn't followed you, you'd be dead now. How many times do I have to tell you to stay off th' street? Th' only place you're safe is inside this house."

"And how many times do I have to tell you I can't do that?" Kirby snapped back.

"Why th' hell not?" King could clearly hear the exasperation in the detective's voice.

"Close your eyes," he said unexpectedly, looking up now at the Osage detective.

"Huh? Why?"

"Just do it. It'll be okay."

Suspicious, Yellowstone nonetheless did as King asked. King said nothing further, so neither did the detective. He quickly became bored with the silent darkness and began shifting his weight back and forth from one foot to the other.

"Okay," Kirby said at last. "Open your eyes."

Yellowstone did so, glancing about to see if anything had changed while he was blind. All seemed as it was before.

"How long would you say you stood there with your eyes closed?" King asked him.

Yellowstone shrugged. "Not long. A couple minutes, maybe. Maybe a little more."

"Forty-five seconds," King replied. Yellowstone shook his head quizzically.

"I told you about being locked up in a cell," Kirby explained. "Well, believe it or not, that was the good times.

"There were plenty of bad times, too…and those always ended with me in solitary confinement. Sometimes for a day, sometimes for a week. Once or twice, for a solid month.

"Those 45 seconds seemed a lot longer than that didn't they, Mr. Yellowstone? Now picture spending 24 hours like that: almost no light, barely room to stand up or lay down.

"Nothing to do, no place to go but inside your own skull: sometimes for days, even weeks at a time." King shook his head slowly.

"If you wasn't already crazy when you went into the box…there was a good chance you would be by the time you got out."

Yellowstone, who had now taken a seat across from King in his easy chair, drew in a deep breath, let it out slowly as he studied the face of the ex-con.

"What was it that got you sent to th' box?"

"Fighting, mostly."

"Fighting about what?"

"Almost everything," King replied with a doleful chuckle. "One guy wants you to be his woman. One guy wants to steal the lousy dessert off your supper tray.

"One guy's just mean…another's just crazy. A whole lot of 'em don't like the color of your skin." Without realizing it, he had begun to clench and unclench his fists.

"And even if you win those fights, you lose the one against the guards who break it up by beating you senseless with their batons.

"Most of them don't like the color of your skin either."

Yellowstone could tell that King had forgotten he was even in the room with him.

"Then you go to the box. And when you get outta the box, there's always someone new wanting to fight." Kirby shook slightly, as if being jerked out of a sleep; looked up at the detective grimly eyeing him.

"And you keep doing it, over and over. 'Cause you figure fighting and going to the box is still better than not fighting and dying."

"Everybody in th' joint feel that way?" Yellowstone asked.

"Mostly. Not all. Not always; some finally do give up."

"And they die," Yellowstone said.

"They die."

"Sounds to me like a man would kill not to have to go back to a place like that," Yellowstone observed.

"Yeah," King concurred. Then a sly smile tugged at the corners of his mouth.

"That what you think I did, Mr. Detective?"

Yellowstone merely shrugged.

"Just one thing wrong with that theory," King said, his deep voice coming out almost like a distant rumble of thunder. "I wasn't facing no fresh jail time *before* the lady D.A. got herself killed, so that wouldn't be a reason for me do it."

"No," the Osage detective nodded. "But it sure would give you a hell of a lot of incentive to want to keep anyone from finding out if you did do it."

"Yeah," Kirby said, sinking into the back cushions of the sofa, "I guess it would."

"And you did hate th' woman, for sending you up th' first time."

"No, I can't deny that, either. There wasn't a day went by that I didn't wish the bitch was dead." Yellowstone tensed, as King stared down at his clasped hands. "Her…and other people."

Neither said another word for several minutes. Finally, Yellowstone pushed himself up out of his chair, barely noticing the light popping sound his abused knees made as he rose; he'd grown accustomed to it in the years since he had left stunt work behind.

He walked to his small and sparsely stocked liquor cabinet, withdrew a bottle of bourbon and a pair of glasses.

"I think I've earned a stiff drink, pardner. Care to join me?"

"Don't mind if I do, boss."

After filling each glass with a stout three fingers of booze, the detective opened a humidor and pulled out a couple of Prince Edward cigars. He neither smoked nor drank much or often, but when he did he usually enjoyed them in tandem.

King gratefully accepted the glass of bourbon, but waved off the offered cigar.

"No thanks, boss," he said. "I don't smoke."

Yellowstone was already clenching the other stogie between his teeth, and he remained bent over King, gazing at him expectantly. Kirby blinked, not sure what it was he was expected to do.

"Thank you for the drink," he said, lifting his glass up.

"My pleasure," Yellowstone replied.

Returning to his easy chair, the detective lit up the cigar, leaning back and blowing a lazy ring of smoke toward the ceiling before taking a sip of his bourbon.

"What do you plan to do with yourself when this is all over, Kirby?" he inquired.

"I don't know," King replied, taking another drink. "To be honest, I haven't given it much thought the last few days. Other things on my mind, y'know?"

"Point taken."

"There really doesn't seem much use in making plans for the future anyway," King said. "Things were all right before I went off to prison. But now we got this thing they're calling a Depression. Jobs are scarce. Admit to being an ex-con, and your prospects get even worse.

"Even before I had this here reward hanging over my head, I was mostly getting along by stretching what I was making cooking by making the rounds of the soup kitchens and missions around town.

"Sometimes, some of the good folk there would slip me a couple bucks for helping out in their kitchens with the cooking and the dish washing. That all together was enough for me to pay for the room I share with the rats at the flophouse.

"But at least that way the only charity I had to take was the meals. That's something, at least. Lets me keep a little pride."

Silence again descended between the two men, as each dwelled on his own thoughts.

"Well," Yellowstone said at last, again pushing up out of his chair, "I think I'm gonna call it a night."

"Mr. Yellowstone?" Kirby asked, keeping his gaze averted from the detective.

"Yeah?"

"Have you ever…even once…have you ever considered collecting that bounty on my head for your own self?"

"No!" Yellowstone exclaimed, genuinely appalled and taken aback by the very notion. "I make it a habit not to make money off of another man's life."

"Mebbe you should," King said, his voice barely above a whisper.

"Are you saying you deserve to die?" Yellowstone probed, thinking he might be about to hear a confession. "That you really did kill that girl?"

"All I'm saying…" Yellowstone heard a catch in the felon's voice, "…is that I'm worth a whole lot more dead than I am alive." He now swiveled his head to look up at the detective.

"I just want you to know, if you do decide to kill me, I won't hold it against you none. You been good to me." He was now nervously twisting his hands around his glass.

"But if you do…would you do me one last favor? I got a kid sister living here in Detroit: her and her little boy.

"If you could see they get just a little bit of the money, I'd be much obliged."

Now standing near the liquor cabinet, Yellowstone stared at King through narrowed eyes.

"I thought you said you didn't have any family, Kirby."

"Yeah. I lied about that, too."

"Why?"

"The reason's not important. Just think about it, okay?" The look in Kirby's eyes, on his face, was that of a supplicant.

"Yeah," Yellowstone said, snuffing out his cigar and finishing off his drink before turning toward his bedroom. "I'll think about it."

But that night, for the first time since long before his current nightmare began, Kirby King would feel safe enough to fall asleep quickly and soundly.

CHAPTER TWENTY EIGHT

Detective Yellowstone and Lt. Hill spent the first half of the following day checking out leads in the murder of Rebekah Nixon, despite Hill's continued assertion that it was a waste of time to investigate anyone other than Kirby King. This day, he proved to be correct.

As usual, none of these so-called leads had any merit: they ranged from a claim that Rebekah was still alive and had run away with a distraught housewife's philandering husband, to a report that the crime had been committed by someone who was a dead ringer for President Herbert Hoover.

One skid row bum, characterized by Yellowstone as being more pickled than grandma's cucumbers, had tried to confess that he was the killer and had taken the ghastly action of trying to cut off his own head in hopes of turning it in for the reward.

Now Yellowstone sat alone at his desk, his partner down at the courthouse waiting to give testimony in one of their earlier cases that had finally gone to trial.

On a hunch, the Osage detective had requested a list of the names of the men who had been brought in for questioning in connection with the fatal car chase of the night before last.

List in hand, he trekked to the department's criminal files to check for any priors among them. Most of the men had no prior arrests; almost all the others were for fairly petty offenses such as drunken driving and public urination.

Unknown to him, as the day began to turn into the first gloom of evening, one of the men on that list was pulling to the curb not far from the detective's house.

Tony Matson smiled as he switched off the ignition. The new set of wheels he'd stolen early that morning had proven to be a smooth and powerful ride. Now bearing a license plate he had purloined from yet another vehicle, he felt secure that there was little chance of his being caught with the stolen car.

He assured himself that he was near the correct address: the one he'd gotten from the driver's license he had lifted off the oblivious detective the previous day.

Where he was parked, he couldn't be easily seen from the house, but he had a clear view of three sides of it. Leaning against the door, Matson folded his arms over his chest and settled in for as long as it might take.

His instincts told him that sooner or later Kirby King would show up here also. And when he did his head would belong to Matson.

Back at the police station, Yellowstone was back at his desk. The sun had slid from view; Lt. Hill had returned from his courtroom duty but left for home after deciding to call it a day. Yellowstone had assured him he would not be far behind.

He had one last file he wanted to go over: one that was by far the thickest of all those that he had perused.

This particular jacket belonged to a man named Anthony Matson. His record was extensive but maddeningly short on details. It seemed he'd been brought in for questioning as part of the investigations into half a dozen cases in nearly as many different states.

It appeared, though, that the only time he had actually been arrested was in connection with a disturbance in a Memphis cathouse. The case had been dropped after a witness failed to show for a hearing and the madam of the house declined to press charges.

The file included a copy of Matson's mug shot, taken when he was booked in Memphis. Yellowstone whistled softly. The face looking back at him was a few years younger, but was otherwise a perfect match for the one sitting atop the shoulders of the man who had bumped into Yellowstone the previous afternoon.

Rising from his chair, Yellowstone arched his neck to look around the squad room. As hoped, he spied the man he was looking for near one of the windows.

Lt. Matt Calahan was the oldest veteran on the force. He'd put in more than enough years to retire at full pension; he'd fully intended to do so until his wife Clare had passed away a couple years back. With his kids all grown and gone, the prospect of an empty house frightened him more than any perp ever had. So he just stayed on the job, and would do so until death or the brass forced him out.

He smiled as he saw Yellowstone approaching his desk. He liked the younger detective; Yellowstone was the only one there who always showed Calahan the respect he felt his years of service had earned for him. In return, Calahan never called Michael Yellowstone Hollywood or cowboy or One Take.

Maybe it was an Indian thing, Calahan figured: respect for the elders of your tribe. Or maybe Yellowstone was just smarter than the other jokers around this place were.

In addition, Calahan loved hearing Yellowstone's stories about Hollywood, even more than Jack Hill did.

"Smoke, Lieutenant?" Yellowstone asked by way of greeting. Lt. Hill had left a partial pack of Lucky Strikes and a book of matches atop his desk when he left for the day, and Yellowstone had snatched up both on his way over.

"Don't mind if I do," Calahan replied, reaching across his desk to pluck one of the cigarettes from its package. He loved the things, yet seldom seemed to carry a pack of his own.

Yellowstone leaned across the desk and lit the cigarette for Calahan, then dropped both matches and cigarettes atop it before planting himself in a chair facing the lieutenant.

"Let me ask you something," Calahan said. "The other day, Jack told me you knew Wyatt Earp. Is that true?"

"It was, yeah," Yellowstone said. "He finally passed away back in '29. But before that he was a fixture on th' movie lots. Directors would bring him in as a 'consultant', but mainly they just wanted to hear him tell stories about life in th' Old West."

"I bet he had some rip-roaring ones to tell, too," Calahan said.

"Hundreds of 'em. Of course, th' old codger liked to embellish them a little. I sat and listened one time while he told John Ford all about some gunfight he'd been in while he was marshalling in Tombstone, him and his brothers.

"To hear old Wyatt tell it, that battle lasted pert near as long as th' Great War did!" He chuckled at the memory.

"And his wife Josie was an even bigger pistol. She's still around; they'll probably have to beat her to death with a stick."

"I declare," Calahan wondered. "And is it as wild out there in movie land as they say?"

"You mean sex? Yeah; for some it is, yeah."

"I bet Valentino got all the action he could stand on a Saturday night," the older detective postulated.

"Oh, he did, all right. Just not th' kind of action you're probably thinking about."

"What do you mean?"

The Osage detective looked around conspiratorially, motioned Calahan to lean in closer.

"I mean th' man was queer as a three dollar bill."

"No!"

"If I'm lyin', I'm dyin'. Oh, he loved th' ladies, all right, he surely did: just not th' way you and me do. And God knows th' ladies loved him; but they couldn't compete with th' men when it came to his real affections.

"Poor Rudy; I think he'd have been happier if he'd just stayed a gardener."

"Holeee cow," Calahan exclaimed. "It just goes to show: you never know, do you?"

"No, you never do."

Calahan leaned back in his chair. "So what can I do for you, Michael?" he asked, his mood warming along with his lungs as they filled with smoke.

"Th' usual thing," Yellowstone replied. "You can give me the benefit of your experience and knowledge."

"We're both on the same team, son," Calahan said. "You don't have to flatter me to get my help." Yet Yellowstone knew he was indeed flattered.

"Just stating a fact, Lieutenant." Yellowstone slid the mug shot of Anthony Matson across the desk. "This face ring any bells for you?"

Calahan lifted the photo, gazing at it for only a few seconds before dropping it as if it had soiled his hands. He chuckled somberly.

"Tony the Torpedo," he said. "Yeah, I know the mook."

"Is he a bad one?"

"Hard to say. No one's ever been able to pin anything on him; but I think so, yeah."

"Bad in what way?"

"Again, hard to say. Some people say he's just another soldier for the

Mob, nothing but a small time hood. Others say he's a stone cold killer.

"Either way, he's a loose cannon. Never stays in one place for long. Rumor has it he's freelanced for families all over the northeast third of the county: the Gambinis, the Lucheses, the Giamattis, the Delvechios.

"He's not loyal to any single one of them; he's not loyal to anyone but himself. But they all make use of him and his special talents.

"So far, no one's been able to pin anything on him that would stick." Calahan frowned.

"If you're going after him, Mike, you'd better be damned careful."

"I'm always careful, Matt," Yellowstone replied lightly, rising to his feet. "You can ask anyone." He tapped the stiffened fingers of one hand to his forehead in a semblance of a salute before turning to walk away.

"Hey!" Calahan called out, holding up the pack of Lucky Strikes. "You forgot your fags, kid."

"Those aren't mine, Lieutenant," Yellowstone replied with a straight face. "Never touch th' things; I'm a cigar man." Now a trace of a smile tugged at one side of his mouth as he winked at the veteran. "They must be yours."

Calahan laughed as Yellowstone moved away, then slipped another cigarette out of the pack and popped it in his mouth.

Returning to his own desk, Yellowstone flipped through the pages of his notebook until he found a specific phone number. He didn't know if anyone would still be in the office this late, but it was worth a try.

His fears seemed to be confirmed after he dialed the phone and heard the other end of the line ring repeatedly without answer. Just as he was pulling the receiver away from his ear to hang up and give up, he heard a click in the earpiece and a woman's voice.

"Who is this?" he asked.

"Who's *this*?" the woman snapped back. He smiled.

"This is Detective Michael Yellowstone from the Third Precinct."

"Oh!" This had obviously flustered the woman slightly. "I'm sorry, detective. This is Gladys Cooper; we've spoken before."

Indeed they had, and she was just who he'd hoped to reach. Gladys had worked as Rebekah Nixon's assistant.

"Were you on your way out, Gladys?"

"Well, yes. It's well after five."

"I know it is, and I won't keep you long, I promise. I just need a little more information from you, that's all."

"If it'll help your investigation, detective, I'll gladly stay as long as you like."

"It's pretty simple, really, Gladys; you may know it off the top of your head. Can you tell me what cases Miss Nixon had on her calendar at th' time of her death?"

A momentary pause followed, accompanied by the sound of shuffling papers.

"Let's see," Gladys said. "We had a drug possession case Becka was hoping to plead out. Whiz-bang, I think. A grocery store robbery we were still deposing witnesses for. And the really big one."

"What one would that be?"

"The Angelo Giamatti trial, of course."

"Th' racketeering charge?"

"That's the one. Jury selection was scheduled to begin next week. We've asked for a continuance, given what's happened."

"Anything else?"

"No…that's all she had on her plate at the moment. Is any of that useful to you, detective?"

"I hope so, Gladys. Thanks for helping me out."

"Any time, detective. Becka was a good girl; she deserved better."

"All th' more reason to see she gets our best work," Yellowstone said before hanging up.

A cold smile pursed his lips. According to Lt. Calahan, Tony Matson had done work for the Giamatti family in the past. Now here he was in town, just as Rebekah Nixon's murder delays Angelo's trial.

Maybe it was coincidence. Maybe Matson had just been drawn here by the lure of the reward for Kirby King; Yellowstone had noticed a recent increase in the number of cars driving around with out-of-state tags.

Or maybe it was something more.

Maybe the detective had just uncovered the first bit of new evidence that could blow this case wide open.

CHAPTER TWENTY NINE

Tony Matson was bored, and he didn't like being bored. He would have much preferred sitting in a bar, or taking his pleasure in a cathouse.

It made him mean.

He'd been sitting in his car for better than two hours, keeping watch on the detective's house. It was fully dark now, but no lights had come on inside the dwelling, indicating the place was empty. He knew the detective had not returned home yet; maybe he should just break into the joint and take a look around.

Matson was reaching for his door handle when a movement at one side of the house caught his attention. A side door leading out of the house's attached garage was slowly opening outward. From within, a shadowy figure slipped out, taking pains to close the door behind him with minimum noise.

Matson's eyes lit, and his soft, crazed laughter filled the interior of the car. That wasn't the detective leaving the house; it had to be Kirby King.

Patting his coat pocket to assure himself of his revolver's comforting presence, Tony the Torpedo looked at the long knife sitting next to him, then exited his stolen vehicle.

He casually crossed the quiet boulevard to put himself on the same side of the street as the man he was stalking. King was no more than a hundred feet ahead of him and ignorant of the gunman coming up behind him.

Matson discretely quickened his pace, as to gradually but steadily close the gap between him and his prey. His breathing quickened, not from exertion but from anticipation. One pop in the back of the head would do it, he expected. A few seconds to saw off his head in the car with a knife that he'd taken from the pawnbroker the other night and the bounty would be his.

The gangster scowled as a new player unexpectedly inserted himself onto the field of play.

It was a little boy, probably no older than eight. He was coming up the sidewalk from the opposite direction, walking toward King. He was carrying a flat stick, which he was running along the slats of the picket fences that fronted most of the houses in this neighborhood. As only a child can, he was deriving great satisfaction from the resulting clack-clack-clack sound he was making.

As he drew near King, the boy looked up at the black man and flashed him a smile. Kirby nodded and returned the smile before passing on.

Moments later, the little fellow smiled at the next man approaching. But this time he was met with a cold and merciless glare that froze him in his tracks and caused him to drop his stick.

Tony Matson leaned down close to him, taking sadistic pleasure in the stricken look on the boy's face: the tears already welling up in his wide and innocent eyes.

"A kid your age shouldn't be out on the streets at night," the gunman growled. "Go on, you little punk...get your ass home."

Knowing sound advice when he heard it, the little boy took off running. Matson watched after him for a moment, giggling as he heard the child give vent to his fear and begin to wail.

When the Torpedo turned his attention back to his prey, he saw King rounding a corner, about to move out of sight.

Matson quickened his pace, only to find his path blocked by a new obstacle. Unnoticed by all, when the little boy had been running his stick down the fencerow, he had inadvertently popped open the latch on one front gate.

That gate now swung open and a dark figure bounded out from the fence's confines. A Doberman pinscher planted itself directly before the startled hit man. Lips curled back over powerful fangs, a menacing growl vibrating within its chest, the guard dog began to advance toward Matson.

The mobster's right hand dipped into his coat pocket, its fingers wrapping around the comforting feel of the butt of the gun riding there.

"I'm sorry, mister."

Matson's eyes left the dog to see a middle-aged man rushing out through the open gate.

"Heel, Hercules!" the man commanded loudly, grabbing the Doberman by its collar. The dog instantly dropped to its haunches, its tongue flicking in and out rapidly as it looked up to its master.

"I don't know how he got out," the man explained. "One of the darn neighbor kids must have opened the gate. No harm intended."

The man flashed an apologetic smile, but like the child before him his melted away before the blazing eyes of the hit man.

"Let's go, boy," he said, practically dragging the Doberman back into his yard.

Snarling like an animal himself, Matson lost interest in both man and beast instantly. His intended target was now completely out of his vision, and he broke into a trot to make up for lost ground.

He slowed again as he reached the corner and rounded it. He was just in time to see a bus pull away from the curb half a block away. With a belch of black fumes, it took off down the street.

Kirby King was nowhere to be seen.

Openly and loudly cursing now, Matson turned and sprinted back to where he had left his car parked. Firing up its engine, he peeled away from into the middle of the street. After hanging a sharp right onto the avenue down which the bus had been traveling, Matson found himself stopped by a traffic light.

Across the intersection, he could see the high-set taillights of a city bus moving away from him.

Right next to an identical city bus.

Matson glanced to his right and saw yet a third bus speeding off in another direction.

There was no way to tell which, if any, of these conveyances had Kirby King as a passenger.

Enraged, Matson slammed the palm of his left hand against his steering wheel, again and again.

When the light turned green, his car didn't move.

CHAPTER THIRTY

Kirby King had no specific destination in mind when he exited the bus near the inner city and set off on foot. He'd experienced one tense moment, when a hardhat riding across from him seemed to be looking at him a little too intently; but the laborer had gotten off two blocks earlier without raising any alarm.

The detective, Yellowstone, would be mad at him for going out alone again; this he knew. But the cop wasn't the one who had to live with a million-dollar sword hanging above his head.

As expected, he found another small cluster of streetwalkers near the same corner where he and Yellowstone had encountered the first three before. It was as if each hooker was merely one part of a single, large organism, he knew; by now every whore in town was keeping her ear tuned to any tidbit of information having to do with this case.

"Look who's back, girls," one of the hookers squealed as Kirby approached and she recognized him. "It's the million dollar baby!" She and her sisters of the night descended upon him in a covey.

But one dove hung back. She called herself Mattie: a slatternly looking white woman of indeterminate age (though probably far younger than one would guess by looking at her worn features). She drew away from the others, and then turned to walk off.

"Where you goin', girl?" a statuesque hooker asked, catching up to Mattie and taking hold of one of her arms. Mattie shrugged and gave her a weak smile.

"I gotta go call my man," she explained, referring to her pimp. "If I don't check in with him regular, he gets awful mad."

The other streetwalker released her arm and nodded sympathetically. She herself knew only too well the consequences of making your pimp angry.

There was a phone booth half a block away and Mattie practically ran to reach it. Slipping a nickel into the slot and dialing rapidly, she stood tapping one foot impatiently as she listened to the phone on the other end of the line start ringing.

"Yeah?" a gruff voice made only slightly less so by the tinny quality of the phone line said at last.

"He's here!" Mattie declared breathlessly.

"What?"

"Kirby King…he's here!"

"You sure?"

"It's him, I tell ya. I can still see him from here. He's with some of the other girls right now. Right on the corner of Third and Muldrew."

There was a brief silence.

"Keep him there."

"How'm I supposed ta do that?"

"Just do it, woman. We'll be right there."

"You'll take good care of me, wontcha, Daddy?" Mattie said in what she hoped would pass for a little girl's voice. "After you do him, I mean."

"Sure, sweetheart," he assured her. "A healthy piece of that reward is going to be yours. We'll paint the town red, you and me. Now get going."

The line went dead. Before hanging up her receiver, Mattie gently touched the mouthpiece, as if by extension stroking her lover's cheek.

Just four blocks away, Roger Sinclair engaged in no such sentimental gesture as he ended his side of the conversation and slipped out of the phone booth.

Sinclair had stayed close to this phone every night since his girlfriend Mattie had confided in him about her and her fellow streetwalkers being questioned by King and an indian detective.

Inherently lazy, Sinclair had felt it would be easier and smarter to use Mattie as both bait and stool pigeon for him than to waste time and effort patrolling the streets actively hunting for King. Besides, doing just that had already gotten some of his cohorts killed and hospitalized.

He smiled smugly as he stepped from the booth. The faces of the seven other men, all of them fellow members with Sinclair of the Ku Klux Klan, turned expectantly toward him.

"Let's go, boys," he crowed. "We've got a buck in our snare!"

Mattie rejoined the cluster of hookers just as Kirby King was about to take his leave of them, having discerned that none of them had yet come upon anything that might be of help to him.

"What's your hurry, big boy?" Mattie said. Fearful of letting him get away, she playfully grabbed him by one arm and turned him back toward the other soiled doves.

"Wouldn't you rather stay here and have a little fun with us girls?"

"No, I'd best be going," Kirby demurred, stammering slightly and hanging his head. Seeing his embarrassment, the other streetwalkers now joined in on seductively teasing him.

"C'mon, handsome," one said, cupping her breasts in her hands, arching her back as to thrust them forward. "You gotta like what you see."

"We could show you a good time like you ain't ever seen before," another promised.

A wide and only partly sheepish smile spread across King's face.

"I appreciate the offer, ladies...honest I do. And I have no doubt you all could turn me every which way but loose, and make me like it." They all tittered in unison at this.

"Every one of you looks fine as cotton candy," he continued. "But right now I'm terrible short on either the time or the money to avail myself of your services."

King again made to walk away, but this time his path was blocked by Mattie's right leg, hiked up in front of him with her foot pressing against the wall of the nearest building beside him.

As the ex-con stared hungrily at the exposed limb, Mattie pulled the hem of her already short skirt up even higher. Doing so not only revealed an enticing flash of thigh...but a metal liquor flask held in place there by a lacy black garter.

As Mattie pulled the flask free from the garter, she also managed to slide the edge of her skirt even more indecently upward.

"The least you can do is join us in a drink before you go," she said, giving him a sly wink. "No charge."

The other girls again circled tightly around him, rubbing his arms and broad shoulders and cajoling the man to accept the offer.

"After you," he said, smiling and motioning toward Mattie. She saluted him with the flask, tipped it up and took a short nip, then handed it to Kirby. After he took a drink, the flask began to be passed back and forth rapidly.

They were all having fun, so none noticed that whenever the flask would make it back to Mattie's hands she immediately passed it on without taking a drink. She craned her neck, anxiously looking for any sign of her boyfriend's arrival.

The next time the flask found its way into King's hand, he was disappointed when he tipped it to his lips and nothing came out. Holding it up for all to see, he turned it upside down and shook it so all could see it was empty. All but one of the doves moaned petulantly. Kirby shrugged and handed the empty flask back to Mattie.

"I got to go, ladies," he said regretfully. "But I'll be back first chance I get. Promise."

They laughed and blew kisses at him as he set off down the sidewalk, showing only the slightest of alcohol-induced hitches in his gait as he did so. Nor was he so impaired as to forget his newfound habit of staying in the shadows as much as possible. He didn't know that this time it would do him no good.

CHAPTER THIRTY ONE

Ice cold sobriety expelled even the mildest traces of inebriation from within Kirby King as a dark car pulled to the curb no more than twenty-feet feet ahead of him and four white men carrying pipes, chains and baseball bats came spilling out.

Fighting the urge to panic, he still wasted no time in spinning on his heels and running off in the opposite direction. He didn't make it far; a second car roared up, jumping the curb and coming to a jarring halt directly in his path. The group of streetwalkers, having nearly been struck by the vehicle, shrieked and took off running in several directions. From this car, four more white men stepped out, armed similarly to their brethren.

At least they didn't seem to be carrying any firearms this time; that was something. Not much…but something.

King backed away from this second band of vigilantes, glancing over his shoulder to check the progress of the first group. They were drawing closer, moving with slow deliberation.

The ex-con backed up against a wall as if to make a stand of it there. Instead, and to the Klansmen's surprise, he pushed off from the hard surface, using it to launch himself out into the street.

The ex-con stared hungrily at the exposed limb...

Horns began to blare and brakes to squeal in protest as he precariously wove his way through four lanes of traffic.

He'd almost made it to the opposite side when a large coupe struck him.

The driver of the vehicle had slammed on his brakes, lessening the impact. Still, it was enough to take King's legs out from under him and flip him up onto the car's front hood.

As he then rolled deliberately to one side off the car, he caught a fleeting glimpse of a black face staring back at him in amazement from behind the steering wheel.

King huffed as he rolled off the vehicle and fell heavily to the sidewalk. Using his hands to push himself up, he resumed running. Each step brought a bolt of pain through his left leg, slowing him down. But he kept moving forward, afraid to look back.

Something else hit him; a smaller object this time, and in the back of the head. He stumbled forward from the impact and fell to the ground.

He turned his head to one side and saw the projectile that had decked him as it rolled away and off the curb: it was an empty whiskey bottle.

Oddly, the principal thought in his befuddled brain was the fact that the bottle was still intact. In the movies, bottles always shattered like thin ice when they were smashed over someone's head.

He'd have to ask Yellowstone about that…if he came out of this night alive.

King yet again forced himself to his feet, though his vision swam and he fell against a wall as he did. He put a hand to the back of his throbbing skull, winced upon touching an egg-sized lump already swelling there.

The hand came away wet with blood.

His eyes teared up and his vision was still blurred, but he could make out the mouth of an alleyway just a few feet ahead. He forced his body to lurch forward and into the gap.

Too late, he saw that the alley, and thus, possibly, his life, came to a dead end.

King leaned against the towering brick wall that barred his path; his head hung down between his shoulders while a sound like a choking laugh spilled from his lips.

As he turned around, he saw all eight of his pursuers already in the alleyway, blocking any hope of escape. They came forward slowly in two ranks, each four abreast. There was no need to hurry, they knew, and they wanted to savor the kill.

One of the Klansmen in the back row suddenly cried out in pain and pitched forward.

All eyes turned in his direction. Behind the fallen Klansman stood a young black man, wielding a length of pipe now stained with blood. Four other black youths stood with him, each similarly armed.

Both groups of men stood silent for a moment, sizing up each other. Then someone, in the confines of the alley it was nearly impossible to tell whom, gave a savage yell at the top of his lungs. Whites and blacks charged in unison.

Kirby King leaned against the back wall of the alley, taking deep breaths and watching the melee erupting before him. At least now his vision was beginning to clear and he could focus on what was happening.

He didn't look upon these new arrivals as rescuers; his nearly fatal encounter of the previous evening had left him convinced that for most men the only color that trumped all others was green. He had no reason to believe that these black intruders had any other motive than to collect the reward for themselves.

But their assault could also provide the means for King's escape.

Leaping forward, he landed on the back of a Klansman who had turned to face the new threat posed by the black attackers. As he rode the man down to the ground, King grabbed his head with both hands and drove his face into the pavement. With a sickening crunch, the white man's nose was pulped by the impact.

The man's hands flew to the bloody mess that was his face as he began to roll back and forth on the ground, sobbing in pain. Doing so required him to release his grip on the baseball bat he had been carrying, and King now snatched it up for himself.

Grateful now for the many hours he spent playing stickball in the streets as a boy, he waded into the middle of the mass of struggling humanity clogging the alleyway.

Both sides were screaming in primal rage. The harsh sounds of bats and pipes colliding were sometimes punctuated with the softer sound of one of those instruments connecting with skin and bone.

At least one combatant was armed with a knife, and flesh could be heard parting beneath a slash or a thrust. Blood sprayed in all directions, its sickeningly sweet odor hanging in the air.

Kirby King was elbowing his way through the tangle of arms and weapons, wanting nothing more than to be free of both factions.

A movement on his right caught his eye, and he saw one of the young black men racing toward him through a momentary break in the jumble of bodies.

King acted without hesitation. Holding the baseball bat in both hands, he thrust it forward like a lance. The wide end of it came up from under to smash into the charging man's chin. His head snapped back and his knees buckled as consciousness fled.

Nearing the outer edge of the fight, Kirby leaped over a fallen body. As he did, he himself became the recipient of a blow from a lead pipe. It caught him in his right side. Ribs broke and shifted painfully under the skin; he dropped his own makeshift weapon as the wind was squeezed from his lungs.

With his arms wrapped tightly around his midsection, Kirby staggered on. The exit from the alley yawned enticingly just feet ahead of him, if he could only keep his feet moving.

He couldn't. His knees turned to rubber and his legs failed to support him. He dropped to his knees, and then pitched over to one side, moaning as the fall jolted his cracked ribcage. The ex-con dragged himself along with just his hands, until he reached a wall and was able to pull himself into a sitting position.

With his left arm draped over his torso, his back literally to the wall, the sound of his own blood roaring through his veins threatened to deafen him. Only when that noise subsided did he realize there was no other sound coming from the alleyway.

King's head lolled to one side, and he saw that only black men were still standing: and a couple of them only with the assistance of their comrades.

As they now slowly walked toward him, their faces showing no emotion save grim resolve, King steeled himself for the worst. He felt even less safe than he had before their arrival on the scene, being now less mobile. He assumed he had merely passed from the hands of one gang of bounty hunters into those of another.

He found the knowledge that the reward would at least be shared by members of his own race was of absolutely no comfort to him at all.

King's eyes lifted as the young man he took to be the leader of this band came to stand over him. A long and jagged cut above the youth's left eye was still bleeding, and one sleeve of his shirt had been torn away completely.

He spoke not a word…but simply extended an open hand to Kirby.

King accepted the hand, and the young man pulled him up off the pavement. Kirby winced with the effort, but found the pain from his ribs, his leg and his head was actually subsiding somewhat.

"We've been looking for you," the young man said earnestly. Then a smile pulled up the corners of his mouth.

"When I hit you with my car, I was afraid I had killed you."

"I'm a tough man to kill," Kirby replied, relaxing slightly.

"And we mean to keep it that way," the youth replied firmly. His companions now gathered around, some slapping Kirby on the shoulders, to his painful dismay.

"We've been driving around the city every night," one of them said, "just keeping an eye out for you. And we're not the only ones, either. There's lots more of us."

"And you saved my bacon," Kirby said sincerely. "But now you need to get outta here."

"Huh?" one man protested. "But we want to help you."

"You have, boy. Even more than you know. But now you got to go, before the police get here and find you standing over a bunch of unconscious crackers."

"Well, you're coming with us, aren't you?" another asked. "You need to be patched up."

"I will be," King assured him. "But it wouldn't do for you to be seen with me. If that happened, it could bring a whole other mob down on our heads. And next time guns and death might come with 'em."

This was met by grumbles and the shuffling of feet.

"Go on," he insisted. "Git."

Slowly, hesitantly, they began to move away. The young man leading them brought up the rear and turned back briefly to again extend a hand to the ex-con.

"We're going, Mr. King," he said, "because that's what you want. But we're going to keep on patrolling the streets at night just the same; keep an eye out for you."

"That's fine, boy," King told him.

"We've all had to swallow at least a little bit of what's being dished out to you, sir." His grip on Kirby's hand tightened.

"And we're not going to just stand by and let it happen anymore."

King nodded but said nothing more as the young man turned and walked away. He wasn't sure if this rising tide of defiance among the blacks would prove to be a good or a bad thing in the long run; and he regretted that he had played an unwitting role in helping to inflame it.

Kirby retrieved his cap from the sidewalk where it had fallen after he was hit by the bottle, slapped it back on his head and set off at a slow, limping walk.

He stopped at the next unoccupied phone booth he came upon: unknown to him, it was the same one the streetwalker Mattie had used to sell him out to the Klan.

Detective Yellowstone, despairing of ever convincing King to stay in hiding, had at least made him promise to check in with the lawman with periodic updates on his whereabouts and doings.

When he failed to get a response from the detective's home phone, Kirby scooped his nickel from the coin return and dialed the second number he had committed to memory. This time, he heard a click on the other end of the line after just two rings.

"Third Precinct, Detective Yellowstone."

"It's just me," Kirby said, his voice sounding just as weary as he suddenly felt.

"Are you all right?"

"Yeah. I had a little trouble, but I'm fine now."

"What kind of trouble?"

"The kind I'd rather not talk about."

"Do I need to come get you?"

"No." Kirby was highly grateful for the offer, though. "I'm just checking in, like you said."

"Listen to me, Kirby." The detective's voice was firm. "Get yourself back to the house as quick as you can. I'll be there soon."

"No argument this time, boss," King said. "I'll see you there."

The Osage detective returned his receiver to its cradle. His right hand moved from it to the dream catcher slide of his string tie, rubbing his thumb across its polished surface. His left hand fruitlessly pushed back the hair off his forehead as he rose from behind his desk.

When he turned, he found himself face-to-face with Lt. Hill.

It was a face grown dark and clouded with anger.

CHAPTER THIRTY TWO

"What are you doing here, Jack?" Yellowstone asked in a voice that sounded far calmer than the thoughts roiling within his brain. "I thought you'd gone home."

"I started to," Hill replied through clenched teeth. "But then I thought: What's the point? I can't sleep.

"So I decided to come back here. I haven't been keeping up my end of this partnership lately, I thought. Been leaving Yellowstone to fend for himself too much. Thought I should try to rectify that."

"That's mighty nice of you," Yellowstone said, trying to step around Hill. "But it's not really necessary."

"Why not?" Hill snapped, grabbing Yellowstone by the front of his denim jacket and roughly spinning him around so they again faced each other.

"You too busy spending time with your *new* partner?"

Yellowstone glanced down at the hand holding him, then back up at Hill. Yellowstone's face looked impassive.

"You need to take your hand off me, Jack." He spoke softly, but there was an edge to his voice that spoke of danger about to be unleashed.

"I heard you talking on the phone!" Hill hissed.

Yellowstone continued to lock his piercing and mysterious eyes with the fiery ones of the lieutenant.

"You need to take your hand off me *now*."

Hill's lips twitched: his grip on Yellowstone's jacket tightened. Then it relaxed and released its grip.

"Now we can sit down and talk about this," Yellowstone declared.

Hill managed to keep his hands and his thoughts to himself as Yellowstone explained to him how he had come to be so closely involved with Kirby King.

"You let the little bastard snow you!" he exploded at last.

"Keep your voice down," Yellowstone admonished, glancing around the squad room to assure himself they were not drawing undue attention.

"The filthy murderer's been playing you for a fool, can't you see that?" Hill asked in an urgent whisper.

"I don't think so," Yellowstone replied. "With or without him, I've been working every angle I can think of in this case."

"Yeah? Well, any trail you followed that didn't lead straight to King was a false one."

"Maybe not, Jack." Yellowstone went on to tell Hill what he had learned about Tony Matson.

"That's it?" Hill snorted. "That's all you've got? Hell, this is Detroit, cowboy. You probably couldn't throw a rock out the window without hitting one of Giamatti's made men out there looking to collect the bounty on King's head. Why wouldn't they? Everybody from Sunday school teachers to bootleggers is."

"Is that why you haven't been bothering to do much digging yourself?" Yellowstone challenged. "You don't have any proof to convict King, so you just sit back and wait for someone to kill him?"

"Sounds like a pretty good plan to me."

"Not to me it doesn't. My job is to help the law do its work, and I mean to do it as best I can."

"By harboring a fugitive?"

"He's not a fugitive from the *law*, Jack, only from those bounty hunters."

"And what will you do if we are able to prove your new best friend did do it, huh?"

"Then I'll slap the cuffs on him myself."

"Are you sure? You've let yourself get personally involved in this case, partner. You sure you could arrest King?"

"If she broke th' law, I'd cuff my own mother."

Hill cocked his head to the side, glaring across the desk with one eye. Then he seemed to relax.

"All right, cowboy. I'll believe you. Not that it matters much; the slimy bastard's doing a pretty good job of staying hidden."

Yellowstone hesitated before replying, and then decided to plunge ahead. "That part's not a problem," he said. "I can lay my hands on him any time I want."

"Really? You're sounding a little cocky now, Hollywood. What makes you so sure of that?"

"Because he's been staying at my house."

Lieutenant Hill's hands snaked out to grip the edge of Yellowstone's desk. He fought the urge to yell, but the effort made his face turn almost purple in complexion.

"What the hell kind of a mess have you gotten yourself into, Yellowstone?" he said at last, his voice calmer than his partner would have expected.

"It just worked out that way, Jack. Besides, it lets me keep an eye on him while protecting him from the vigilantes."

"That's not your responsibility."

"It's my responsibility to uphold the law, Jack; just like it is yours. I've made this town my home and I won't have it turned over to thugs and bounty hunters."

Hill exhaled loudly, leaning forward in his chair. After staring at the floor for what seemed like a long time, he straightened back up, running both hands through his hair.

"Do you know where King is now?"

"He should be on his way back to my place."

Hill rose to his feet and smiled tightly. "Then that's where we should be, partner. Three heads are better than two."

"You mean it?"

"I do. But just so there's no misunderstanding: I'm still convinced he did it, and I still mean to see him fry."

"I wouldn't have believed you if you said you felt any different, Jack."

"Just so we're clear." Hill patted the pockets of his shirt and jacket.

"But let's stop at a store on the way. I seem to have lost my cigarettes."

CHAPTER THIRTY THREE

Tony the Torpedo rubbed his eyes sleepily, shifting uncomfortably in the car seat he had occupied for the last few hours.

When he'd lost Kirby King's trail, he had driven back to the spot where he could resume his surveillance of the detective's house. But the mobster had few good traits, and patience was not among them. If something didn't happen soon…

He jerked upright, grown suddenly alert. There were no street lamps along this boulevard, but even in the gloom he could make out the figure of a man slowly approaching the detective's house.

As before, Matson saw the side garage door open, this time to allow entry into the house. Moments later, a pale light illuminated one window of the dwelling.

The hit man remained where he was, eyes locked on that window. It was nearly half an hour later that the light within blinked out. Moments later, the light in another room came on; this time it went out only a few minutes later, leaving the entire house in darkness.

Matson giggled softly; he worked best in the dark and the shadows. And the smell of blood kept this watch from seeming so tedious.

Giving whoever was in the house (and he felt certain it was King) time to relax and possible fall asleep, the Torpedo left his car and the long blade lying on its seat and sprinted in a crouch to the side of the darkened house.

Matson tried the garage door through which his target had entered, but found it locked. He was sure he could easily pick the lock, but didn't want to risk stumbling through a darkened garage filled with who knew what. The element of surprise was what he sought.

Staying close to the outer wall of the house, he slid around to its back side. As expected, the dwelling had a rear door. This should serve his purposes perfectly.

Extracting a pair of picks from his inner coat pocket, Matson set to work. It was no surprise to him that a cop had no shoddy, dime-store lock on his door, but it still took no more than a minute for the hoodlum's dexterous fingers to get the job done.

Returning the lock picks to their resting place, Matson pulled his revolver from his coat pocket and slowly opened the door inward.

It led into the kitchen, which was even less well lit than the outdoors. The hit man crouched as he closed the door behind him, remaining still then as his eyes adjusted to the darkness.

As his vision became adapted to the gloom, he could make out the open doorway that appeared to lead from the kitchen to the living room, as well as shapes and forms well enough to avoid colliding with anything. He moved forward.

In the near total silence, he could hear his own footsteps, the slight creaking noise as his weight bore down on the linoleum flooring. But he knew there was little chance anyone else would hear such a faint sound. He moved through the doorway, gun thrust out before him.

Strong hands closed down tightly on his right wrist.

Matson felt himself being pulled almost off the floor; flipping and falling to his side as a large weight fell atop him.

When Kirby King had entered the house a short time earlier, his first order of business had been to doctor his various wounds and injuries. Yellowstone's medicine cabinet had yielded most of what he needed.

First his knee and then his midsection he had wrapped as tightly as possible in wide bandages. The wound in the back of his head had clotted closed; after washing away the dried blood, he had poured nearly half a small bottle of mercurochrome over the lacerated area, hissing as he felt it burn. Gauze and some tape covered up the wound nicely.

Even when the burning sensation had subsided, the pain and swelling from the blow remained. After filling an ice pack in the kitchen, he had turned out the lights and reclined face down on the sofa, leaving the cold compress on the back of his head.

He hoped he might doze off, but the aches and pains fought against the solace of sleep. In the quiet, the sound of someone lightly jiggling the back doorknob carried sharply to his ears.

There was no reason for the detective to enter his own home from the rear, but every reason for an uninvited intruder to do so.

King rolled quietly off the sofa, crawled to the doorway that led into the kitchen. Risking a peek around the frame, he saw the outline of a man through the shade covering the glass partition set in the upper half of the door.

He pulled his head back and pressed his body to the wall. He let his ears serve as his eyes; he heard the door open and close, the slow and deliberate footfalls across the floor. Then he actually saw the gun, and struck.

King kept his grip on Matson's wrist as the two men began to roll back and forth across the floor. They crashed into a nightstand, sending it toppling over and the lamp atop it flying to shatter against a wall.

Matson managed to get his knees under him and rise up off the floor. King came with him, never relinquishing his hold on the mobster's wrist.

Like two Greco-Roman wrestlers, they stood toe-to-toe, each struggling for an advantage. Matson had added his left hand to his right to counter the weight of his prey's muscular arms, but this was only enough to keep them in stalemate.

A swath of white against King's dark skin caught Matson's eye, and he hazarded a quick glance down; saw what appeared to be bandaging around the black man's middle.

He took the chance of dropping his left hand down, balling it into a fist before driving it into his opponent's side. King gasped loudly in agony as the blow to his broken ribs brought a world of pain crashing down upon him.

Kirby's legs buckled and he fell to his knees. As he did, he brought the mobster's right arm down with him which had the effect of aligning the barrel of Matson's revolver directly with King's forehead.

Grown stronger by desperation, King pushed up with his legs. Matson's gun hand was thrown upward and he stumbled back. King added impetus by throwing an elbow into the gangster's chest. He released his grip on Matson's arm, leaving him to stagger under his own momentum.

The small of Matson's back slammed into the liquor cabinet, toppling it. He went down along with the cabinet and its contents, accompanied by the sound of breaking glass.

As he tried to push himself up off the floor, the palm of Matson's left hand came down on a jagged shard of one of the broken bottles. He cursed, jerking his hand away and rolling over.

That left hand brushed against the cloth of a curtain, which he grabbed and used to pull himself upright. The curtain material ripped under his weight and allowed moonlight to spill into the living room.

Matson's face twisted in anger as he saw an even larger oblong of light. This was coming through the now open front door of the house.

Kirby King was on the run.

CHAPTER THIRTY FOUR

Traffic was fairly light as the Osage detective drove his roadster along Grand Boulevard. This route would take him to his home in the shortest time, on its way to the railroad yards and finally to the Detroit River. In the passenger seat, Lt. Hill maintained the sullen silence that he had kept throughout the drive.

In glancing over at his quiet partner, Yellowstone found he could also see the upper floors of the towering Maccabees Building, the top two floors of which housed the studios for radio station WXYZ. He could make out the station's sign sticking up from the middle of the roof: the twin broadcast towers jutting upward from either end of the building could be seen from miles away.

Yellowstone looked at his watch and realized Stacy Lord would be ending her nightly news program just about now. He reached out to switch on the car radio, which he always kept tuned to her station. He braced himself for whatever bit of inflammatory rhetoric he would hear coming from his fiery girlfriend.

As soon as her voice came over the air, though, Yellowstone detected a more reserved, even conciliatory tone to her voice, and his ears perked up.

"...that's why I urge everyone within the sound of this broadcast," she was saying, "to fight whatever temptation you might be feeling to try to claim the reward on Kirby King. A reward, I remind you, offered by an unknown source whose own motives may be less than moral. Certainly, they are less than legal.

"What should we do, then? We should let the law and all its duly appointed agencies continue to work in the way that they are supposed to.

"I urge each and every one of you to ask yourself the same question I now do: do we want to become a society where the power over life and death derives not from the law, not from our noble American traditions, or even from our common code of human decency – but from the pocket book and the barrel of a gun?

"A country where individuals are freely allowed to take the law into their own hands...in the end will become a country that has no law.

"I don't know about you, but that doesn't sound like the country I grew up in. The country I love.

"That's why I wanted to take this time tonight to apologize to all my listeners, one especially, if I've said or done anything to foment the lawlessness that has threatened to turn this beautiful city into an ugly den of iniquity. That was not my intent."

Yellowstone felt the beginnings of a smile tug at the corners of his mouth.

"We still should be outraged," the sharp voice coming from the radio continued, "by what happened to Rebekah Nixon, a hard-working and dedicated servant of the people. No woman, nor man nor child, deserves the horrible fate that befell her."

Yellowstone noticed that Lt. Hill had turned his head and was staring out the side window at the passing buildings, as if trying to ignore what he was hearing.

"And we should continue to press the agents of the law and the legal system to pursue this case diligently; as long as the animal who did this is still roaming our streets, none of us is safe.

"But we mustn't allow our righteous indignation over this horrible atrocity to become simply unthinking rage nor seek the powers reserved to the legal system for ourselves.

"If, God help us, the day ever comes when it really is necessary for us to do so…we'll have far worse problems facing us, and far more to fear, than Kirby King.

"I'm Stacy Lord. Good-night, and stay well."

The instant the woman's voice ceased, a new voice took its place; a male one, speaking with rehearsed smoothness.

"You're listening to Detroit's own WXYZ. Be sure to join us every Monday, Wednesday and Friday at 8:30 for the thrilling adventures of that masked rider of the plains…the *Lone Ranger*…sponsored by *Silvercup*, the world's finest bread!"

It was at that point that Lt. Hill impatiently reached out and shut off the radio.

"That dame's become as big a bleeding heart as you are, One Take," he griped.

Yellowstone said nothing in reply, but at the moment he was feeling proud of his little firecracker.

As Yellowstone's automobile pulled to a stop in his driveway, Lt. Hill stepped out and fired up one of his habitual Lucky Strikes. But his eyes narrowed and the cigarette drooped from the corner of his mouth as his partner walked around the front of the car to join him.

"Do you usually leave your front door hanging open, cowboy?" Hill asked.

"Never," Yellowstone replied tersely. The two detectives exchanged a knowing glance. Simultaneously, each flashed a hand beneath their jackets and came back out holding their service revolvers.

As Yellowstone slowly moved up the front steps, Lt. Hill hopped up on the porch at one end. Reaching the top step, Yellowstone jumped to the left side of the gaping doorway, pressing his back to the wall. Hill took up an identical position on the opposite side.

At a nodded signal from Hill, Yellowstone leaped into the house, crouching with his gun pointed to the right. Hill came in standing, gun aimed to the left.

"The place looks empty," he said.

"Let me get us some light," Yellowstone offered. He felt his way to a familiar lamp and switched it on.

It didn't take a trained professional to interpret the signs revealed by the light. Overturned furniture and broken glass bespoke clearly of the struggle that had transpired here.

Yellowstone bent to lift a small clock that had been knocked to the floor. He quickly observed that the hands of the broken instrument had stopped moving no more than three minutes earlier.

"Whoever did this might still be close by," he told Hill, holding up the broken clock.

"We'd better hope so," Hill replied. He lifted a section of torn curtain and Yellowstone nodded grimly as he spied streaks of blood staining its fabric.

The detectives stepped back out onto the front porch and looked about. They saw nothing untoward: the normally quiet neighborhood seemed undisturbed.

"I'll go east," Hill said tersely. "You go west."

The Osage detective nodded and the two of them bounded from the porch, setting off at a run in opposite directions.

Though unspoken, each carried the thought that they might already be too late.

CHAPTER THIRTY FIVE

Kirby King, naked from the waist up, was already running out of steam as he staggered into the Grand Trunk railroad yard. As he leaned against a parked railway car, he sucked in great gasps of air. As he did so, he also inhaled the maritime smells issuing from the river, not far to the east.

Every such breath brought ripping anguish through his ribcage as his lungs expanded. His head pounded like someone was using it for a bass drum at a Salvation Army rally, and his bruised and beaten knee screamed at him for relief.

King cried out and threw himself to the ground as he heard the report of a gun, followed by a pinging wail and a burst of sparks as a lead slug ricocheted off the skin of the railway car, after narrowly missing his own flesh.

No more than fifty yards away, he could see the man who had tried to kill him minutes earlier inside the detective's home. In the man's right hand was a gun. In his left hand was a long knife. Kirby's blood ran cold.

Matson had quickly closed the distance between himself and his intended target, but stopped now to take more careful aim after seeing his first snap shot go wide of its mark.

King rose slightly up off the ground, scuttling crab-like across the gravel of the train bed and between two of the parked cars. Inches from his heels, a second shot kicked up pieces of the gravel.

Some distance to the west, Yellowstone was standing and listening. He wasn't sure that he had heard a gunshot until the echo of the second one came floating to his ears. Coming from the opposite direction to the one in which he had been moving.

Without further hesitation and drawing his service revolver, he broke into a dead-out run in the direction of the railroad yard.

Tony the Torpedo was moving more cautiously now, having lost sight of King. As he drew near the site where the black man had scrambled out of view, Matson began to walk in a crouch that enabled him to see under the railway cars, scanning for any sign of King between the rails or standing on the other side of the stationary cars.

There were at least twenty of these empty cars parked in a line here, and the mobster approached each one with equal caution. Any time he reached a car that was open, he would quickly leap from one side of the portal to the other, in case King had taken refuge inside one of them and was waiting to pounce on him if he dropped his guard for even a second.

The one place the wary Torpedo did not think to look was up.

Kirby King had managed to pull his exhausted body to the top of one of the parked cars and was now lying there flat, mostly hidden from the view of anyone below.

As he had done when the killer stalked him in the house, King now relied on his hearing to save him. There was no way to walk silently across the gravel bed of the railroad tracks, so he used this noise to measure the progress of his stalker.

King closed his eyes, trying to mentally calculate where the killer was in relation to the ex-con's hiding place.

When he gauged the sound of the footsteps was close enough, King launched himself from the roof of the rail car, aiming for the spot he calculated the gunman to be. *Just like Mr. Yellowstone himself would have done* Kirby thought as he hurtled through the air.

Of course Yellowstone would have done it *better*.

Too late, Kirby realized he had leaped out too far and would overshoot his mark. Helplessly in the grip of gravity now, he could neither halt nor alter his trajectory.

As he saw the gunman look up and start to react, though, Kirby was able to slash downward with one leg. His foot caught Matson in the right shoulder, spinning him to the ground and sending the revolver flying from his hand.

King was able to land mostly on his left shoulder and roll, but the impact with the ground still sent such shock waves of pain through his battered body that he feared he would pass out.

Fighting off that plunge into oblivion, he pushed himself to his knees. He saw in the instant that his would-be killer was between him and the spot where the gun had landed. Already, Matson was scrambling to retrieve it.

Kirby had no choice but to force himself to stand and take off running again.

Tony the Torpedo scooped his revolver off the ground, dropped his knife from his left hand, and then cradled the gun for a moment in both hands as if it was his precious baby.

He smiled wickedly as he turned and saw his prey limping away from him, but did not immediately pursue. In truth, he didn't want another physical confrontation with King. That wasn't his style; he'd never wanted to be just some dumb muscle for the mob, didn't like to get his hands dirty either literally or figuratively.

Nor, odd as it might seem, was Matson an exceptionally good marksman. He'd never needed to be; he'd always stalked his victims with stealth, often striking them from behind. Always at close range.

So now he took his time rather than snapping off another quick shot at the fleeing ex-con. Planting his feet firmly, holding the revolver with both hands, Matson sighted down the barrel of the gun.

Kirby King had managed to stagger far enough away that he actually heard the crack of the pistol a split second before he felt a blow as from a hammer punch him low in the back. He was knocked off his feet and thrown forward, his face ripping as it skidded across the gravel alongside the train tracks.

His brain screamed at him to get back up, but the flesh at last was too weak to obey the spirit. Tears stung his eyes and he emitted a choking sob as he tried to rise only to fall back flat on the ground.

He resigned himself to his fate as he heard the crunch of slow footsteps coming up behind him. There was no need now for the killer to hurry; his victim was helpless.

Kirby's eyes widened as the sound of giggling reached his ears. It was almost like that of a child, but with a maniacal edge to it that no innocent could ever produce.

A hand slid under his chin and roughly pulled his head back and up off the ground. He felt hot breath in his ear and the sting of a knife's blade against his neck, followed by a voice that could have frozen the fiery lakes of hell.

"The lady D.A. put up a better fight than you did, boy!"

The hit man was kneeling astraddle his intended victim. Kirby felt the knife to slit his throat just under his Adam's apple.

Kirby jerked involuntarily as a gunshot rang out but he felt no pain. Someone grunted loudly but it wasn't him.

Matson spun off King, driven by the slug that had entered his own back. He dropped the knife. He flopped to the ground beside King, who saw the gunman's body convulse upward once and then lie still.

Dumbfounded, Kirby rolled onto his back and propped himself up on his elbows. No more than ten feet away, Lt. Hill stood staring at him. A curling wisp of smoke still trailed upward from the detective's pistol.

Hill didn't lower his gun as he began to walk toward the prone ex-con, but rather kept it trained directly on him. He didn't stop his approach until the end of the revolver was mere inches away from King's face.

"Don't think for a minute that I saved your sorry ass, you murdering sonofabitch," Hill hissed. "I just wanted the pleasure of killing you myself!"

The veteran detective's finger began to tighten on the trigger.

"Don't even think about it."

The warning was accompanied by the pressure of yet another gun barrel against the back of Hill's head.

Very slowly, Hill raised both arms out to his sides before dropping his revolver to the ground.

Panting for breath, Michael Yellowstone kicked the fallen weapon out of reach.

"It's over now, partner," he gasped.

Lieutenant Hill straightened. Arms held above his head, he turned. Yellowstone winced as he saw a smirk on Hill's lips.

"Oh, I'd say you're deluded if you believe that, Hollywood." He jerked his head back toward where King still lay on the ground.

"Even if your boy survives his wounds, he'll still be the prime target for every glorified bounty hunter in the country." The smirk on the detective's lips grew more pronounced.

"And your only other viable suspect is dead…out of your reach."

As if intending to contradict Lt. Hill's assertion…Tony the Torpedo Matson let out a long, loud groan.

CHAPTER THIRTY SIX

Twelve hours later, Detective Yellowstone was sipping his tenth cup of hospital coffee as he sat in a small waiting area on the ground floor of St. Mary's. He'd spent the night there.

His features twisted in disgust, either from the lousy cup of coffee or from the sight of Lt. Hill entering the room.

"How's your buddy doing?" Hill asked.

"As well as can be expected," Yellowstone replied. "They got the slug out of his back pretty quickly; I sent it on to th' lab boys.

"But he had a lot of internal injuries, internal bleeding. It was touch and go for quite awhile; the poor slob's been through th' wringer."

"Yeah, yeah. Cry me a river, Hollywood."

"I spoke to his surgeon just a few minutes ago," Yellowstone continued, choosing to ignore his partner's sarcasm. "He's out of surgery and in recovery. Barring complications, he should pull through."

"Maybe," Hill quipped venomously. "Unless some nurse decides to collect the reward on him."

Yellowstone flung his cardboard coffee cup aside and leaped to his feet, fists clenched. Hill took a step back and braced himself.

"Detective!"

Both Hill and Yellowstone turned at the call to see a uniformed

He spun off King, driven by the slug that had entered his own back.

police officer approaching them. As he drew near, he extended one hand, clutching a manila file folder, toward Yellowstone.

"I was told you wanted this as soon as it came down," the cop explained as he handed off the folder.

"Thank you, officer," Yellowstone said.

The uniform looked back and forth at the two detectives, feeling the tension virtually crackling between them. Deciding that whatever was going on here was probably above his pay grade, he wisely turned and walked away without saying another word.

Yellowstone sat back down, opening the file and reading the contents of the report within. He ignored his angry and impatient partner. Finally, he closed the file and handed it to Hill.

"You can read it for yourself, but I'll give you th' gist of it, Lieutenant. That's th' forensic report on th' bullet they took out of Kirby King's back last night."

"It's a perfect match for the ones taken out of Rebekah Nixon's body."

"What?" Hill exclaimed, opening the file to see for himself.

"You heard me," Yellowstone said sternly. "There can't be any doubt. Tony Matson murdered Miss Nixon...probably on orders from Angelo Giamatti, as part of a scheme to keep him out of prison for as long as possible."

Lt. Hill seemed not to hear him, instead poring over the lab report to allay his own sense of disbelief. He'd had time to read it word for word at least three times by the time he finally closed the file and tossed it back to the Osage detective.

"Looks like you were right after all, cowboy," the grim-faced Hill reluctantly conceded. "It's all over, now."

"No, partner, I was wrong," Yellowstone replied, shaking his head sadly. "It's just begun."

CHAPTER THIRTY SEVEN

In a large, luxurious but lonely estate in the Saint Claire Flats residential district, former judge Malcolm Nixon sat alone in his den.

Having just heard Stacy Lord break the news to her radio audience that Kirby King had been exonerated in the matter of the death of his daughter, Nixon found the stout Scotch he had poured himself could offer no solace.

Setting the glass down, he buried his head in his trembling hands and began to sob uncontrollably.

+++

The dinner crowd at Toretelli's was a good one, and the waiters and busboys were being kept constantly on the move.

At a large corner table always kept reserved for him, Angelo Giamatti was holding court with eight of his "associates," all in the midst of a sumptuous meal.

"How'd I know he was a Hebe?" the crime boss said, finishing off a tasteless joke that nonetheless drew hearty laughter from his dinner companions.

The smile vanished from the face of the man closest to Giamatti, one of the two bodyguards seated on either side of him. Angelo noticed the sudden change in his demeanor and glared at him until the bodyguard motioned with a jerk of his head for his boss to turn and look elsewhere.

Detective Michael Yellowstone was walking toward Giamatti's table. Close behind him strode four uniformed officers.

The entire restaurant had grown quiet. Some of the diners nearest the front door had thrown cash down on their tables and were making a quick exit.

Angelo Giamatti merely smiled.

"Good evening, officer," he said in oily tones. "Would you and your colleagues care to join me for dinner?"

Yellowstone's only response was to grab the mobster by the collar of his expensive jacket and jerk him roughly out of his chair and onto his feet.

Giamatti's bodyguards leaped up as well, hands dipping toward their shoulder holsters. The uniforms were faster, and had revolvers drawn, cocked and aimed before the mob soldiers could clear leather.

"*Basta*! Hold it!" Giamatti barked at his men and they lowered their hands, empty. "Killing's bad for the digestion," he told them. Clearly he was not worried by the situation.

"I hope you enjoyed your meal, Angelo," Yellowstone said. "I hear they serve spaghetti in th' Big House, too...but th' wine there's lousy." He enjoyed hearing the distinctive sound of metal on metal as he cuffed the mobster's hands behind his back.

"What the hell do you think you're doing?" Giamatti demanded.

"I think I'm arresting you, tough guy."

"Arresting me? On what charge?"

"Try solicitation of murder."

"What murder?"

"Th' murder of Assistant District Attorney Rebekah Nixon," Yellowstone said, taking the mob boss by one arm and starting to lead him away from the table.

"Hey, Frankie," Giamatti called out to one of his men. "Call my mouthpiece and tell him to meet me at the police station." Yellowstone could see that the arrogant and assured smirk had returned to his prisoner's lips.

"The rest o' you stay and enjoy your dinner. I'll be back in time for dessert!"

+++

Inside his shabby basement apartment, Roger Sinclair was now feeling doubly miserable.

Bad enough that he could barely hobble around. In the melee between the blacks and he and his fellow Klansmen, his right knee had been virtually shattered by a blow from a baseball bat. His entire leg was now encased in a stiff cast, from ankle to thigh.

And now came the news that the bounty being offered for the death of Kirby King had been withdrawn. Already, the infamous wanted posters bearing King's likeness were being taken down all over town.

He looked around at his comrades as they listened to the latest radio news report. Several of them also bore the wounds of their recent alleyway battle. All looked as glum as he.

So Sinclair began to laugh.

The other men turned to fix him with baleful stares, but he met their puzzlement with a broad smile and outstretched arms.

"Hell, boys," he cackled, "we don't *need* no reward to go coon hunting!"

He laughed again, and now the others joined him.

+++

In a spacious office suite of a building on Woodward Avenue, attorney Virgil Lowery was meeting with officers of the Detroit chapter of the NAACP.

He had already told them that the police department had issued a formal statement clearing Kirby King of any involvement in the murder of Rebekah Nixon. He held up one of the reward posters.

"Within a few days," he said, "the only ones of these that will remain will be those that people keep as grisly souvenirs."

"I think we should keep one," said Harold Morton, president of this chapter of the civil rights group. "As a reminder."

"I spoke briefly to Kirby, too," Lowery told them, "at the hospital. He told me flat out that, while he appreciates all we tried to do for him, he wants nothing further to do with our organization." Lowery absently shuffled a few papers.

"That's not surprising, really," the lawyer said, "considering he was nearly killed by two of our own people."

"Any further word on them?" Morton asked.

"None. I think it's safe to say we've heard the last of them. But because of them, and possibly other factors, Kirby now just wants to be left alone."

"It's perfectly understandable that Mr. King would feel that way," Morton agreed. "I don't blame him. But maybe he'll change his mind, in time."

"I hope he does," Lowery said.

"Meanwhile, the board has agreed to pay the man's hospital bills," Morton said. "At least he won't have those hanging over his head.

"And I think there is a bright side to all this ugliness.

"It's brought the entire Negro community together in a common cause. Look at all the good young men who gathered of their own volition to try to protect King.

"And look at you, Virgil. You've worked so hard, yet refused to accept a dime from us in payment. Even returned your retainer."

Lowery tried to shrug this off. "It seemed like the right thing to do."

"That's all we need," Morton declared earnestly. "Men who are willing to do the right thing." He looked at the others assembled there, smiled.

"This affair has given us something upon which we can build, gentlemen and we mustn't let that opportunity slip away from us."

CHAPTER THIRTY EIGHT

Triplicate.

Why did everything have to be filled out in triplicate, Lt. Hill wondered. It was like the police department didn't run on manpower and investigative skills but on paperwork.

He looked up from the stack of forms cluttering his desktop to see Detective Yellowstone walking across the room toward him. Behind him strode two men in plain suits that Hill did not recognize.

He knew the type, though: more detectives.

Hill couldn't read the expression on his partner's face, so he leapt to no conclusions. His guts twisted slightly, however, in anticipation of the worst.

"You been out recruiting, One Take?" he asked. His vague smile was not returned.

"I just thought you'd like to know that Angelo Giamatti is downstairs being booked right now, Lieutenant. And even as we speak, several of his lieutenants and foot soldiers are being picked up, too."

"Good. Can we make it stick?"

"I think so, yeah. Ever since he got out of surgery and found out that we had him dead to rights on th' Nixon killing, Tony Torpedo has been singing like a canary about Giamatti and every other mob boss he's ever performed jobs for."

"In return for some sort of…special consideration, I assume," Hill said.

"Of course," Yellowstone replied. "In return for turning state's evidence, Matson won't have to face th' death penalty for his own crimes. And he'll serve his jail time as far away from Detroit as they can get him."

Hill lit up a Lucky Strike and exhaled. "I don't mind telling you, cowboy, I'd rather see Matson fry right alongside Giamatti."

"So would I," Yellowstone concurred.

"But," Hill sighed, "I suppose I can accept the way things have turned out instead."

Yellowstone nodded. "Th' girl's father…Judge Nixon… also signed off on accepting the plea deal. He says he's satisfied."

He stopped talking then, but remained standing stiffly, staring down at the lieutenant.

"Go ahead and drop th' other shoe, Hollywood," Hill said at last, snuffing his cigarette out in an overflowing ashtray.

"I'm sorry, partner," Yellowstone said.

"Just do it," Hill replied. "Say what you came to say."

"All right. Matson insisted on one other condition before he started spilling his guts about his mob connections."

"What condition was that?"

"He made the District Attorney promise that he'd also be called in as a material witness…at *your* trial."

"What the devil are you talking about?" Hill snarled. He looked like he'd been hit between the eyes by a two-by-four. He'd anticipated some sort of reprimand for his actions, but not this.

"You're being placed under arrest," Yellowstone reluctantly informed him. "For intent to commit murder. Matson and King will both testify as to what you planned to do the other night before I stopped you."

Yellowstone could practically hear his partner's teeth grinding together; feel the heat of his anger. But then Hill seemed to relax, his eyes twinkling above just the trace of a confident smile.

This made Yellowstone feel even more uncomfortable, for the new expression on Hill's face bore an uncanny and unsettling resemblance to that worn by Angelo Giamatti at the moment of his arrest.

"Do you really think there's a jury in the land that'll convict a decorated police officer based on the testimony of an ex-con and an admitted hit man?" Hill asked.

The Osage detective shook his head slowly; his expression was one of pity.

"Don't forget," he said. "I was there too, remember? At th' railroad yard and that night at the safe house.

"That's when you planted this on King, isn't it?"

Yellowstone pulled a small, shiny object from his jacket pocket and slid it across the top of Hill's desk. It was the engraved cigarette lighter he had found a few days earlier in Kirby King's jacket.

Kirby King…a man who didn't smoke.

"I believe this is yours, Lieutenant," Yellowstone said grimly. It really hadn't been that hard for him to discover the identity of the lady friend of Hill's that his neighbor lady had told Yellowstone about. After that, and in light of Hill's actions throughout the investigation of this case, the pieces fit together nicely.

Lt. Hill reverently placed his hand upon the lighter. He stared at it in silence for a long time before speaking in a resigned voice.

"Rebekah left it at my place the last time she was there," he said softly.

"So we add hindering a police investigation and planting false evidence to th' charges against you," Yellowstone declared. "It doesn't look good for you, partner."

Hill looked up at Yellowstone; his eyes now glistened with tears.

"It was because I loved her, Mike," his said, his voice quivering with emotion too long kept in check. "I loved her so much."

"I know you did, Jack."

"And I just wanted to make sure she received a little justice for what happened to her."

"Sure. And while you were trying to do that…you just lost your way, that's all."

Hill nodded. As he then rose to his feet, he slowly removed his badge and his service revolver, placing both atop his desk.

"They won't let me keep this, either," he said, holding the engraved cigarette lighter out toward Yellowstone. "Could you hold onto it for me?"

"It'd be my pleasure."

Hill said nothing further, and offered no resistance as one of the other detectives performed the task Yellowstone couldn't bring himself to do: placing handcuffs on a brother officer.

He watched in silent sadness as the two plainclothesmen led Hill away to be booked.

At the very least, Yellowstone thought, a long and otherwise honorable and distinguished career would be over. That's the way it had to be.

But he couldn't help hoping that his former partner would be spared from the worst of the possible consequences of his actions.

With all he'd already lost, and all he was about to lose…for a man like Jack Hill, that should be punishment enough.

CHAPTER THIRTY-NINE

Kirby King fidgeted nervously in his wheelchair, looking anxiously down at his wristwatch for at least the tenth time and realizing it had only been three minutes since the last time he had done so.

It had been two weeks since he had been admitted. A tube was still funneling fluids out of his belly, and he couldn't walk unassisted for more than a few steps. But he was eager to leave this place behind him and the doctors had agreed to his release.

He looked up at the sound as the door to his hospital room flew open and Detective Yellowstone entered.

"Sorry to keep you waiting so long," Yellowstone said, "but apparently a hospital consumes even more paper than th' police department does. I had to do everything but pledge my first born to them before they'd agree to let me spring you from this joint."

"But they did, right?" King said anxiously. "I can get outta here now?"

"You betcha." The detective's face now grew more serious. "I hate to sound like a broken record, Kirby, but I'm gonna say it again.

"Things are still pretty hot out there, and will be for awhile yet. After you're all better, all healed up…I still think it might be wise for you to leave Detroit."

"It will cool down, boss, and I think I've decided to stay after all," King replied, also not for the first time. "This is where I grew up. This is where the few friends I have live. For a…for a man like me, it's the same everywhere, anyway. I'm gonna stay."

Yellowstone nodded; he'd say no more on the subject. Instead, he pointed to a small potted plant King was holding in his lap.

"Got yourself a secret admirer while you were laid up, did you?"

Kirby smiled. "Ah. You know this is from my sister Delia. She come to see me nearly every day I been here. I tried to talk her out of it, but she insisted on me coming to stay with her and her little boy till I get back on my feet."

"I visited with her a bit one evening, as she was on her way out," Yellowstone told him. "She seems like a nice young lady."

"She is, Mr. Yellowstone. Real quality."

"But maybe you could clear up something for me."

"What's that?"

"Just out of curiosity, I've been reviewing th' files of the case that landed you in the joint."

"Why would you do that?" Kirby asked, clearly growing tense.

"Like I said, just curious. Some of the details were a bit hazy, though they do contain some references to your sister as well."

"She had nothing to do with it."

"Still, I'd like to hear th' whole story."

"Why? What difference does it make? It's all done and gone now."

"C'mon, Kirby," Yellowstone said. "After all we've been through together? Don't you owe me that much?"

King sat staring at the tiny plant in his lap, and then raised his eyes to the detective.

"If I tell you…you won't never tell nobody else?"

"Nobody."

King drew a deep breath before beginning.

"I told you I was an automobile mechanic…before. I was a whiz at it, too; I truly was. I loved working with my hands and I loved that it paid good enough for me to take care of Delia.

"She was just sixteen years old then: the only family I had left. A beautiful little girl. You know that, boss; you seen her.

"She's smart, too. A lot smarter than me. She was bright and happy then; the future looked good. I loved her more than anything. Still do.

"Sometimes, she'd come down to the garage and bring me my lunch before going back to school. Sometimes, she'd meet me there at the end of the day. After I'd clock out, we'd go to dinner together: tell each other how our day went.

"The shop was run by a white man named Jerry Slate. Behind his back, most of us fellas that worked there called him 'the pig'. That's partly 'cause he looked like one: all fat and jowly. Partly, though, it was 'cause he acted like one.

"That ol' pig took a shine to Delia. Whenever he was around her, he'd make all kinds of nasty remarks; the kind you shouldn't never say to a girl.

"You can imagine, that made me mad as the dickens. But Delia would beg me to just ignore him, same as she tried to do. She was afraid if I made trouble, Slate'd fire me. Even then, good paying jobs weren't plentiful, 'specially for a colored boy without much schoolin'.

"And to my everlasting shame…I listened to her. I did nothing."

King stopped talking for a moment, turning the potted plant slowly in his hands. The Osage detective didn't press him.

"One day," he resumed at last, "Slate sent me out late to give one of the garage's regular customers a jumpstart. By the time I got back, the shop was empty; everybody else had gone home.

"But Delia was there, standing all alone outside the front door. I could tell right off that something was wrong. She looked upset, had her arms wrapped around herself, a'trembling like she was freezing cold. Her eyes was all red, like she'd been crying.

"When I asked her what was wrong, she told me she was coming down with something and made me take her home.

"After that…she stopped coming around the garage." Kirby paused to look at Yellowstone: saw by the detective's eyes that he still wanted to hear the whole story. King swallowed hard before continuing.

"Delia just drew more and more inside herself, until she wasn't hardly talking to me at all. That went on for weeks; so I finally sat her down and made her tell me what happened.

"That night at the garage, she'd showed up while I was still out. Everybody else was already gone…except for the pig.

"Old Slate was all smiles, inviting Delia to come have a seat in his office while she waited for me to get back.

"Once he got her in there, though, he started pawing at her like the animal he was. When she tried to push him away, he backhanded her: knocked her down on his sofa.

"He locked his office door and started taking off his clothes. Delia told me he was still smiling as he come at her, telling her he knew she really *wanted* what was about to happen. She was sixteen years old: just a baby."

Kirby choked on those words. Yellowstone made no comment, but in his mind he was recalling that moment when, during the police questioning of him, King had reacted so strongly to the rape allegation being leveled against him: why he had seemed even more adamant about professing his innocence of that crime than he had been of the murder of Rebekah Nixon.

The very thought of rape had been so abhorrent, so repugnant to him, because the same atrocity had been committed against his beloved sister.

"I didn't let her tell me no more," the ex-con said, resuming his narrative. "I'd heard all I needed to hear: all I could bear.

"I must have looked like a madman as I headed for the front door. Delia was near hysterical, clutching at me. Begging me to do nothing foolish: to wait to hear all the story. But I was beyond listening then.

"I admit it, Mr. Yellowstone…I was in a killing rage by the time I got to Jerry Slate's apartment. I didn't bother to knock; I just kicked the door open.

"I could barely hear Slate's wife screaming as I stormed into the place; it was like my head was under water.

"Before Slate could do much more than ask me what the hell I was doing, I had my hands on him. I threw him halfway across the room, causing him to crash right through the top of a coffee table.

"I pulled him out of a pile of broken wood and glass and starting working him over good with my fists."

"Did you mean to kill him?" Yellowstone asked.

"I didn't want to just kill him; I wanted to punish him, make him suffer good for what he done. I wanted to beat him so far into the ground it would o' took a steam shovel to dig his fat ass up."

"What stopped you?"

"Not what: who. The only thing that kept me from killing him with my bare hands was the arrival of some of his neighbors. They heard Mrs. Slate's caterwauling. They managed to pull me off o' what was left of that pig and held me till the police arrived.

"I didn't have enough money for bail or a lawyer of my own, so the court appointed me some public defender fella. He told me that Slate had pressed charges against me and that I'd be tried for attempted murder.

"Long about then's when I first had the honor of meeting a newly-minted, lady District Attorney by the name of Rebekah Nixon.

"She called a meeting with me and my lawyer, and offered me a deal. If I pled guilty, she'd recommend that the judge sentence me to no more than five years, with the provision that I had to serve the full term.

"'Sounds good to me,' my so-called lawyer said. What did he care? He was probably overworked; definitely under qualified.

"'Sounds good to *you*?' says I right back at him. 'It ain't you who's gonna be locked up in no pen for five years!'

"I told the both of 'em that I shouldn't be charged with nothing. Not after what Slate did to my baby girl.

"'Will your sister corroborate that story?' the lady DA asked me.

"'Sure she will,' I told her.

"'Are you sure you want her to? It'll mean making her take the stand and testify in open court about what happened to her.' It was the first thing she said that made her sound like a real human being to me, but I felt I had no choice.

"'She'll do it for me.'

"'Well,' Miz Nixon says, spreading her arms like so, 'if you want to take the chance that a jury will believe you and your sister over Mr. Slate, that's your right and your choice. My offer remains good for 48 hours: no more. After that, I go for the max.'

"After she left the room, my lawyer laid it all out on the line for me. We'd be facing a young, attractive and well-intentioned lady. She was short on experience, but that just made her even more eager to prove she deserved the job some people said no woman should hold and that others said she'd only gotten in the first place by virtue of being a judge's daughter.

"Me, on the other hand: what was I? An uneducated, low class Negro who would likely be facing an all-white jury, under the rules of an all-white legal system. And my only hope was that they would take the word of two colored people over that of a white businessman.

"That being the case, my fine public defender, also a white man, again pressed me to take the plea deal. That left a bitter taste in my mouth

"'You ain't much of a lawyer, are you?' I said to him.

"'No, I'm not,' he admitted. 'But I'm all you've got.'

"They let Delia come visit me the next morning. Just like I thought, she told me she'd be glad to get on the witness stand for me. But I could tell she had something more to say to me. Sure enough, she broke down crying and told me what she tried to tell me the night I went off on Slate."

"She was pregnant," Yellowstone surmised. King nodded.

"Yeah. Carrying the child of the pig that raped her. But I told her not to worry about it. I told her everything would be all right.

"And that afternoon, I talked to my lawyer: told him about Delia. That's when he did the only thing he ever done right for me. He went to talk to Slate: to make him an offer.

"Slate gave Delia a thousand dollars to help see her through her pregnancy and I agreed to plead guilty and serve the time, without a trial.

"That way, what Slate done would never come out in court. His wife would never have to know. He'd be spared from public humiliation and so would Delia."

"That's a helluva price to pay for another man's crime," Yellowstone said.

"But that's the way it went down, boss," Kirby insisted. "Honest to God. Delia begged me not to go through with it. But what else was I gonna do? Like the lawyer man said to me: I was all she had. If I didn't look out for her, who would?

"Now she's got the sweetest little boy in the world, and a good job with good people." King gently stroked one of the waxy leaves of his potted plant.

"If I had to do it all over again, even knowing what I do now about the Joint...I'd do it in a heartbeat. No regrets."

Looking down at King intently, Yellowstone chose to believe him.

"I've got what may be some good news for you," he said.

"What's that, boss?"

"Well, I never told you this, but I love cars near as much as you do. A holdover from my Hollywood days, I guess.

"So I've been talking to an auto mechanic buddy of mine; owns his own shop over near Fort Wayne.

"He told me that if you're as good with automobiles as you claim, he might have work for you after you're all mended."

King's face brightened instantly. "You really think he'd do that? Does he know he'd be getting an ex-con?"

"He knows. Matter of fact, he's an ex-con himself: has a soft spot for them." Yellowstone tapped the side of his nose with one finger. "Just don't tell my bosses I consort with riff-raff like him and you."

Kirby nodded.

"Oh, and one more thing," Yellowstone said, smiling crookedly. "You know this means I'll be expecting free tune-ups."

"Any time, boss," King chuckled. "Any time."

"But for now, we need to get you out of here. I'll go get my car and bring it around to th' front. A nurse will be here in a minute to wheel you down to th' exit."

"Will we have to go through a bunch of reporters?" King asked.

"We probably would," Yellowstone replied, giving him a sly wink. "If I hadn't leaked word to them that you'd be leaving here *tomorrow*."

King grinned broadly as the detective turned and headed for the door leading out of the room.

"Mr. Yellowstone?"

"Yeah, Kirby?" the detective said, standing in the open doorway.

"Thank you." King's mouth opened again, but all the other words he wanted to say wouldn't come out. "Just…thank you."

Equally stoic and employing the silent language men often use between each other, Yellowstone merely nodded, then left the room.

CHAPTER FORTY

The smile returned to Kirby King's face as he heard the door to the hospital room opening; he assumed it was the nurse come to take him downstairs.

The smile faded when he saw instead a corpulent old man enter. At first, Kirby thought he might be another of the hospital's patients, as he did not look well and walked slowly.

"Mr. King?" the old man said, not bothering to remove the expensive fedora atop his head.

"Yeah?"

"My name is Judge Malcolm Nixon."

King's eyes grew cold and his jaws clenched.

"What do you want, old man?" the black man said.

Nixon tentatively stepped closer.

"I wanted to tell you how sorry I am, for all you've been through."

"Is that all?"

Nixon flinched at the icy tone of King's voice. "I also wanted to offer my help, if you'll have it."

"You got nothing I want, Mr. Judge."

Nixon's face twisted in anguish. "You have to understand. She was all I had left, son. All that really mattered to me."

Kirby could see the pain in the old man's eyes: the kind that went far beyond the mere physical. He felt his own heart soften, just a little.

"I'm sorry for your loss, sir," he said, with a sincerity that mildly surprised him.

"I know from experience how hard it can be to let go of grief and anger... but you got to do it."

"Tell me how," the dying old man pleaded.

"You might be able to do it, or at least start to do it, by putting that money of yours to some *good* use. Here's what a good man would do..."

Humbled as he had never been before, Judge Nixon nodded and dropped his gaze to the floor.

+++

Downstairs, Yellowstone pulled up short as he stepped out of the hospital. Stacy Lord had been approaching from the opposite direction and also came to a halt.

He hadn't spoken to her since the night the case had reached its climax in the railroad yard. He didn't think he wanted to talk to her now, either, and started to walk on past her.

"No comment, Miss Lord," he said brusquely.

"Some detective you are, Yellowstone," she replied tartly. "Do you see a microphone anywhere?"

In truth, she was alone: no assistants, no engineers, and no equipment of any sort. He looked at her rather sheepishly.

"I have very good sources, though," she said, "and they told me you'd been spending quite a bit of time here; so I thought I'd take a chance." The rather haughty manner she liked to affect mellowed before his eyes.

"I just wanted to talk, Mike. Face-to-face."

"That's always th' best way," he replied.

"I'm sorry, Mike; really I am. I let this whole Kirby King story get the better of me and let it bring out the worst in me."

"Oh, not completely, Firecracker," the Osage detective assured her. "I caught your broadcast th' night we took down Tony Matson. It was a real humdinger."

"It was just the truth," she said reflectively. "Which is all that a reporter should ever say."

"Amen to that, sister."

"And I let it drive a wedge between you and me, too. That hurt me the most, you big galoot. More than I knew it would."

"That's all right, darlin'." Yellowstone thought back on all those who had reacted far more badly to the chain of events just passed; not the least of which was his own partner.

"This case pushed a lot of people down a lot of paths they wouldn't normally have followed."

Stacy reached out and placed a hand on his arm, looking up at the detective with earnest eyes.

"Does that mean you'll be able to forgive me and move past this?" she asked.

"Woman, you're lookin' at a man who was once kicked in th' head by a horse," he replied, smiling wryly and patting the tiny hand that rested on his sleeve.

"I can get past damn near anything."

CHAPTER FORTY ONE

In a small, tidy house in Virginia Park, Amanda Carpenter sat and looked out her front window.

Her two oldest children, Peter and Sally, were engaged in a vigorous game of tag with some of the other children from the neighborhood.

Playing the way children should: without a care in the world.

Watching the little ones at their games almost never failed to make her smile, but today the best she could muster was a wistful look of longing.

Her head turned away from the window at the sound of racking coughing coming from one of the bedrooms. She started to rise, and then stopped as the coughing spell did.

That would be Midge, her youngest. She'd never played a game of tag: never would. If the doctors were right...she'd be gone within the month.

Amanda's gaze fell to her lap, where the letter from the Michigan Mutual Insurance Company rested. She read it for the fourth time, as if hoping repeated readings would change the message it bore.

The letter was to inform her that her claim had been denied; her husband Sean had allowed his life insurance policy with them to lapse two months before his death.

She thought again of what a horrible and pointless death it had been. Her nights were haunted by grotesque visions of the husband she had loved so dearly lying broken and bleeding on the cold pavement.

All because he had tried to kill another man and collect a bounty. Because he had grown so desperate that he saw murder as his best, possibly only, way to help his family.

Instead, the poor, hapless man had only made things worse.

Amanda had gone straight from her parents' house to Sean's, as an eighteen-year-old bride. She had no skills, except those she had needed to be a good wife and mother.

It had taken the bulk of their meager savings account simply to pay for a decent funeral for Sean.

Looking ahead now, Amanda Carpenter saw nothing but darkness.

She and her children had nothing: no husband, no father, no money... no hope.

She crumpled the letter in both hands, pressing it to her bosom as she began to weep. Her face was averted from the window now, so she did not see the children stop their playing to stare at the long, sleek touring car that was pulling up to the curb.

Amanda straightened at the sound of a knock at her front door, frantically wiping away her tears. It was probably just another bill collector, but she was too proud to let them see her in distress. She moved quickly to the door and opened it.

She didn't recognize the old man standing there. He was a very large but well-dressed gentleman, with very sad eyes. He looked chastened and contrite, and was nervously twisting the brim of an expensive fedora in both hands.

"May I come in, Mrs. Carpenter?" Judge Malcolm Nixon asked softly. "I won't take but a moment of your time. You see, I have several additional stops to make today in order to correct some...terrible mistakes...I've made.

"I'd like to talk to you about your husband...and about your future."

-THE END-

ABOUT OUR CREATORS

THE AUTHORS

R. A. JONES - is a native of Oklahoma (originally Indian Territory) where he still resides. R. A. has been a freelance writer and editor for the past thirty years.

His credits include newspaper and magazine columns, articles and short stories. He has been a movie reviewer and commentator in newspapers and on radio. He assisted actor Gary Lockwood (*Star Trek; 2001: A Space Odyssey*) in the writing of Lockwood's autobiography, *2001 Memories: An Actor's Odyssey*. With Michael Vance, R. A. co-wrote the syndicated comic book and comic strip review column *Suspended Animation* for five years.

The readers of *Comic Buyer's Guide* magazine voted him "Favorite Writer About Comics" in 1985, and in 2006 he was inducted into the Oklahoma Cartoonists Collection Hall of Fame.

He has scripted more than 100 different issues of various comic book titles in his career. Among the more noteworthy are Wolverine and Captain America for Marvel Comics; *Harlan Ellison's Dream Corridor* for Dark Horse Comics; and *Star Trek: Deep Space Nine* for Malibu Comics. He also co-wrote, for Image Comics, *Bulletproof Monk*, which served as the basis for the 2003 movie of the same title.

His comic book stories, "Cold Hard Facts" and "Three On A Match" which originally appeared in the magazine *Metal Hurlant*, were short films in France.

His novels include *Deathwalker, Global Star* (written with Michael Vance and Mel Fox), *The Equation* (co-written with Michael Vance), *The Steel Ring*, a superhero book based on characters from one of the earliest publishers of comic books, Centaur. He also wrote the Western thriller, *Gun Glory*.

MICHAEL VANCE - was born in Oklahoma City, Oklahoma. He was first published in "The Professor's Story Hour" chapbook at the age of eleven. He has been published in dozens of magazines and as a syndicated columnist and cartoonist in over 500 newspapers. His history book, *Forbidden Adventure, The History of the American Comics Group*, has been called a "benchmark in comics history". It was reprinted in *Alter Ego* magazine #s 61 & 62.

His magazine work has been published in seven countries, and includes articles for *Starlog, Jack & Jill* and *Star Trek, The Next Generation*. He briefly ghosted the internationally syndicated comic strip, *Alley Oop*, and created and wrote his own strip for five years called *Holiday Out* that was reprinted as a comic book. Vance also wrote comic book titles including *Straw Men, Angel of Death, The Adventures of Captain Nemo, Holiday Out* and *Bloodtide*. Artists with whom he has worked include, Wayne Truman, Richard "Grass" Green, and Dave (Alley Oop) Graue.

His work has appeared in several comic book anthologies, and he is listed in two reference works, the *Who's Who of American Comic Books* and *Comic Book Superstars*. His thirty short stories about a fictional town called "Light's End" have been published in numerous magazines. They have also been recorded by legendary actor William (*Murder She Wrote*) Windom. One of these stories was nominated for the international 2004 SLF Fountain Award for Best Short Story.

These short stories were the foundation for a trilogy of novels published by Airship 27: *Weird Horror Tales, Weird Horror Tales: The Feasting,* and *Weird Horror Tales: Light's End.*

With novelists Mel Fox and R.A. Jones, he co-wrote *Global Star*, a tabloid in a world where werewolves and babies born with bowling balls in their stomachs are reality. He co-wrote *The Equation*, a suspense-thriller about the impending financial collapse of America, with R. A. Jones. Airship 27 also published Vance's novel, *Young Nemo and the Black Knights* about Jules Vern's Captain Nemo as a young man of eighteen years of age. *The Thief of Two Worlds* is Vance's Middle Grade, Christian SF novel about a trip back into time to recover a 'jewel' of infinite value.

MICHAEL VANCE (L) AND R. A. JONES, THE AUTHORS OF MOTOR CITY MANHUNT, STANDING IN FRONT OF THE APARTMENT BUILDING WHERE LESTER DENT BEGAN HIS CAREER. DENT CREATED AND WROTE ABOUT 180 DOC SAVAGE NOVELS.

Vance's weekly comics review column, *Suspended Animation*, was continuously published for more than twenty years in fanzines, newspapers, and on over eighty websites. At its peak, it was read by approximately 4,000,000 readers a year. It was the longest, continuously published, comics review column in the world. In his career, he worked in newspapers for twenty-two years as an editor, writer and advertising manager, creating three successful newspaper magazines. He also worked as an advertising copy writer, journalist, novelist, historian, graphic designer, in public relations, as a grant writer, cartoonist and columnist.

Vance also created the Oklahoma Cartoonists Collection housed in the Toy and Action Figure Museum in Pauls Valley, Oklahoma, and was a keynote speaker at the "Uncanny Adventures of Okie Cartoonists" exhibit at the Oklahoma Historical Museum in Oklahoma City. He is a Christian.

THE ARTIST

JESUS ANTONIO HERNANDEZ RODRIGUEZ - a.k.a "Portaveritas" Architect, Illustrator and Penciler from México, being published in many countries like Spain, Italy, UK and USA. In his country is a Cover Artists of many magazines and one is also an expert of Lucha Libre Ilustrating and designing artwork for Luchadores in his country. Right now working a secret project for the Canadian Market.

https://www.facebook.com/Portaveritas-ART-363531623736248/
http://portaveritas.deviantart.com/
https://es.pinterest.com/portaveritas/

From Michael Baron, the award winning creator of Nexus and Badger, comes a tale of terror and suspense set against the backdrop of the Outlaw Biker culture.

Josh Pratt is an ex-con turned private investigator. A woman dying of cancer hires him to find the son she gave up as a baby. The child's father is a sadistic sociopath named Moon who has vowed to kill her for abandoning them.

Josh is the BIKER, caught up in a race for survival against a human monster on the road between heaven and hell at the end of which lies either salvation or damnation. Baron spins a tale of unrelenting suspense and horror that moves across his narrative landscape like the roar of a chopper's engine. Creating memorable characters and authentic backgrounds, this is an amazing, quality crime thriller unlike anything you've ever read before. The man who shook up the comic industry with his revolutionary stories now turns his limitless skill and imagination to the world of crime fiction and the result will blow you away.

Featuring illustrations by artist Joseph Arnold and designed by award-winning Art Director, Rob Davis, BIKER is a punch-to-the-gut reading experience even the most jaded thriller fan will be cheering.

"Hard-boiled. Hard-edged. Hard-core. Hard to put down until you get to the last page." Charles Saunders, author of Imaro and Damballa.

www.ingramcontent.com/pod-product-compliance
Lightning Source LLC
Chambersburg PA
CBHW071238250626
47163CB00001B/233